*Also by Elizabeth Daniels Squire
in Large Print:*

Kill the Messenger
Memory Can Be Murder
Remember the Alibi
Who Killed What's-Her-Name?

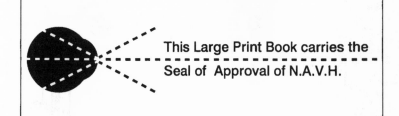

This Large Print Book carries the
Seal of Approval of N.A.V.H.

WHERE THERE'S
A WILL

Elizabeth Daniels Squire

Thorndike Press • Waterville, Maine

Published in 2003 by arrangement with
Luna Carne-Ross Literary Agent.

Thorndike Press® Large Print Paperback Series.

The tree indicium is a trademark of Thorndike Press.

The text of this Large Print edition is unabridged.
Other aspects of the book may vary from the original edition.

Set in 16 pt. Plantin by Minnie B. Raven.

Printed in the United States on permanent paper.

Library of Congress Cataloging-in-Publication Data

Squire, Elizabeth Daniels.
    Where there's a will / Elizabeth Daniels Squire.
        p. cm.
    ISBN 0-7862-5246-4 (lg. print : sc : alk. paper)
    1. Dann, Peaches (Fictitious character) — Fiction.
    2. Women detectives — North Carolina — Fiction.
    3. Inheritance and succession — Fiction.   4. Memory
disorders — Fiction.   5. North Carolina — Fiction.
    6. Cruise ships — Fiction.   7. Large type books.   I. Title.
    PS3569.Q43W46 2003
    813′.54—dc21   2003041303

LT-M

WHERE THERE'S A WILL

Acknowledgments

I'd like to thank the many folks from Dorothy L. for sending me the lyrics for, and lore about, "The Tattooed Lady," and especially for the lore connected with the renditions of that song by Groucho Marx. You folks inspired a new wrinkle in the plot.

The Blue Ridge Parkway staff in North Carolina and members of the forest service were extremely helpful as I put together the scenes at Linville Falls State Park. Shauna Dixon at the Linville Overlook, Bob Hewett, ranger, and Blanche Purcell at the main office were among those to whom I'm grateful.

The nice folks at the *Avery Journal* in Newland, North Carolina, steered me to their microfilm files in the Avery County Library, which contained stories of a murder trial involving the alleged pushing of victims from a mountain overlook. Debbie McLean of the library staff found the story I wanted to mention.

Jennifer Wren of the Western North

Carolina Mushroom Society gave me information about Amanita (Destroying Angel) mushrooms, among others, and where they might be found.

Mary and Rich Freedman of Hatboro, Pennsylvania, who were visiting Linville Falls and watched me pace off the murder scene, sent me a snapshot they took of the falls from just the right angle.

I would like to thank the staff of the ocean liner on which I crossed the Atlantic — a lovely kind of research. I will not mention the name of the ship because in *Where There's a Will* the staff is sometimes nasty. On the real ship, they were a delight.

Miss Kitty and Amanda of Sky People Tattoo in Asheville graciously showed me everything I needed to know about tattooing, body piercing, and kindred arts, which I would rather write about than actually experience.

Clothes Encounters consignment shop in Asheville not only made a good backdrop for my sleuth to learn more about the Groucho Marx connection, but also led me to find a really wild necklace. Thanks.

Ske and Kitty Boniske lent their environmentally hep house to Winnie.

My writing group: Dershie McDevitt, Geraldine Powell, Peggy Parris, Florence Wallin, and Jan Harrow made a great many invaluable suggestions. Also thanks to Lisa Franklin, Julie Burns, and Gigi Derballa.

Many thanks to my editor, Judith Palais, and my agent, Luna Carne-Ross.

My son Worth, the poet, sometimes supplied the right word, his special talent.

My husband Chick Squire was most helpful of all. He has always encouraged me as a writer, put up with my near-to-deadline quirks, and has been generous with his time and good sense in every way. I dedicate this book to him.

CHAPTER
1

MONDAY, JULY 14

"I made a video of the reading of the will, Peaches," said my friend Marietta. "At least I got the others to agree to let me do that. I knew there must be some catch when I heard that Uncle Hiram left money to us." Even now, nearly ten months after the fact, her voice held wonder.

"Uncle Hiram hated my brother and me and all our kids. We were poor relations. Of course, at the end he hated everybody. I suppose he wanted to be sure his dirty millions couldn't possibly go to Suzie. That's his ex-wife who always thinks she knows more about everybody's business than God does. Hiram hated her worst of all."

Marietta has never looked like anyone's poor relation. She has smart eyes in a thoughtful oval face. Not beautiful, but nice to look at. With dark curly hair. She went to high school with me. Class of

1961. She knew how to protect herself even then. I'd get mad at someone for being arrogant or bossy. She'd pierce them with a quip. Like the time Margaret Smith said she should get the lead in the school play because she was better looking than Marietta. Marietta said they needed to save Margaret till they really needed her, for the lead in a play about dumb blondes. Don't mess with Marietta. Now she has a nursery for herbs and plays the violin. Her words stay pungent.

"My family let me tape the will, but with strings attached: we keep the tape in the house that Uncle Hiram left us," she explained. "God knows what good it did to make that rule," she said, "but it was my brother Wingate's idea, and Wingate, poor soul, liked to set conditions."

So that's why, on a sunny day in June, about ten months after her uncle Hiram had died, Marietta and I had come to the big empty house with the Gothic arch over the front door. That, and because she believed I could help her.

Strange, I thought, that here in the mountains of North Carolina where the backroads folks can be dirt-poor, rich people feel at home. The Vanderbilts had built a magnificent castle here in the

1890s. For a fee you can tour it and see priceless art, foreign architecture, and top-of-the-line 1890s furniture and plumbing. Uncle Hiram's house, with its parquet floors and mahogany-paneled walls, was not quite a castle, and not quite that old. The dark walls drank light.

I followed Marietta into the huge living room, past wine-red brocade chairs and couch, complete with lion's-claw feet and hand rests, past the glassed-in bookshelves, the wrought-iron lamps — all maybe vintage 1920s. Past a clock on every wall. Uncle Hiram collected clocks of all sorts — antique steeple clocks, cuckoo clocks, whatever. We beelined toward a large modern television set on a bent chrome stand, entirely out of keeping with everything else in the room.

We were about to view canned memory. The words I'd hear would shock me — that's what Marietta had said. Also we could replay any part of that tape about Uncle Hiram's will that we felt we'd missed, even two or three times. Wonderful. Better, I admit, than the memory tricks that I collect. Those range from the method of *Loci* that Cicero used to remember his orations, down to my own systems for not losing my car keys. They are

13

all in a book I wrote called *How to Survive Without a Memory*, now in paperback. But I mustn't let my mind wander.

Marietta plugged in the TV. "This room is still exactly as it was when my uncle died," she said as she began fussing with the set. "In fact, it's mostly like it was when Uncle Hiram inherited the house from his first wife, Amanda. He'd added clocks, of course, and that elaborate coat of arms in red and blue and gold. He said that was from the family of an English earl we're all descended from. He gave himself airs about that."

It was a fruity-looking coat of arms, with lions rampant and roses. Almost camp.

"But the furniture has stayed the same," Marietta said. "Uncle Hiram didn't like changes. Except for changes that made him richer. Or changes in girlfriends. That's why his second wife left him."

A picture on the TV set came into focus. "Good!" said Marietta. "Here's Ellington Foxworth, my uncle's lawyer. I wouldn't trust him for a minute. I think of him as the Fox."

Yes, I thought, his face on the screen was even triangular — wide forehead, pointed chin. His eyes were bright, like a fox's, or like a man who knew how to grab hold of a

14

buck quick. *What the Ell is the Fox worth?* Good way to keep hold of his name. I anchor new names with tricks like that.

Marietta had stopped the tape. "As you can see, the Fox sat in that chair," she said, pointing to a red one near the set, and turned sideways so that the person who sat there could look at the TV or the watchers with a turn of his head. Marietta sat down in the chair. "The Fox had his papers on this little table." She tapped a round mahogany table next to the chair. "You sit here on the other side," she said.

So I sat and was amazed how comfortable that red brocade chair could be. Indestructible, but proportioned right. The fabric was firm but not coarse, smooth, in spite of the woven pattern, but not slick. The red arms, ending in mahogany lion's claws, invited my arms to rest on them. Wealth, even someone else's, has advantages. I could watch in comfort.

Marietta clicked the remote control, and the picture moved to show the assembled heirs as the Fox said "good morning" to them, rather wryly, I thought. Marietta stopped the tape again so I could study the heirs.

"There's my daughter Goldie and her two kids next to my empty chair. I was doing the filming," she said.

I knew Goldie, but not as well as I knew Marietta. Goldie was as blond as forsythia in the spring, even now at around forty. Had been since she was fourteen and found out about hair dye.

"And next to her is Wingate's son, Rich." Rich was dark and quiet, a high-school teacher with a sense of humor much like Marietta's, more like his aunt than his father, I'd always thought. Now his nickname was going to fit. Rich.

"Yes, go ahead and make a chart," Marietta said. She knows me well. A pencil is my best friend. "My brother Wingate looks so hopeful there on the couch," she said. "Poor Wingate with his one-track mind. He was thinking, 'Money! Hoorah!'"

"This was an incredible moment for us all," Marietta said. "We were amazed to learn we were in Uncle Hiram's will, and God knows we all needed the money. I had even been worried about how I was going to pay the taxes on the farm."

Two frown lines formed between her eyes. "Goldie had a job waiting tables, but she's never been able to hold onto two cents. She got a notice they might repossess her car. So as soon as she heard she might inherit money, Goldie looked like the cat that . . ." Marietta stared at the screen. Yes, Goldie's eyes flashed with triumph.

"Goldie has always pined for luxuries." Marietta sighed, as if that mattered now. "Cashmere and silk instead of polyester. You see how she wore all her jewelry to the reading of the will, even though it was costume jewelry. Ready for a trade-in, I guess. I bet Goldie was spending the money in her head and maybe thinking that Bill — that's her ex-husband — would be sorry he'd divorced her."

Appropriately named, that girl, I thought, not just because she was blond. Gold was her goal.

"My cousin Poo, Hiram's other niece, is the one sitting a little off by herself. I have to admit none of us liked Poo. She never bothered to be nice. Very unsouthern. Behind her back we called her Eeyore. She was a chemist, and as I told you, she drank herself to death the next day."

"Bad timing," I said. I shivered. Poor woman. Imagine drinking yourself to death the day after you inherited fifteen million dollars! At least I wouldn't have to remember her name. She was out of the picture.

Still, I was impatient. "You brought me

here to hear the will," I said, "because you said I wouldn't believe how outrageous it was unless I heard it with my own ears. So don't make me wait. Later we can replay the family's reaction."

Marietta shrugged and nodded and started the video again. Ellington Foxworth reappeared on the screen. His eyes were sly — by habit or just for this occasion? "Now that we are all together," he said in rounded mellow tones like caramel sauce, "I will let your benefactor speak for himself." Was there a hint of sarcasm in the way he said "benefactor"? I wasn't sure. Marietta listened as intently as if she'd never heard this before.

The Fox had a remote for the TV in his hand. I realized Marietta and I were going to see a tape within a tape. A box within a box. We were going to see and hear Uncle Hiram tell his heirs that now that he was dead, they'd get his money. Oh, the miracles of modern technology.

He appeared on the screen sitting in one of the lion's-claw chairs. I wondered if it pleased him that the lion's claws matched the coat of arms he'd hung on the wall. Though the chairs with claws must have been in the room first. Hiram was too small for his chair, which was a shock, somehow. He was not so much short as scrawny, dried out, partly bald. Inside his red flannel shirt and red plaid pants, he was a stick figure. But his eyes glowed feverishly in his wizened face. As if almost all of him but his spite had burned away. What was he dying of? Cancer, I seemed to remember. I didn't like him.

He looked straight into the camera. "I have been aware," he said breathily, "that you all have believed that I failed to make the most of my money and let it turn me into an unpleasant old man." He raised one wispy eyebrow. He smiled. His teeth were yellow. He pointed at the watchers with a gnarled hand that looked as if it had been burned and healed and scar tissue held it clawlike. "You all believed I should have done wonderful things for you, and instead I was a miser. Admit it. That's what you thought, damn you." He stuck out his chin belligerently.

The assembled heirs blinked and squirmed. This was evidently not what they'd expected, even from their uncle Hiram. Wingate was clenching his teeth. He had sparkling white teeth in a broad mouth, and earnest eyes. Somehow that added up to good looks, perhaps because his lashes were so long and his dark hair curled in such a boyish way. He wore a serious coat and tie as if he hoped to sell only the best and most expensive homes.

"Wingate looks like he's going to burst and talk back," I said. I should have kept my mouth shut. Marietta stopped the tape again.

"Don't worry," she said. "Wingate would put up with anything in order to get that money. He'd made bad investments. He was scared he couldn't pay his mortgage. It was that bad. You'll see his fingers twitching for the cash. Besides, Wingate and Goldie have always been alike. Goldie should have been his daughter instead of mine. Ready to spend up a storm. Wingate was extravagant" — tears came into her eyes — "but he was generous, and never mean."

She swallowed hard and pushed the play button. Whereupon her uncle Hiram pointed at the camera and shook his finger. He must have imagined his family all assembled. "Not one of you understood that money is hard to handle," he accused. "It turns the people around you into gold diggers." He looked from one side of the screen to the other, as if taking in his relatives, the gold diggers. "It makes your small mistakes be big mistakes in the eyes of the vultures who watch. It makes them watch. Look what money did to Howard Hughes, one of the richest men in the world." His voice rose in protest. "His millions turned him into a sick and eccentric hermit." He gripped the arms of his chair with those claw hands. "Probably without the best medical care. Perhaps it made him die sooner." He glared as if the viewers were to blame. "And look at that Du Pont heir. Money undoubtedly hastened his insanity."

That's what Hiram wanted to think, I told myself. How would he know? What a strange man. The video played on:

"Who will tell a rich man he's losing his mind? People say what a rich man wants to hear, at least to his face. Until perhaps he's killed a man. So Du Pont was convicted of that." He glared around again, and the camera panned around at the heirs. Goldie was smirking, not believing a word.

"I had to be blunt to make up for yes-men, for toadies, so you didn't like me," Hiram said defiantly. He pointed a claw finger. "Not one of you had the good sense to find out who I really was, or why I was angry."

He paused, rubbed his chin, and broke out into a great big grin. "I know that for a fact because I had you watched."

The heirs all sat up in shock, wondering, no doubt, where this was going to lead.

"Yes," he said, "I hired a detective."

No man can stand up to an investigation. Some famous statesman said that.

"Just like the old bastard to snoop," Marietta said dryly. "He got that way toward the end."

"I wanted to see which of you deserved to be my heir," the taped Hiram said importantly. "I don't know why I bothered. Wingate, you had the nerve to insult me right on your car phone, which anyone can easily listen in on. They even listened to Prince Charles talk to his paramour. He was a fool, too. You said I wouldn't lend you money for that big real-estate deal near Pisgah Forest because I was a stingy old skinflint who squeezed every penny till Lincoln yelled 'help.'

"But that's not the worst. Marietta, you told Goldie that I was losing my marbles, and that slaphappy kid of yours agreed, with no evidence at all. Just because I thought someone was stalking me and hired a bodyguard. You said I was paranoid."

Marietta winked at me. "He *was* paranoid."

"And Winnie lectured me on doing good works," Hiram added.

Goldie and Rich both glanced sideways at Wingate's homely daughter, Winnie, as if to say, Yes. She does that. God preserve us.

"You're all a bunch of losers and you don't even know it," Hiram spat. He began to shake. "And you're the only family I've got, damn it. You need to learn a lesson, and I, by God, am in a position to give you just what you deserve!"

Goldie winced as if her uncle had been real, not just a picture. Wingate kept his face blank. He knew how to keep a poker face when things looked really bad. The others looked alarmed. What were they heirs to?

"I'm going to let you find out what it's like." Uncle Hiram shook his fist. "I'm going to make you very rich!" He laughed in delight. "I wish I could be there to see just how you handle that, just what fools you make of yourselves. Because not one of you has the gumption to make the most of fifteen million dollars."

The camera panned back to the heirs. They gaped. The young man next to Goldie gasped out loud. Marietta stopped the tape.

"We certainly hadn't expected that much," she said. "In fact, the way Hiram was talking, he could have left it all to Planned Parenthood and the Red Cross. That's Goldie's son Brian who gasped," she said with a sigh. "He was most stunned of all." I hadn't seen Brian since he was a preteen with a mop of red-blond hair. Brian the Lion — that nickname was a joke. He had such a soft voice I had to strain to hear it, and he wore a surprised look on all occasions, especially in Marietta's video.

"Brian was too young to cope with all this," she said. "He's just eighteen. He wants to be a poet or a priest, except he can't resist the girls.

"His sister Lil is the one next to him, looking pleased. She thought she could handle this fine. She's always been determined to get what she wanted from the day she was born and yelled to be fed every two hours. My jet-propelled granddaughter, Lillian."

Yes. *Lil* with the strong *will*. I remembered she kept winning contests. She'd won the advertising jingle contest for some kind of pork sausage, and a trip to Disneyland for selling the most of some magazine, and I forget what else.

"Lil was not broke," Marietta said. "She had a beginning job with an advertising agency and never spent more than she earned, which is more than I can say for her mother."

Damn it, I must not be diverted. *Lil* should not stop the *will*.

"Please," I said, "let's finish the tape and then talk."

"I'm sorry," Marietta said. "I watch this, and my thoughts swirl. But I want to say one thing. There was just one member of our family who was mature about all this. Thank God for my nephew Richard. How can Rich and Goldie be cousins and be so unlike each other? There he sits in the chair on her left, and she's grinning like a fool, and he is solemn as the pope. I think he knew from the first minute that millions would change our lives in ways we couldn't even imagine. Rich agrees with me that this whole money thing is just surrealistic. Beyond belief."

Well, he was a high-school teacher. That should sober anyone. But I looked at dark, quiet Rich on the tape and I thought his eyes had a mocking twinkle. Marietta's sometimes do. It was as if Rich thought this whole reading-of-the-will thing might turn into a farce.

"All right, all right, back to the will," Marietta said. She clicked, and her uncle Hiram came back to life, angry eyes and all.

"You'll destroy yourselves," he scolded with a sneer, "and then you'll know how hard it is to be as rich as I was. And to get no help at all from those who should care."

For a moment I thought the tape had stopped running again. Then I realized that Hiram had finished his spiel from beyond the grave, and from the heirs I was hearing a stunned silence.

After a dramatic pause the Fox read out the exact terms of the will. First, a strange provision. In order to inherit, the heirs had to agree to travel together to the English village where the earl had lived, the earl with the coat of arms on the wall, ". . . and see your heritage. See that I had noble blood, and so do you. You have to do this within a year of my death or lose my money, and you have to return together on the *Ocean Queen*. That's the cruise ship where my Amanda and I spent our honeymoon. It was the ship's maiden voyage. Where we were happy before we discovered she had leukemia. If you take that trip, perhaps it will dawn on you what I lost, the sweetest girl in the world."

Amanda, Hiram's first wife, had paid for such a luxury honeymoon, I figured. Marietta said her uncle had been an investment counselor before he married a rich woman. Amanda left him the money that grew into his fortune. He should complain. And yet I'd rather be loved than rich. I shouldn't be a cynic.

The heirs squirmed, so who cared about the earl? Who cared about the old miser's honeymoon? They were waiting for the good part. But next came a provision that if any heir should die within a year of Hiram's death, half of that person's share would be divided among the other heirs, with the remaining half going to his children, if any. How strange when they were all relatively young and healthy. They squirmed more. Next came a cash bequest: ten thousand dollars to Hiram's housekeeper, Annie Long.

"She was home with the flu," Marietta told me. "I bet she'd hoped for more."

Then the Fox smiled. "Now, as to you folks here . . ." As Hiram had said, each heir got about fifteen million dollars. The house he left jointly to them all to dispose of in any way that they all agreed upon. By now I was getting a feel for old Uncle Hiram and I could see the house bit was a joke. He didn't think they could agree on anything. So maybe that bit about the earl was a practical joke. Hiram had envisioned how his newly rich heirs would hate a trip together — would want instead to do their own thing.

And yet, except for Uncle Hiram, I liked this family, especially Marietta — I'd known her best and longest. Her family wasn't coldhearted. They were just ordinary less-than-perfect folks. Or so I thought.

On the tape, Winnie smiled. Let's see, that was Wingate's daughter, about thirty years old, and dour. I'd met her when she came around raising money for good causes. She'd made it clear by little mannerisms and sighs that she felt unloved. She would have been more lovable if she washed her hair and her clothes fit. She did good deeds and made herself see the best in people in a kind of a belligerent you-should-do-this-too way. She smiled and said, "I guess we misjudged Uncle Hiram, even if he does talk that mean way. We should be grateful to him."

"Poor girl," Marietta commented. "She isn't very smart about people." At least this time Marietta didn't stop the tape.

"He did leave you fifteen million dollars each," I said dryly.

But I must watch the canned memory. "Fifteen million dollars," I heard Brian the Lion say in that soft, wondering voice of his.

"To make us miserable," crowed Wingate's gravelly voice. He stood up and jumped into the air and let out a rebel yell — Wingate the dignified real-estate man. "Miserable!" he cried, and then he began to laugh. There was something catching about his laugh, or maybe the family were all in shock and a little bit hysterical. First, Goldie, the jewelry gal — I was sure I heard it clank as she laughed. Then a childlike "hee-hee," which must be Brian the Lion. Finally a chorus of "ha-ha-ha," so infectious that as I watched those taped laughers I began to laugh, too. So did Marietta, though her eyes stayed sad and she kept catching her breath, struggling to stop. We couldn't help roaring with belly laughter. We shook till we almost fell out of those solid, dependable chairs. We laughed till our throats hurt.

Marietta turned off the tape. "It sucks you in," she said. "The sound of it gets you. Like having your feet tickled, only much worse. Even when we know we need to be serious and wise."

"I understand," I said. "You need to find

out what really happened, and I've some-times managed to shed some light on crimes. But I think that was luck. I hope I can help this time."

"You're my friend," Marietta said. "You won't just tell me, like the law did, that there aren't enough clues to be positive there was foul play. You'll help me find out what happened." She paused as tears came to her eyes, and she blew her nose. I went to her and put my arm around her.

"Because one thing is sure," Marietta said. "My brother Wingate, who was afraid of heights, who stayed away from heights, fell or was pushed off a mountain overlook two weeks ago and died. Two weeks ago, at nine o'clock in the morning." She was trembling hard. "And I believe that Win-gate's death was somehow caused by Hiram's will."

CHAPTER
2

TUESDAY, JULY 15

I went right home and fixed my backward calendar. That's something it took me a while to figure out. If you can put something you want to remember in the future on your calendar, why can't you use those nice little write-in squares for things in the past? You can. Depending, of course, on how far back your calendar goes. In the niche for Friday, June 27, I put *Wingate. Fell to death, about nine a.m.* right above *Dentist 9:30.* If I ever needed one, I had an alibi because the dentist is more than an hour away from Linville Falls. Then on Tuesday, July 15, future division, I wrote *To Linville Falls with Marietta.* That was nine a.m., too. I'd agreed to go look at the place where Wingate fell or was pushed to his death.

We met at my house, and I drove. My husband, Ted, who has a talent for such things, highlighted the map before he went off to teach summer school.

"So your uncle Hiram predicted that after you inherited his money, things would go wrong," I said as I turned onto Route 19-23. "And two of the eight heirs are dead within a year. That seems weird." I was not tactful. Marietta and I have always been open with each other.

"Uncle Hiram wasn't always so bitter," she said. "He got mad at the world when he got sick, and turned nasty. Before that, he was a cross between a bad boy and Santa Claus. He chased girls even when he was married. He was unpredictable. But he often helped us finance business deals and projects. He had no children. We were his kin."

"You'd expected him to die?"

"Oh, yes. A year before Hiram went, the doctor said he had three months to live. He was a fighter. In some ways Wingate was like him, a skirt chaser. But Wingate could charm the birds out of the trees. I really miss my brother." She swallowed hard.

We passed a truck marked PREFERRED BEVERAGES.

"But you don't miss the cousin who drank herself to death," I said thoughtfully. Marietta is not usually cold-hearted. "How did that happen?"

"Cousin Poo. Yes. The night after the reading of the will — when we found out we were going to be filthy rich — Wingate invited us all to a celebration. I think we were all in a slight state of shock. Who else but the other heirs would understand how it felt? Heady, but a little scary. Sort of unreal. Because, knowing Hiram, he could have left it all to the Red Cross or the Sierra Club. But he left it to us. So we all went to Wingate's party. Wingate even invited the Fox and Annie Long and Cousin Poo, who rarely went to parties. She was one of those people who just can't relate to anyone. In fact, if she showed up when you'd had a stroke of luck, she'd point out that *she* hadn't, and so it wasn't fair. Like when Lillian's poodle won first place in a dog show and Poo said that her own dog had been hit by a truck. And the worst thing was that she whined in B-flat minor."

I'm not musical, but that sounded bad. "Still," I said, "in this case she had good luck, or what most folks would call good luck, inheriting all that money."

"At Wingate's party, she laughed and drank toasts and was downright human. She drank so much it killed her. Acute alcohol poisoning, the doctor said. That was ten months ago."

I was quiet thinking that something that ought to help a person bloom — like fifteen million dollars — could actually help kill her.

"I didn't sleep last night," Marietta said. "I kept lying awake trying to think why anyone would be so angry at Wingate that they'd push him off a cliff. I mean, he could be annoying — like the time he stood me up on my birthday because he got diverted. But he always made up for it. He was like that." She yawned. "I might take a catnap," she said. So I enjoyed the beauty of the Blue Ridge Parkway by myself.

She woke up as we drove into the parking lot for Linville Falls. An American flag was waving from a pole. It was a big lot with tall trees all around it, but largely deserted. Only a battered blue car and a red pickup truck were parked along one edge, and this was at nine o'clock in the morning. I parked near the weathered wood reception shed, and we disembarked. Marietta had a grim look around her mouth and sad eyes as she scanned the lot. Familiar Marietta in jeans and a man's shirt over a red T. Only change from the usual was a pair of binoculars around her neck. She walked resolutely into the shed.

Along one wall were maps of trails and overlooks. "We have to walk a ways," she said, and led me through the building to a metal bridge with three-tier railings, over a stream the color of tea. We crossed to a wide path lightly shaded by trees, with ferns and wildflowers along one side of the path, a steep rise on the other. The air had a wonderful woodsy smell, like mushrooms but fresher.

This was a long walk, but even when I almost tripped over the exposed roots of trees that snaked across the path, I felt drawn into the charm of the place. Some of the trees along the path were huge, hemlocks so tall I almost got a crick in my neck looking up to the top. They'd be old enough to go back to the days of Hiawatha with his murmuring pines and hemlocks. That was in Longfellow's poem that I learned in the sixth grade.

"Why would Wingate take such a long walk with his killer?" I asked out loud. "Gunpoint would risk discovery by tourists. He must have come of his own free will."

Marietta kicked a pebble, which arced into a patch of fern. "I don't know," she said angrily. "We haven't seen any tourists yet, and it's the same time of day. They could arrive at any moment. Maybe someone had a concealed gun. Or maybe Wingate thought he was with a friend." She began to cry quietly.

I reached over and squeezed her hand. "We'll find out what happened."

Finally a path went off to the left. "That leads to the top of the falls," Marietta said. "We want to go much higher, to the very top of the gorge overlooking the falls."

Now the path was rockier, the going harder, but before I was entirely out of breath, we came to the overlook. It was down some wooden steps, with a fairly flat stone floor and a low rock wall on three sides. And here were tourists!

A pretty dark-haired girl in white shorts was sitting on the low wall at the edge. A smiling young man backed up onto the stairs and took her picture with the view in back of her. And what a view!

To the left, far below, was the white spray of falls, coming from halfway down a sheer stone cliff. The falls had plainly worn the cliff away. In back of that casually perched girl was the drop to the gorge. I shivered.

I was relieved when she jumped up toward us, off the wall, and boy and girl left arm in arm. Perhaps on their honeymoon.

That dramatic view beyond the low wall where the girl had been perched must have been the last thing Wingate saw. Had the condemned man enjoyed his last view? I remembered Wingate could describe a house for sale and make it sound colorful and intriguing and well built, as if it was all that mattered in the world. Had he cared about nature? Was that why he came here?

I went to the edge of the overlook wall and shuddered to discover that the cliff plummeted almost straight down. I thought of that girl sitting there, and my skin crawled. The young do not expect to die. I made myself look over the edge. My stomach rose into my mouth. The distance was so great. First came a rugged stone cliff, down, down, down. I felt dizzy. I felt as if the suction of the drop might grab me and pull me over. I stepped back and shuddered. Wingate would never — ever — have been careless at the edge of a drop like that. He wouldn't, for example, step onto the wall. Would he?

"Wingate's head burst open on a rock ledge. His bones were broken. It was horrible," Marietta said.

I could imagine.

"And all this happened just a week ago," I said, "while I was off visiting my father in

Tennessee." I pulled the newspaper clipping about Wingate out of my pocketbook. Anything to take my eyes off that drop. I read it out loud.

WINGATE SCOTT DEAD IN FALL, the headline said. " 'Wingate Scott, 60, of Asheville, died of a fall into Linville Gorge at around 8:50 a.m. on Monday. Two tourists from Maine told rangers they saw the body falling from an overlook. They called the Watauga County Sheriff's Department. Scott's car had been parked in the Linville Falls parking lot when the tourists arrived, and it appeared that he was at the overlook alone when he fell.' "

"Alone, my foot," said Marietta. "Somebody must have pushed him or brought him here at gunpoint. He was afraid of heights." She pointed toward the gorge. "At least no one would fail to notice his red Cadillac convertible in the parking lot. That's what he took his last drive in. So he must have been in a good mood. He drove his black Ferrari when he felt out of sorts. He bought three cars when he got the money." Tears came to her eyes.

I read on. " 'No witness has been found who saw anyone else at that overlook on Monday morning, a deputy sheriff said, adding that while there were no immediate indications of foul play, his department was investigating every angle. The death occurred a few miles from a spot where two women fell to their deaths in 1988.' "

I vaguely remembered. One woman's husband had been accused of murder, but he'd been acquitted. Then I remembered one of those little details that stick in my mind when I even forget my best friend's name. Strange. A pathologist had said both women's legs were injured in a way that suggested they'd stepped off the ledge feet first. Which didn't sound like being pushed. That probably convinced the jury.

Why did they step off to death? By mistake? To kill themselves? Two people together? In my mind, I heard their screams fade as they fell into the void. "So, suppose someone wanted to lure Wingate here, how would they do it?" I asked Marietta.

Before she could answer, two teens came running up the stone steps and joined us. "Yeah, there was a man killed right here," said the boy excitedly. "Can you imagine that?" The girl shoved him, and he screamed. They were not too near the edge, but I gasped again. When it comes to heights, I'm a sissy.

"You kids stop that, or I'll call the ranger," Marietta barked, and the two chased each other back onto the path, laughing wildly.

"A height like this is a tried-and-true death spot," Marietta said, looking down into the gorge below us. "The sheriff says that anybody would figure that this would be an effective place to jump." She hugged herself.

"All you've got to do is look," I said. "Waterfalls, like that one" — I pointed to Linville Falls — "are beautiful, but they're seductive. Like sirens. So tourists get killed wading in the river just above the falls, or climbing on slippery rocks, or climbing over the safety walls at overlooks. Heedless as those kids." I remembered a book Ted had about photographing North Carolina waterfalls. It said something like: "If you step over the overlook wall to get a better picture, at least have the courtesy to tell the ranger ahead of time so he can arrange for divers to find you and bring a body bag." Yes, there were accidents. "But this place isn't seductive like that," I said. "The edge looks dangerous."

"Wingate would never have taken chances on the edge of a cliff," Marietta said. "Everybody who knew him said that. And he would never kill himself. He had everything to live for."

"Why did the sheriff favor suicide?" I asked.

"Because he's a lazy dolt." Marietta bristled. "Because there were no easy clues to murder."

"And maybe," I said, "because he gathered evidence that he thought showed murder once, and then the man was acquitted. Maybe he didn't want to go through that twice."

"I don't know." Marietta stood with her back to the gorge. Easier not to see the drop. "But I do know Wingate would never have jumped on purpose." She clenched her fists. She walked over and sat down on the lowest stone step and looked more thoughtful. "You see, he'd begun to discover how great it felt to be a philanthropist. He discovered it was more fun than buying new cars. I mean, how many cars can one man drive? But he could make a difference in a lot of people's lives and feel good about so many thank-yous. So Wingate was in hog heaven." Marietta turned unhappily toward the gorge. "On top of that, he was too squeamish to take a chance on crushing his head like that, even if he wanted to die." She sighed. "Wingate would have killed himself in some neater way, perhaps with sleeping pills. He would have wanted to arrange for an obituary that mentioned his generosity, not a news story about falling."

Personally I could not imagine that jumping off a mountain was a good way to go. Suppose you changed your mind halfway down?

I borrowed Marietta's binoculars and knelt, leaning my arms on the stone wall. The stone terrace was hard on my knees, but my center of gravity was so low I felt safe. Straight down below there was a rocky spot. Had Wingate died instantly as he hit? I hoped so.

"So you're not happy with the Watauga County sheriff's investigation," I said as I studied the underbrush. Nothing to see but some broken twigs.

"Not when he assumed this was suicide," said Marietta. "And he did, until we yelled and screamed so loud, and had the best lawyers in the mountains yell and scream loud. Then he felt he had to go through the motions of an investigation."

I stood up and handed her back the binoculars.

She began to pace up and down the overlook. "Mostly the sheriff has just questioned us. Maybe because we're from over the line in Buncombe County. Nobody else. Some investigation — just a little over a week!" She stopped suddenly. "He isn't trying." She glanced over the edge of the overlook. "I hate this place. It's beautiful, but I still hate it."

"Come on," I said, "we don't have to stay here by the falls. Let's go walk." We found a map of trails on a signpost and drove to a likely one with an overlook right by the road. We hiked off among the flat green leaves of rhododendron bushes, steeply downhill.

"It sounds to me as if your family members are all too busy spending money to have the time to kill anybody," I said. I could say that to Marietta. She'd told me she'd paid her taxes, put a third of her money in a community foundation to handle good works, given two thirds to a money manager to take care of, and gone on living almost as she did before she got the money. Except that she could hire someone to do more of the work at the nursery, and that gave her more time to play the violin.

"Since Hal died" — that was Marietta's much-older husband — "I've realized I'm no good at running a nursery business," she'd told me. "So I've hired a business manager, which is wonderful." Every

43

woman to her own luxury.

We passed a man and woman and a child of about six with a bunch of wildflowers in her hand. Hey, she wasn't supposed to pick those.

"How is Goldie's house coming?" I asked. Goldie was building a huge house with a pond and an island in the middle, and a fountain on the island. She'd invited me by to see it, and I was so curious I went. But that was in the early stages when all she had to show were tentative plans.

"It will look a little like the palace at Versailles," Marietta said. Marietta does exaggerate. "But you're right — it keeps her busy. That, and buying clothes. Her son Brian says he hopes the largest rooms in that house can be turned into closets. Brian wants to travel. He seems kind of lost. He's so young. I worry about him. Wingate's son, Rich, is very busy setting up his educational foundation. It's a lot more work than he thought. Yes, we're all busy. Wingate's daughter, Winnie, has even had a nose job and a tummy tuck. She's spending her money on that thug who showed up out of nowhere and says he loves her. But she's happy for now. Even her father's death didn't throw her for a loop. Unfortunately I think my granddaughter Lil is suffering from money overload. Lil liked figuring out how to get what she wanted. Now she can have anything anytime, and that seems to bore her. She's drinking too much. But that wouldn't make her want to kill Wingate, for heaven's sake."

"So what is happening in the family that doesn't make sense?" I asked.

"Brian has invited Annie Long to travel with him and be his social secretary, more like his mother," Marietta said. "He's very hush-hush about that but he told me."

"Annie Long?" The name sounded vaguely familiar.

"Oh," she said, "don't you remember? She was in the will. She was Uncle Hiram's housekeeper. Had been for years. She was home in bed with the flu when the Fox read us the will or she'd have been there. She got ten thousand dollars outright from Uncle Hiram. She was at Wingate's celebration, looking better."

Yes, it all came back. "You need to talk to her," Marietta said. "Annie knows more about Uncle Hiram than anybody else in this world. She's worked for him for thirty years. Maybe she even knows why he wrote his will that way. Though he'd be pleased, no doubt, to know that we could all be suspects in the sheriff's eyes, because, under

45

the terms of the will, we all inherit part of Wingate's money."

"And Brian has hired Annie Long. You think that's strange?"

"For my grandson, who's just nineteen? Yes, I do think it's strange to pick a fifty-five-year-old woman to travel around the world with."

But it didn't sound like a lead to Wingate's murder — if indeed it had been a murder.

"Anything else odd?" I asked Marietta.

"Yes. Goldie thinks she's being stalked. But when I ask her what she's seen, she says nothing. It's just a feeling she has. I think she's getting paranoid, like Uncle Hiram."

Odd, though, that they both got paranoid in the same way.

"It does seem as though Hiram arranged to create trouble no matter what happened after he died," I said. I could imagine him preplanning Wingate's murder with a killer hired before he died. Suspicion to fall on the rest of his heirs. But that was too far-fetched even for that angry old goat.

"So if not a family member, who do you think pushed Wingate?" I asked Marietta.

"I can't imagine," she said. She hesitated. "But something is wrong. When

Goldie told me she has the feeling that someone is stalking her, I thought it was her imagination. Because Hiram had said someone was stalking him, and I think that suggested it to Goldie. She can't give me a single concrete example of something that could only be a stalking. She says it's just a feeling she has, that she's being watched. But occasionally I've felt the same way."

I shivered. I realized I had the same eyes-on-my-back goose bumps. Was I suggestible? We'd been walking briskly down the trail and were a good ways down the side of the gorge.

I looked up. Someone was standing on an overlook near the edge, looking down at us. It wasn't the overlook we'd been at before, because the incline below this one was very steep, but not too steep for a path to wind along. From this distance I couldn't see the face clearly, especially since the person wore a baseball cap. The face was in dark shadow. I looked at Marietta. "So you've felt that someone might be following you?" I asked.

"Occasionally," she said, "but maybe it's my imagination."

My eyes went back to the person at the overlook. But I couldn't see — the sun was in my eyes. I couldn't even be sure if it was an adult or a child. He or she picked up something from the wall and threw it toward us. A rock hit the ground with a loud thump a short distance from us. Since it hit on the path and bounced along, I could actually tell which rock it was. It was quite a small rock, the size of the end of my thumb. But if that rock had hit one of us from so far above, we'd be hurt badly.

"Good Lord!" Marietta cried. "What idiot threw that?"

We both looked up, and no one was at the overlook.

"The moon is full," Marietta said. "That's why kids are acting crazy." Her voice shook.

"That's possible," I said. "It's also possible that someone hated your uncle Hiram so badly that they've transferred that hatred to his heirs. That's you. So let's hope it's crazy kids — but be careful."

My stomach puckered inside.

CHAPTER
3

HEAT

Marietta picked up the rock and turned it over in her hand. It was a pinkish granite with a streak of clear quartz, roundish but rough. It fit in the palm of her slender sturdy hand. She looked at the rock with a puzzled frown, then anger swept the frown away. "Damn it! Who threw this?" she yelled, and began to run up the path to the overlook, still clutching the rock. I ran right after her up the long and winding path, which left us out of breath.

I was not surprised that when we got to the overlook, it was deserted. Marietta seethed. "Yes!" she said. "Somebody has it in for us!"

Now, I have to admit there's a side of me that says, *On the other hand . . .*

"It could have been a crazy kid," I said. "Wingate could have fallen. We don't know. But the more strange things happen, the more we need to find out why."

"Yes, and there's so little time," she said as we approached the car. "Let me drive," she said. "That'll be good for my nerves. I'll feel like I'm doing something."

It took a minute after we were in our places for what she'd said about time to sink in. "There's so little time for what?" I asked.

"In three days we all leave for England," she announced as she swerved around a curve.

"England! Why on earth haven't you told me that before?" I groaned. "Exactly what's going on?"

Marietta looked sheepish. "Remember when the Fox read the will? Remember how we all have to go to England together and visit the damn dead English earl's village? Or else we lose the money? Well, we haven't gone yet. Everybody's been too busy. Or too pigheaded or something. And the time is nearly up. So while my poor brother Wingate was still in good health, I arranged for us to go over on the Concorde, the fastest plane in the world. Then I've laid on a bus to the village. We'll all come back on the *Ocean Queen*. We'll have it over with and be back in less than a week. Everybody liked that plan because they didn't have to do anything but just go. And the will said they had to go to keep their money. So we all agreed. We've also agreed not to let this tragedy stop us. We need to get this over with."

"And how do you expect me to talk to everybody before you take off?" I asked. "How do you expect me to look into Wingate's death?"

"I haven't been thinking clearly," she said. "I've had so much on my mind that I simply figured what doesn't get done before we leave can be done when we get back." She stopped and sighed.

"Maybe I should go with you," I said, letting myself daydream. "That would be a luxurious way to try to find a killer!"

She looked taken aback. "We'll only be gone a few days, and there's a lot you can find out here."

I felt I had a nerve asking to be taken on a cruise.

"Evidently this is not my travel year," I said, embarrassed. "Ted and I were all set to go to Peru for a vacation — we even had our passports updated — and then he fell and pulled a tendon in his right leg." When I'm embarrassed I do rattle on. "I've always wanted to see the Aztec ruins, ever since I read a book about them last year.

But it would have been no fun to go if Ted couldn't walk."

Marietta stuck to her point. "I hope you can talk to some of my folks before we leave. And then ask around here. I hope you won't be embarrassed if I say I'd like to pay you for your time."

"Pay me in herbal advice," I said. "And when you're more on an even keel, remember to tell me what I need to know related to Wingate. But you really mean to go on this trip now? With Wingate just dead?"

"Yes," she said. "Maybe it will help to get away. And we can grieve anywhere."

I shrugged. It wouldn't look good. If the sheriff got suspicious, he'd get more suspicious.

"I'll start asking questions," I said. "Who should I talk to first? And meanwhile slow down. A speeding ticket won't help." I expected her to say talk to Goldie. After all, Goldie thought she was being stalked.

Marietta didn't hesitate. "Go talk to Winnie and meet her boyfriend. He wants her money. And he'll never be satisfied that any amount is enough." She flushed with anger just talking about the man. "I won't tell you any more, except he just loves the idea of sailing on the *Ocean Queen*. He's a gold digger. Winnie's acting like a fool. But go find out about him for yourself." She slammed on the brakes to avoid a crow eating a dead possum in the middle of the road. I think she enjoyed the *whump* when she hit the possum. Almost as good as a slap, and who could she slap? Not me. I was being helpful.

Winnie was thirty years old, and, as far as I knew, no member of the opposite sex had ever given her a tumble. She'd not only acted like a wet blanket, but also she'd looked a little like one. Shapeless and droopy. Except for her nose, which was too big. Real wet blankets have no mouths, though, and Winnie had self-righteousness spewing out of hers. Not a sexy combination. And yet there'd been something touching about Winnie. She'd tried so hard to prove she was a good person. She'd obviously wanted to impress her father, but he had treated her as if she wasn't there. Now he was dead.

But Marietta said that Winnie'd had a nose job and a tummy tuck. She was making an effort to look good. And evidently somebody cared about her. So why not be glad?

"They bought a house out in Bent Creek," Marietta said. "That is to say,

53

Winnie bought the house, and Alexander lives there with her. Up in a clearing in the woods. Winnie is not interested in building houses. In fact, she's not interested in houses at all, except to be sure they're energy-efficient and all that. She found one where the last owner had put in solar heat. Although she hardly needs any added heat with that boyfriend." Marietta raised her eyebrows so high I was afraid she'd knock her cap off. She smirked. "Just the two of them alone in the woods. Wait till you find out all about him!"

But on the way home along the winding parkway, she refused to tell me more about the man. Marietta believes in the impact of learning about things firsthand. In fact, she talked about her herb farm and how she wished her thyme would grow faster and suchlike. She gave me a lecture about gingko tea. She was shocked, she said, that I wasn't drinking it to improve my memory.

"Why, Asheville is full of gingko trees," she said. "You could just pick a few leaves as you wander around downtown. But if everybody did that, the trees would be bare, so I'll bring you some tea, and you must drink it every day. For years gingko has been known to improve memory. You're behind the times."

So, okay, I hadn't done much with herbs. Marietta would reform me.

Meanwhile we drove past breathtaking views and gentle clumps of wildflowers. Yes, I thought, the views would really be *breath*taking if you fell off the side of the mountain. Luckily not many places were dangerously steep. Finally we came to downtown Asheville, with its few tall buildings and many interesting ones, like the pink rococo city hall built in the 1920s and the simple mirror-glass-and-stone building by I. M. Pei. That wonderfully stark and modern structure reflects a colorful older building complete with gargoyles. Asheville has a way of interweaving the new and the old and coming up with the unexpected.

We wound through town, and eventually I dropped Marietta off near her car in the downtown parking lot. I drove on toward the Biltmore Mall and stopped for a late snack at McDonald's near the mall. I hurried on to Winnie's, which is farther down that road. I read the number on the mailbox, the only clue that this was the right place, and drove up a long winding gravel driveway into a clearing. Hey, I liked her house. It sat in a sunny space, and daisies bloomed at the edge of the woods around it.

Not a house that matched the Winnie I remembered. No boyfriend in sight. No neighbors in yelling distance as far as I could tell.

The house was modern and also old-timey. There was weathered board-and-batten siding and a fieldstone chimney. There were also lots of large glass windows. Around the side, I could see solar panels in back of the house. I parked in a gravel area bounded by old railroad ties and noticed as I got out of the car that the far side of the parking area was the top of a small cliff. I went to the edge and looked over. The drop was tiny compared with Linville Gorge. But the reminder made my stomach clench.

I hurried up a flagstone walk to the front door. Nobody was in sight. I hoped I hadn't outsmarted myself by not calling ahead. I'd thought the surprise factor might be fruitful. I knocked. Long wait.

I thought about the Winnie I remembered — asking me for money for good causes. For the shelter for battered women or the Friends of Animals or suchlike. She always emphasized the horror story. The woman whose husband had polka-dotted her with cigarette burns. The dog who'd been abandoned in a pen without water and food when the family moved away. And something in her manner always suggested she had a lot in common with those victims, though she never said so. So how was she coping with good luck?

I couldn't see anyone through the windows, but a large freestanding fieldstone fireplace hid parts of the room. I had almost given up when Winnie opened the front door, slightly breathless, as if she'd been rushing. To get dressed? She was buttoning the top button on her white blouse.

She was obviously dressed to please in what looked like designer jeans, a slinky white knit blouse that buttoned down the front, and red sandals. She'd lost at least twenty pounds in the right places, and her face was carefully made up with lipstick to match the shoes. I wanted to say, Good for you! On the other hand, she did not appear to be a woman overcome with grief for the father who'd just died.

"Hi," I said. "This is a lovely house. Excuse me for dropping by unannounced."

"The house is very efficient," she said flatly, and eyed me as if I might be some kind of spy. No, she hadn't been taking lessons in charm. But wow, she'd sure been to the beauty parlor. Her hair was almost as blond as Goldie's and piled in disheveled curls on top of her head. This was obviously on-purpose disheveled. The I-have-just-been-laid look. Possibly accurate this time, judging by my long wait.

"I was so sorry to hear about your father," I said.

Manners prevailed. She led me past a large wrought-iron frame full of firewood, around the stone fireplace, and into the living room. The huge fireplace was open in two directions, like a square tunnel. "It heats both ways," Winnie said as she caught me staring. "Also, those things that look like andirons are water pipes. The fire heats water that circulates under the floor. That helps heat the house." The pride in her voice was a good sign. She was forgetting to be suspicious. God bless the fireplace. No fire on such a warm day, of course.

And where was the warm boyfriend?

"I wanted to talk to you about your father," I said. "I visited the place where he died."

Was that grief that softened her face? But then suspicion quickly sharpened it again. "Aunt Marietta took you there!" she accused. "She has some silly notion he was deliberately killed. She riled the sheriff till he gave us the third degree. We don't need that!" she said. "I don't believe my father was pushed." Her voice began to climb. "Heights made him dizzy." I could feel her edging me back toward the door. "That's why he fell."

I thought: *The idea that he was pushed is very frightening to her.*

Marietta had sure set her off.

"I just wanted to talk to you about what he was like as a person," I said, "and I also hoped you'd show me how the solar heat works in this remarkable house." Heat was the subject that calmed her down. Calm was better than being thrown out. "I wanted to talk about how your father was enjoying his life. I gather he gave to good causes. I saw his face in the paper a lot."

She nodded and smiled shyly, and indicated I should sit down on the long couch that faced the fireplace. Good.

"He enjoyed helping people," she said. "He even helped me. I don't think he really liked me before." She frowned. "We didn't have much in common. He wanted me to be a pretty little girl, and I wasn't." Sadness in her voice.

But now you are *pretty,* I thought, and I realized that the nose job gave her face a cheerful, pert cast. She'd become appealing by a nose. I wondered how it felt to know that someone liked you not because of what you could do but because of what a surgeon could do and what the best hairdresser could do. Wouldn't that make you mad?

"All of a sudden my father and I had the same problems to solve," she said, and smiled with satisfaction.

Off to one side of the room, a man appeared and stood quite still, listening. He looked as if he belonged on the cover of a romance novel. He had brown curly hair, slightly long around the ears, limpid eyes, and a chest span that suggested steroids. He wore tight jeans and a white shirt unbuttoned down the front to show some of that magnificent chest. He seemed happy for me to admire him. Winnie, who was turned toward me, didn't seem to see him.

"You know it's a lot of work, having money," she said with a sigh. "I never knew that. I have to be sure it's all invested in a socially responsible way. I have to give it to several money managers so that if one is stupid I won't lose everything. I have to double-check what they do." She sighed again.

I was tempted to laugh and say she could give it to me, but I restrained myself.

"And, after the first month, when he

went a little crazy and bought everything in sight, my father was careful with his money, too. By then I'd done a lot of research. I could give him suggestions."

The gorgeous man winked at me and grinned. Quite plainly he meant that Winnie could go overboard on suggestions.

I opened my mouth to call Mr. Handsome to her attention, to ask to be introduced.

What Winnie said next stopped me.

"My father was not like Aunt Marietta, who has just one money manager and lets him do what he pleases. Marietta doesn't want to bother with money, or with double-checking, and I think she's being robbed blind."

"You think her money is being handled by a crook?" I was alarmed. I could see right off that Marietta could ignore money and be robbed.

"Exactly," Winnie said. "That's hardly fair to her daughter."

Fair. If Winnie was into fair, she had reason to be mad about that, too. "Do you think it's fair that half your father's money will be divided among Uncle Hiram's other heirs because your father died in less than a year after your uncle?" I asked. What a strange provision of that strange will.

"*I* resent it!" cried Mr. Handsome in a mellow, sexy voice. Winnie turned, startled. "It's not fair to Winnie," he complained. Then his voice went hard. "And personally I think old Wingate was pushed."

"This is Alexander Flint," Winnie said. Her eyes said, Isn't he wonderful? And he's mine. I half expected her to melt into a puddle of sheer joy.

As for Alexander, he thought he was great. Alexander the Great. But he probably had a heart as hard as flint. Alexander Flint-heart the Great.

He sauntered closer, broadcasting the aroma of expensive aftershave. "May I have the privilege of sitting between you two lovely ladies?" He raised my pulse even while he annoyed me.

"This is Peaches Dann, Marietta's friend," Winnie told him. "She's actually helped solve a couple of murders, which impresses Marietta. Peaches is forgetful, so she's written a book called *How to Survive Without a Memory.*"

Alexander burst out laughing. "So you're an amateur detective who can't remember! That's rich! Hey, if you find a killer, can you remember his name?"

"Anyone who can't remember has to be

a detective," I said. "I've had practice." I stared him down.

"I understand the sheriff says Wingate may have jumped," I said. "I promised Marietta I'd just try to find out about his state of mind before he died." I wasn't being tactful. I had the distinct feeling that Winnie wanted me to vanish.

"My father seemed fine," she said. Her inflection said, So that's all you need to know. Go away.

"He was interested in this house, for instance?" I asked.

She mellowed. "Oh, yes. It was his idea to use photovoltaic cells."

Alexander the Great yawned. He ran his hand lightly up and down Winnie's back. Her color heightened. But the photo-whatever cells had her in thrall. "They are in that panel on the roof of the garage," she said, and pulled me outdoors to see the panel on a slanting shingle roof. Alexander came, too. "NASA developed them to make power from sunlight in space," she continued. "We make so much power that way that we are not even connected to the power company. The extra power is stored in batteries in the garage."

Alexander the Great nuzzled her cheek. He was not interested in extra power. Except his own. He massaged the small of her back. He was not inhibited.

"We conserve power, too," she said. "We have special lightbulbs —"

"Winnie doesn't want to think someone pushed her father," Alexander interrupted. "She'd rather think about lightbulbs. But personally, I'm a realist." He turned to Winnie. "If someone did push Wingate, we don't want that person to profit from murder, Winnie." He hugged her and at the same time he gave me an I-need-you-too smile.

If he had killed Wingate, he wouldn't keep saying that Wingate was pushed, would he? Or was this an act for my benefit?

Winnie was pointing to the far end of the parking area. "But my father wouldn't even go near the edge of our little drop-off. It made him so dizzy."

"So he wouldn't go near Linville Falls unless someone kidnapped him and took him there," Alexander said.

As we walked back into the house, I asked Winnie, "Who was angry at your father?"

"No one was angry enough to kill him!" she said. "There were some people who wanted to give a huge gift to endow special purchases at the art museum. The name was Markham. Then they discovered the museum didn't invest its money in special socially acceptable funds, and for some reason the museum board refused to guarantee they'd always do that. The museum people said they had to have flexibility. So the Markhams canceled their gift. Wingate told the museum he'd replace it. The Markhams were in a rage. They wrote letters to the editor like you wouldn't believe."

Actually I remembered them. They called Wingate a contributing factor in the self-destruction of the human race.

"They said Wingate encouraged the bottom-line philosophy that is destroying this country," Winnie explained.

Mr. Handsome patted Winnie and said, "This gal has a very fetching bottom line."

Now Winnie smirked. Then she was serious again. "Of course, those people had a point. But the art museum said they'd keep the money in socially acceptable funds unless those began to pay much less than the going market rate. Did you know that socially responsible funds, where they screen their holdings for bad labor practices and pollution and stuff like that, do just as well? Did you know —"

But I needed to know about Wingate.

"Who else was angry at your father?" I asked as we came back inside.

"He began to look into giving money and he said some of the charities around town were protecting their own turf and duplicating services," she said. "He said it when the newspaper did a story about him after he helped the art museum. That annoyed some folks."

I could see a headline, PHILANTHROPIST KILLED FOR BEING PICKY. I didn't think it would fly.

"Your mother and father were divorced, right?" I said.

"My mother died five years ago."

"Did Wingate have a girlfriend?"

Winnie squirmed. "He had a lot of girlfriends," she said. "After Mother died he was secretive about some things. He used to go off for vacations by himself. Lately I've wondered if he was really by himself. He was whistling a lot as if he had a happy secret. I didn't see him the day before he died. Rich says he was depressed that day." She glanced at Alexander the Great and started to melt again. Now she understood what a force love — or at least physical attraction — could be.

Alexander looked at his watch. "I have to go pick up some things," he said. He meant I should leave. "Come back any-time." So I walked with them toward the door, where he took car keys off a hook, kissed Winnie a passionate good-bye as if he was off to the moon, and we both went to our cars, Alexander first. At the end of the driveway I carefully turned in the opposite direction from his. I drove down the road a mile, then turned around and came back. When I arrived at the door, Winnie opened her mouth in surprise. That red mouth that matched her shoes. Before she could say anything, I said, "I forgot my pocketbook." First time I ever forgot it on purpose.

She opened the door grudgingly. I made a show of looking around for the pocketbook. Actually I'd set it on the floor against the end of the couch. Since my pocketbook was tan and the couch was tan, and the floor was tannish wood, the pocketbook had almost vanished. While pretending to search, I said, "You must have other ways to save energy, too." Keep her helpful.

So she told me about the special fluorescent lightbulbs that cost more than the regular kind but last much longer to make up for it. "They use much less power." That didn't give me an excuse to visit the rest of the house. There was nothing in the living room but a couch and a few chairs and a very large television set. Also a framed poster of a tremendous old tree with a motto: SAVE PAPER TO SAVE TREES.

I could see through to the kitchen, which seemed like any other kitchen, with stove, refrigerator, cabinets. Winnie's house looked almost conventional. And there were no personal clues: no books being read or special-interest magazines lying around. No phone numbers jotted down by the phone. I was plotting how to get in the bedroom when she saved me the trouble.

"We have a wonderful free way of lighting closets," she said. "Come see." So I followed her into the room at the other end of the house. Yes, it was a bedroom. Complete with unmade bed. Two bedside tables and two long bureaus along one wall. One bedside table sported an ashtray, a pack of cigarettes, and a lighter. Must be Alexander's side. A novel with a place marked sat on Winnie's side. She opened the door to a spacious walk-in closet. A round hole in the ceiling let in bright light. "A skylight?" I asked. Nothing new about that, and yet the light seemed unusually bright.

She laughed. "There's another bedroom upstairs that I use for an office. And a closet above this one. So this is a tube that goes right up through that closet to the sky. The tube has mirrors in it that concentrate the light down here. Clever, isn't it?"

The clothes so well lighted in the closet were hers on one side and his on the other. More his than hers, I noticed.

He had silk shirts in luscious colors and jackets that looked sexy to the touch. But nothing about those clothes gave me a hint except that he was sensual and vain about his looks.

On the bureaus were baskets that held personal effects. Winnie's hairbrush and comb and makeup. He had more jewelry, I noticed. Even a pair of gold cuff links. "Do people still wear cuff links?" I asked. I picked them up, which was pushy of me, but I noticed they had initials on them.

The initials were *H.R.L.*

"They belonged to Alexander's father," Winnie said quickly. Her eyes were wide with fear. She realized she'd let me see something I should not have seen. Winnie was not good at lying.

"His name is not Alexander Flint," I guessed. "If these were his father's, they prove his last name isn't Flint."

Winnie glared at me. "You have to snoop

into everything, don't you? Well, don't bother to look into Alexander. I already know he's been in prison and I don't care. He told me himself. He's paid for his crime and he has a right to start over."

"What was his crime?" I asked.

"A very common crime," she said, and now her voice was pleading, asking me to agree. "He killed his wife when he found her with another man. It was a crime of passion. Not the sort of thing he'd do again. He was so young, just eighteen years old."

"And he was on steroids," I said, "which lowered his self-control."

She didn't deny it. "He's never taken steroids since."

"Does the sheriff know he killed his wife?" I asked.

"Not that I know of," she said. "But if he finds out, it won't be the end of the world. If people find out and get ugly, we'll have to go and live somewhere else, that's all."

"I probably won't tell for now," I said, "because there's no proof it had anything to do with what happened to your father. But I'll put all the information I find in a safe place, where it will be found if anything happens to me."

"That's ridiculous!" she cried. "And you

don't need to try to prove that Alex killed my father," she said angrily. "He has an ironclad alibi."

"I'm glad of that," I said. "Have a great time in England. And watch your back."

I admit I intended to make her mad. Anger often makes a person more likely to spill the beans. I waited for her to tell me about Alex's perfect alibi and trusted that it would develop cracks.

CHAPTER
4

TUESDAY AFTERNOON, JULY 15

"So how did Alexander kill his first wife?" I asked.

"You put it so crudely," she said. "They had a fight. She hit him first."

I thought of his steroid-enhanced chest span and worked hard not to laugh.

"Unfortunately they were on the fifteenth floor of a building in Miami. He got into a blind rage, he says, when he found her with another man, who was a coward, of course, and ran away, but his wife began to yell that he neglected her, so she had a right. He pushed her so hard she fell off the balcony."

I caught my breath. "He pushed her off!"

"Get that look off your face!" she said angrily. "Don't think you've found a pattern. I told you Alex has an ironclad alibi for the time my father was killed. Besides, he liked my father, and my father liked him."

Yeah. I could imagine Wingate liking Alexander the Great. When pigs fly.

"There is absolutely no way Alexander could have pushed my father," she said. "You can't crack his alibi. He was in jail."

I sat down on the couch. I studied Winnie. She was besotted with love or lust or whatever. "And you're pleased that he was in jail?"

"At the time I was upset, but it's turned out for the best, hasn't it?"

"How did he get into jail?" I asked.

"He is high-spirited," she said. "He was driving too fast, and that's why I was upset with him. When they stopped him for speeding the evening before my father was found dead, he couldn't pass the blood-alcohol test. I was out, so Alexander couldn't reach me to bail him out."

"But why?" I said. "I don't understand."

"You see," Winnie explained, "about ten o'clock that night I got a phone call from someone who said my father had an accident and was in Memorial Mission Hospital, and I should come right over. Naturally I did. But he wasn't there. Nobody knew anything about him. I called his house, and there was no answer. I called

St. Joseph's, and he wasn't in the emergency room there either. So then I waited at Mission in case he showed up. I fell asleep on the couch in the waiting room and didn't wake up until the next morning. By the time I got home, they'd found my father was dead." She sniffed and blew her nose, but quickly came back to her lover's alibi. "Of course, I left Alex a note. But that didn't do him any good in jail."

"So someone wanted you out of the way," I said. "Or maybe they wanted you to have an alibi because you were in the hospital waiting room. Could you prove anybody called you?"

"No," she said. "But if you mean to imply that I might have deliberately created an alibi for Alex by seeing that he stayed in jail because I couldn't be found to bail him out, that's ridiculous. I might point out that there was no way Alex or I could count on his being arrested."

She had a point there.

"Winnie," I said, "I believe you didn't kill your father. But something weird seems to be going on. You might even be in danger. I promised Marietta I'd try to look around and see what the problem could be. I'd like to be your friend, too. Will you let me know if anything else odd happens like that phone call?"

For the first time she allowed herself to drop her guard. She shivered. She said, "Yes. I'm scared." I gave her a quick hug and said good-bye.

CHAPTER
5

LATER ON TUESDAY, JULY 15

I figured I'd better pick up something good for supper and get on home. I was feeling lazy, so I stopped at Laurey's Catering and got Cornish game hens. That would please my Ted. His car was already in the driveway when I drove up to our square-cut log house near Beaverdam. Our house is set back from the road with woods in back of it. Nice and quiet.

Ted was sitting out on the stone terrace, sipping a cool drink. "So I suppose Marietta has you laid on to find out what happened to her brother," he said in a cautionary tone. "You realize this is a precedent. She's not your relative. You don't have to get mixed up in this." He knows I feel that if a relative asks my help, I should say yes. That's old-fashioned southern. Also old-fashioned mountain. So maybe I'm old-fashioned. And God knows I have enough relatives to sink a ship. One more couldn't hurt.

"Marietta is like kin," I said. "After all, we were thick as thieves all through school. We used to trade clothes and double-date in high school. Then we went to Chapel Hill together. I haven't seen her much in the last few years because we've both been so busy, but I think we're honorary kin!"

He raised his glass as if he was about to make a toast. "Speaking of relatives," he said dryly, "your life is about to get more exciting, even without Marietta." He had that wry twinkle in his eyes that usually goes with some remark about the absolute preposterousness of life.

"Oh?"

"Your father, the recent bridegroom, is about to arrive from Tennessee in a stew, complete with sitter. He says Azalea left him."

I sat down. My father is eighty-six years old and in fragile health. That's why he needs a sitter — his arthritis is so bad he can hardly do anything for himself. Even so, last year he married a wild but cheerful character named Azalea Marlowe, no spring chicken herself. They moved to Tennessee, renovated an antique house, and, in the face of all logic, seemed set to live happily ever after. Happily ever after could be too boring for Pop. He likes action, even though he's bound to a wheelchair, and now and then his mind takes a U-turn.

"But his house here is all closed up," I said. "They weren't due to come for two more weeks, after it was opened up and aired out."

Ted grinned a devilish grin. "He's coming to stay here."

My heart sank. "In *our* house? With us? When?"

"He called on his car phone and said it would be about half an hour. That was ten minutes ago."

I shut my eyes and tried not to picture what this was going to be like. Pop in the guest room, trying to run everything. Sitters around the clock so we'd never have a moment alone. And, of course, Pop would want to be the center of attention. "So he's coming in twenty minutes," I said weakly, "but I'm not going to sit around and listen to his troubles." Somehow, I knew before I heard the facts that I was going to be on Azalea's side. I love Pop, but he is irrepressible and absolutely unpredictable. At least the guest room was all made up and ready to go, and the sitter could stay in the small room off the kitchen.

"The sitter can fix him canned soup," I said firmly, looking at my two portions of game hen from Laurey's. Actually, Pop is very fond of canned clam chowder, and since I like it, too, I keep some on hand.

I was not going to go into big preparations. Surprise visitors should take what they get. I spent the twenty minutes till blastoff — or should I say blast-in — filling Ted in on what I'd learned from Marietta.

"I swear," Ted said, "you might guess that Pop heard about Wingate and how he was either pushed or jumped. I have to admit I told him when he called this morning that you were off with Marietta, looking into that question." He shook his head sadly. "I apologize. I figured he was safely off in Tennessee with a new and loving wife, and he'd be interested in the news but nothing more."

Interested was hardly the word. Whether I was ready or not, I heard a car, looked up, and there Pop was, waving from the window of a white Cadillac, white shock of hair tossed back, eagle nose raised at a jaunty angle. The sitter was driving, and she pulled into the driveway, got out, and began removing a folding wheelchair from the trunk. I hurried over to the car and said hello. Not enthusiastically.

"You are my mainstay, Peaches," Pop said. "When catastrophe strikes, I know I can count on you." He gave me his Franklin D. Roosevelt smile, proving he still had his own teeth and that he still knew how to butter me up. Then he and the sitter and Ted were so busy getting him in the wheelchair that the conversation stopped.

We wheeled him into the guest room, which is, fortunately, downstairs. Pop announced he was thirsty, and I went to get him a glass of iced tea while the sitter freshened him up from the trip. Turns out I had to make hot tea and pour it over ice and add more ice, and when I finally got back, Pop was lying on the bed sound asleep.

"What happened?" I asked the plump, middle-aged sitter.

She was a new one I didn't know. Maxine, she said her name was, Max for short. "I always wanted to live in Asheville," she said. "I'm a weaver in my spare time. I specialize in linen. I hear this is a great place for weavers." She had that pale hair that people call flaxen, cut short and loose. How appropriate. I could remember her as *Max* who used *flax* to weave linen.

"What happened to bring my father here?" I repeated, getting back to basics.

She said she didn't know. Someone called the agency and asked if there might be a sitter who would like to drive a patient to Asheville, and since Max was standing right there and had just broken up with her boyfriend, she jumped at the chance. She could work for the branch of the agency up here. Lord knows the branch up here knew all about Pop — at least until he'd moved to Tennessee with Azalea.

So we had to wait until Pop woke up to learn the facts, at least from his point of view.

When Pop was up and sitting with us at the terrace table, the story began to dribble out. "It's a sad day," he said, "when a man's own wife, who he's stuck by through thick and thin, throws him out."

Thick and thin was one year. I waited patiently for the details.

"Azalea has grown crazy over being young again," he said wistfully, eyes in hungry hound-dog mode. "Someone gave her this book about how you can make your brain — and even to some extent your body — young again, and she's hell-bent to do it."

"So why does that upset you?" I asked.

"She wants me to come, too, and pay for the whole shebang for both of us. Thousands of dollars to go to Arizona, stay in a hotel, and go to this miracle doctor. I can't afford that."

Actually, he could. He started out in life as a have-not, but he'd been so clever in investing his money that he could do what he pleased now.

"But what does that have to do with her throwing you out?" I asked.

"If I won't come, she's going alone," he said. "So she said I should come stay with you while she's gone, and then she said that when she's young and full of ginger and I'm still old, that won't be any fun, so why don't I just stay up here. She was mad."

"She's just trying to pressure you to come along," I said, crossing my fingers that that was true. "What is this doctor like? Is he on the level?"

Pop smiled his cat-eating-the-canary smile. "I brought his book so you can see for yourself," he said. "Azalea is going to be wild that it's gone!"

He handed me a book that turned out to be about improving memory, even for folks who were almost around the bend. "Hey," I said, "this is right up my alley. And this man went to Harvard. Why don't you go see him and tell me what it's like? I'll try his methods, too, if it works for you."

"I'm too exhausted from the trip here to go anywhere right away." Pop sighed. "If Azalea comes back young, I'll reconsider." He perked back up quickly. "Ted tells me Marietta is getting you to look into her brother Wingate's death. I remember Wingate so well, though I don't believe I've seen him since he was ten years old and the family moved away from next door. Poor Wingate."

I sent Ted a why-did-you-tell-him? frown. Ted shrugged. Pop is awfully good at worming things out of people.

"I may be able to help you," Pop said magnanimously. "Besides, I have a project here in Asheville. You have a psychic here who is so talented that they talk about her all the way to Tennessee. I am going to see this Crystal next week. It's all arranged." He paused as if a great idea had just come to him. "While I'm there, I'll ask her who killed Wingate."

Crystal, I thought, as in crystal ball. I pictured her looking into one. I bet that Crystal was not what her mama named her. But that was a good name for a psychic.

Trust Pop to explore anything new and interesting — if it suits him — and sure enough, Asheville is becoming a New Age center. Someone told me we're the new Santa Fe. Asheville is an amazing town, with conservative Christians constantly writing letters to the editor quoting the Bible, and an artistic community where members celebrate the full moon. And, yes, we were acquiring New Age healing centers and suchlike, though I hadn't heard of Crystal. But there's no reason that I would. She could have been around for years, and I might not have known.

"Why did you decide to visit this psychic?" I asked.

"I'd like to know my future," said Pop, who is eighty-six. At least he's never dull. "I could live to be ninety or a hundred, Peaches," he said, "and I'm curious." Then his eyes went sharp. "Now tell me all the dirt about Wingate."

Actually, Pop can have good ideas in among the wild ones, so I told him about the will and about the place where Wingate fell or was pushed and even about Winnie's boyfriend.

"A good-looking man is just what Winnie needs," Pop said. "I told her so."

"You *what?*"

"Sure," Pop said. "I haven't seen Wingate in years, but Winnie used to come around trying to collect money for good causes. Because I knew her father, she'd always tell me what he was up to. Smart. Then I felt more likely to give her something."

"So what do you know about Wingate that might help?" I asked, just on general principle.

"Winnie thought her father was sleeping with old Hiram's housekeeper," Pop said.

I almost dropped my iced tea. "Winnie said that about Wingate — her own father?"

"Oh, no. But she had such spite toward that woman. She said her father didn't realize what a dreadful woman she was. Didn't realize that she was a massage-parlor hostess before she went to work for Hiram. She said her father was too nice to that woman. So I figured . . ."

It was always possible Pop might be right. If so, had Hiram known it? And what then? He was dead. But somehow Hiram still seemed to be influencing the action.

"You need to go talk to Annie Long," Pop said. "Outsiders who worm into families know the most."

I figured it was worth a try. It would be great if Pop's visit to the psychic would solve the whole thing. But it's been my experience that work is more dependable than miracles, though not always as much fun.

CHAPTER
6

WEDNESDAY MORNING, JULY 16

Annie Long hadn't put up any curtains, so I could see through the floor-to-ceiling glass into the apartment from the outside. There stood Marietta with her back to me. What was she doing here?

The front door was around the other side of the building. I knocked, and Annie opened the door almost immediately. "Good morning," she said. I thought slightly warily.

Annie Long impressed me. She had presence. I would have thought she was a successful older actress, not someone's former housekeeper. She had coal-black hair with one white streak that curved back dramatically from the center of her forehead. Under arched black eyebrows, her green eyes were carefully made up and sharp at the same time. I felt she took me in at a glance. For a woman of fifty-five, she was downright sexy, firm, and uplifted, probably with a super-bra, and not a bit overweight. Because she stood straight, she gave an impression of height. Actually, she was just a few inches taller than I. About five feet four or five. The same height as Marietta.

"Come in," she said pleasantly as she opened the door to her apartment. "I hope you don't mind talking to me while I finish packing for our boat trip. This country girl is going to see the world. Or at least the ocean." Her mouth smiled. Her eyes were wary.

Why was *she* going? She wasn't a member of the family. Also, she sure didn't look like a country girl even if she grew up as one. The outside of her building was downright modern, all poured cement with broad balconies, flowers blooming on almost every one, and a car parked in front of virtually every unit. Not country at all. No tobacco-barn sag and not one pickup in the parking spots.

But my gut said the building went with Annie. It looked open and welcoming but wasn't. It was two stories high, with stairs to each upstairs apartment, which meant no indoor corridors. This was not a place where people met each other in the hall.

Annie could be private.

She ushered me into a light and airy room with glass sliding doors to a balcony. No sign of Marietta. Was she in the next room? And why so silent? The room was almost bare except for a deep-pile soft blue rug. The kind that makes you want to take your shoes off and wiggle your toes on it. One couch with big throw cushions. One chair, one bookcase. Pictures leaned unhung against the wall. All sorts, from rhododendrons blooming on the mountainside to museum prints of famous art. I recognized Goya's *Naked Maja.* My cousin Alice, who fancied herself an artist, had big books of pictures with all sorts of nudes, male and female. When we were preteens we used to look at them and giggle. Nudity had seemed wicked to us. That challenging look in the *Naked Maja*'s eyes as she lay back on a couch had impressed me even then. It said, I am what I am. So what?

Annie gave me the same look. "I haven't had a chance to hang the pictures," she said. "I'm the pig's tail. I'm only half moved in here, because I've been in Hiram's house. I took care of it. But now they have a college boy. He'll live there and mow the grounds. And here I am getting ready to go off on a trip when my packing boxes here are still half-full." She turned her back and pointed to a cardboard box that stood next to the chair.

And there, it seemed, was Marietta. Of course, Annie and Marietta didn't really look alike — but the height was the same, the dark curly hair, the way they stood slim and straight. "You look like Marietta from the rear," I said.

"I've been mistaken for Marietta," said Annie, "until I turn around. Then I'm just the hired help." So Annie held on to resentments.

My eyes went to a picture of a pig over against the wall. It was done in colored pencils, cartoonlike, but still arresting — an arrogant pig. The little eyes were full of scorn, and yet that pig seemed pleased with itself. It made me want to laugh even while it reminded me of my cousin Lon, who believed that nearly everyone he knew would go to hell. Unlike Lon, who went bareheaded, the pig wore a cap. And the cap seemed to suit it. The cap said HIRAM across the front.

"What an interesting picture," I said. "Is that what Hiram seemed like when you knew him well?"

Annie shrugged. "I draw a little," she told me. "Do cartoons. Get things out of

90

my system. He was a real pain in the ass toward the end. Sick people are no fun."

Then she beckoned me to follow her into a sparsely furnished bedroom that also had sliding glass doors to the balcony. More cartoon pictures against the wall. A chicken with cunning eyes, which seemed browbeaten all the same. Its feathers were awry, and some floated free. I studied it. "Hey, that's Winnie!" I said. An eagle in another picture seemed confused, its pigeon-toed feet clutching a branch. Its eagle eyes seemed to be asking for approval, but the stance of head was proud. "And that's Wingate!" I said. She didn't comment.

"Your pictures satirize all the people you know?" I asked. I was intrigued and a little horrified.

"I do cartoons instead of getting mad," she said, "and sometimes I do them at fund-raisers or church fairs." I assumed those were kinder. But then I hadn't come to find out about her artwork. I did wonder why she was a housekeeper if she had this talent. Maybe she wasn't quite good enough.

"What can I tell you?" she asked as she opened the sliding doors to a large closet, pulled a brilliant green blouse off a hanger, and began to fold it to pack. What Annie lacked in furniture and rugs and picture hooks, she made up for in clothes. She saw me staring at the tightly packed closet. "I get attached to things," she said. "I never get rid of my old clothes." She shrugged and frowned as if she were castigating herself. At a glance, none of the clothes looked old. Or country. The colors were bright. A lot of silk and suchlike shimmered.

A large suitcase with wheels on the bottom was open on the bed. She put the blouse in that and went back for a pair of white slacks.

I decided she wasn't the type who would appreciate beating around the bush. "Marietta has asked me to look into exactly what happened to her brother Wingate," I said. "Did he jump? Was he pushed? In either case, why? And somehow I have the impression that whatever happened may be related to his relationship with Hiram Scott." This sounded far-fetched as I said it. I half expected her to laugh.

Annie Long put the slacks in the suitcase on top of the folded green shirt. She gave me a level *Naked Maja* look. "I think you are exactly right! You can bet somebody pushed Wingate. Something is wrong in that family."

"What?" I asked.

She stopped packing and considered. "I think Hiram was out of his mind at the end. But nobody wanted to hear what I thought. And nobody was willing to have him declared incompetent. Not even when he reached the point where he was crazy as a bedbug. There's absolutely no telling what he may have done or arranged the last few weeks of his life." She grabbed a pair of tan pants from the closet and folded them briskly, as if she were angry at them.

"Who did he see those last weeks?" I asked.

"His doctor, whom I absolutely trust. He's true blue. Ask anyone in town. Dr. Humphrey is wonderful. And Ellington Foxworth redid Hiram's will, I believe. I don't know much about that. It happened when I was out. I wouldn't trust Ellington as far as I could throw him. But if he tried to twist Hiram some way, I wasn't there to protect him. Yes, I advised Hiram a lot toward the end, but he got secretive as a pregnant mole, even with me." Annie crammed the pants into the suitcase, then turned to me, stood perfectly still, and spoke plaintively. "He gave me days off and told me to go out and stay away. He

93

did that even after he was almost too weak to get to the bathroom by himself. And he managed to do that right almost till the end."

"Were you helping to nurse him?" I asked, surprised.

"No," she said. "I'm not patient enough to do that. He managed with a visiting nurse. He had incredible will to manage on his own. I did bring him food and things to drink."

"So what do you think he was up to?"

"God only knows," she said darkly. "He was a master manipulator. He could make a cow lay eggs. He knew all about greed. He could put together deals by persuading two different CEOs that they were getting the best of each other and of him. Then he came out on top of the heap. Ellington helped him do it. And he always talked it over with me. I was his housekeeper, but I was more than that. Why did he stop trusting me? Somebody turned him against me!"

I could see I needed to talk to the Fox. I also needed to get back to the subject of Wingate.

"Did Hiram trust Wingate?"

"He had a fight with Wingate, just a week before he died. Hiram was looking better, and Wingate came by to see him with a briefcase chock-full of something. I don't know what happened, but I heard yelling. I heard both voices, but I couldn't make out words." She glanced over at the cartoon eagle. Was she avoiding eye contact?

"You heard something," I accused, "and you don't want to tell me."

She glared at me and didn't comment.

"So who do you think pushed Wingate?" This gal seemed to respond best to brutal questions.

"I have no idea," she said, still looking away from me. "I don't know what's wrong. I just know things aren't right."

"What was Hiram Scott like before he got so secretive at the end?" I asked. "How would you describe him, not as a businessman but as a person?"

She went back to folding and considered. Her face softened, and she sighed. It was as if suddenly I were talking to a different woman. "In a way he was simple," she said sadly. "He believed money could buy anything he wanted. And it did, just enough that he was mad and confused when money wasn't enough."

"How do you mean?" I asked.

"Well, take that actress he liked."

I'd heard he was a womanizer, even in his old age.

"Hiram gave her more presents than you could shake a stick at. He paid big money for her apartment. When she cheated on him, he was crushed. People don't love you because of money," Annie said with sudden passion. "They love you or they don't. If they love you and you give them presents, they are pleased. If they don't love you, they are tickled to death and try to figure out how to get more. I told him that."

"Did you love him?" I asked.

"Yes," she said. She stared me down defiantly. "But not like you think. He couldn't love just one woman. He was like a bull in rut. Or maybe he was like a dog that wanted to be patted by every person that came by. Or both at once.

"I was like a mother after his mother died, even though I'm about thirty years younger than he was. He was a brilliant man, but he was a child. I loved the child."

"But Hiram became more and more eccentric, didn't he?"

"That's when he needed me most," she said. "Because he couldn't trust anyone else."

"What did you think of his will?" I asked.

"Foolish," she said. "He could have left his money to one of those foundations. He could have been remembered as a great giver. He trusted me until he got so crazy. I could have helped him with that. He could have died knowing that once he was gone, people would admire him for his good works."

What an odd idea, I thought, that all you have to be to be admired is dead and generous.

"I thought you were a housekeeper," I said. "Were you more of an office manager?"

"I was his adviser," she said. "I never managed his office, but I gave him advice about who to hire and fire." Her eyes flashed at me as if she thought I might not believe it.

"Yet he only left you ten thousand dollars," I said.

She flinched. I could see that ten-thousand-dollar bit had upset her. "He paid me well," she said. "I have money in the bank. He knew that."

"So you weren't lovers?" I demanded.

"That," she said, "is none of your damned business." Her words were a challenge, but I had the impression that she wanted to cry.

CHAPTER
7

WEDNESDAY, AFTER LUNCH

"I wanted to bring you a good-bye present," Marietta said. She handed me a small bottle with a medicine-dropper top and a larger bottle, about beer-bottle size, with a cork in the top.

Pop was out on the terrace with me, sitting at the glass-topped table. "Why, Marietta!" he cried. "I haven't seen you since you were a little kid! You've grown into a good-looking woman! What have you got in those bottles? The elixir of youth? Come sit down."

"My own herbal extract," Marietta said. "This is gingko. It improves the circulation in the brain, and that improves memory." She sat in one of the wrought-iron chairs between me and Pop.

"Did you bring some gingko for me?" he asked, eyeing the bottles I'd set down on the table in front of me.

"I brought it for Peaches to try," Marietta said, "but I bet she'll share. I make this extract myself from gingko leaves and wine. You put twenty drops in a little water and take it twice a day. You may not notice a difference for a few weeks."

"What's the difference between the two bottles?" I asked.

"The larger one is for refills," she said. "The smaller one is to measure the drops. Now I've got to run. I have lots to do before I leave."

I walked her over to her car.

"Have you found out anything yet?" she asked.

I shrugged. "Do you think Annie Long was Hiram's lover as well as his housekeeper?" I demanded.

She looked startled. "He had girlfriends," she said, toying with the handle of the car door. "If she was his lover, she was more tolerant than I would be. So I never thought of that."

"Did you know that Winnie's lover pushed his first wife off a balcony in Miami?" I asked.

She opened her eyes wide and gripped the door handle as if she needed it to hold her up. "You do worm things out of people!" she said. "I thought he was trying to exploit Winnie. But I didn't know — so you think . . . ?"

"He has an ironclad alibi when it comes to Wingate," I said. "He was in jail for speeding and driving drunk. I checked."

"Still, I'll watch him like a hawk," Marietta said. "Winnie hasn't got common sense about men! I wish we didn't have to go on this trip right now. All of us together. Suppose he . . . ? Suppose one of us . . . ?" She shuddered.

"Marietta, watch your back," I warned. "Whoever threw that rock at us must have been aiming at you."

"Believe me, I'll be very careful," she said soulfully. But I knew it was not in her nature to be very careful. She was too trusting.

She drove off as the first raindrops hit. I hurried back to the table on the terrace where Pop was quivering to ask what Marietta said. I grabbed the gingko bottles just as the sitter came running out and wheeled him into the house.

I diverted Pop with gingko and the explanation that Marietta just wanted to know what I'd found out. We all went into the kitchen, and I got out two glasses, put a little water in each and then twenty gingko drops. I handed one to Pop and raised mine toward my lips. "Stop!" he yelled as I was about to drink it down. My hand stopped in midair.

"What's wrong?"

"That's got poison in it," he said dramatically.

"Oh, come on," I said. "Do you think Marietta would poison us?"

"When Marietta was a kid, her toys all got stolen because she didn't keep them locked away."

"So what has that got to do with poison?"

"Marietta may lock her front door, but she's not the type to keep the windows locked. Anyone could sneak into her house and poison herbal extracts."

That seemed far-fetched, but it ruined the gingko for me. I set it down, and then, more to myself than to Pop, I said, "How can we find out?"

"If you are sure it's not poisoned, you can feed some to the cat," Pop said. "He'll prove it's good to drink."

I picked up the cat and hugged him. "And if it was poisoned, we'd have one dead cat."

Dern Pop. He can do that to me. I didn't believe him, but I didn't dare take a chance.

Ted joined us right then. My good professor husband has odd spaces between classes, especially during summer school. He pointed at the ants, making a trail down the end of the counter where some sugar had spilled. "Mix gingko extract with honey," he said. "That will bring the ants running to try some. I don't imagine you'll mind if it kills the ants."

Better the ants than my cat! I pulled out a jar of honey in the comb that a beekeeper neighbor had given me. I took out a few drops and mixed it with gingko drops. "The ants should be so lucky with honey and wine."

"If it's made with wine, the ants may get drunk," Ted said. "I've never seen an ant stagger." So he wasn't taking this too seriously.

I put the gingko honey on the counter near the sugar. The ants helped themselves and walked off as more ants arrived. They did not stagger.

"Okay," I said, picking up my glass of gingko, "the ants are fine."

"No! Stop!" said Pop. "You know perfectly well there are slow poisons. Besides, I've heard that ants go back to the nest to die."

It's true there are slow poisons. But I

was annoyed. Still, I put the gingko honey in a canning jar laid sideways, and when the ants went in I put a piece of cheese-cloth that I keep for making jelly over the mouth of the jar with an elastic band. "Now," I said, "we'll know if they live or die." I did not expect them to die. Poison would not be a likely murder tool for someone who liked to push folks off cliffs. Besides, why target me? I didn't know anything yet. But then, on the other hand, if there was poison in the extract, the target might be Marietta. Should I call and warn her? Why? I had no proof at all of any poison. Yet I realized I had begun to suspect it was there.

Pop was quite pleased with himself. "It pays to be suspicious," he said. I took that as a warning that he was going to get himself mixed up in Wingate's demise, no matter what.

The doorbell rang, and I went to answer it. Old curious here can't wait to know who's arriving.

"Hi," said a sad voice. It was Brian the Lion, standing by the door as if he were too shy to come in, eyes darting about under that mop of red hair. I remembered that Marietta had said her grandson was still confused about life. His T-shirt, jeans, and sandals would have done for a poet, except they were too squeaky-clean. Poets should look a bit disheveled, that's my prejudice.

"I need to talk to you," he said in a conspiratorial tone. "I need to talk to you alone."

"Has it stopped raining?" I asked, and answered my own question by going past him out the door and holding out my hand. The sky was still overcast, but not a drop of rain fell. Mountain rain can be like that — quick to pass through. It blows on into the next valley. So I came back inside and grabbed a handful of tissues, then went back outdoors and wiped off two of the chairs at the glass-topped table on the terrace. The house was at our back, and the lawn stretched in front of us down to the road, with woods on the other side.

"This is nice and alone," I said.

He blushed. He stammered, "The — the week before he died, Uncle Hiram called me up and asked me to come see him."

Actually, Hiram must have been his great-great-uncle, but the whole family just seemed to call him uncle regardless of the number of greats that would be appropriate.

"Yes," I said in an encouraging tone of voice.

"He asked me for a favor, and he said if I'd do what he asked he'd leave me a lot of money in his will. That seemed kind of neat." He smiled cheerfully. He evidently still thought so.

"What he wanted me to do didn't sound like it could hurt anybody, so I agreed." His smile went flat.

"What did he ask you to do?" I asked. Obviously, although he liked the money, something about what Hiram had asked worried Brian now. Why else had he come to talk to me alone?

"Uncle Hiram made me swear not to tell, so I can't." He blushed again. He took his glasses off and put them on again.

I refrained from asking him why on earth he was here if he couldn't tell me. "Perhaps you can give me a hint of what it is — about what Hiram asked you to do — that makes you uneasy now," I said. "He may have been out of his mind that last week. Annie Long, his girl Friday and house-keeper, thinks so."

At her name Brian flinched as if I'd hit him. "But a promise is a promise," he said, "especially to a dying man."

On this overcast day the woods across the road, half pine, half maple and oak, looked dark and secret. No breeze now.

Each tree was still. Was Brian going to be like that?

"But perhaps since my grandmother is afraid somebody killed Uncle Wingate — though I almost can't believe that — but anyway, perhaps I can tell you one thing that might matter if that's true." He cracked one knuckle and looked at his hand, surprised, as if he hadn't expected the crack.

I leaned forward encouragingly. "You can count on the fact that I won't tell anybody what you've said unless it seems to relate to a threat to someone's life."

He got up from his chair, walked over to the edge of the stone terrace, and stared off into the woods. He came back and sat down decisively.

"Okay. What he made me promise means that Annie Long will be with the family when we go to the village in England where our ancestor came from, and when we spend five days on the ocean coming back." He hesitated a long time. "And he never even hinted at this, but do you suppose Annie Long could be related to us? I mean in some secret way. Maybe his father shacked up with her mother and he knew it? And so he wants her with the family on this trip? And maybe she's in danger, too?"

Brian had imagination, I'll say that.

"No," I said. "If she was related and he cared about that, he would have left her more in his will, don't you think?"

He nodded and looked relieved. "Yes," he said, and then shrugged. "So I shouldn't have told you."

"You should have told me," I said, "because you never can tell how facts will fit together. This may be a clue in some way that you and I can't even imagine."

He smiled. "And you won't tell," he said. "It's funny," he went on nervously, looking left and right with those magnified eyes, and even back at the house. "I have this feeling like Uncle Hiram is still watching us somewhere and isn't really dead."

"Didn't you go to the funeral?" I asked.

"Yes, but the coffin was shut. They didn't have him out to look at. Not ever. People complained." He blushed till his ears were positively neon. "But we wouldn't have this money if he wasn't dead."

"And what did you promise?"

He swallowed hard. "He said he knew I liked to go places, like the time we went to Myrtle Beach. He said the world was full of places to go, like England and France, and he named a lot of others. He said I was really still a kid and I had to promise that the first year after he died, if I went anyplace out of the country, I'd take Annie Long with me. Then he said something that just sounded silly at the time. He told me I had to do that even if I went with the whole family. He made me sign a paper about that, and I guess he gave it to the Fox."

Was Hiram crazy or just eccentric, I asked myself, *or did he deliberately want to complicate things after he was gone?*

CHAPTER
8

THURSDAY MORNING, JULY 17

I went to the airport with Marietta to see her off, but I kept an eye on the rest of the group and had the feeling they kept an eye on me.

We have a small airport, but it's new and perky. The plane was scheduled to take off from one of the departure gates upstairs. Marietta and I arrived first, and the family members trailed in, Goldie in a zebra-striped pant suit with enough luggage to sink a ship. "I can't count on what the weather will be like," she said. "I have to be ready for anything." Her son Brian checked one of her bags as his so she wouldn't be over the limit. Everything he'd brought fit in a small backpack.

Marietta, who hadn't traveled much, had a new bag on wheels, small enough to fit under the seat, she said. Winnie and Alexander the Great had twin wheelie-bags. Winnie wore what I'd seen in the catalogs advertised as a travel jacket with all sorts of secret pockets, and Alexander wore a travel vest that gaped over his steroid chest.

Richard counted heads like a good high-school teacher and announced that his sister Lillian hadn't arrived yet. "Neither," said Brian, "has Annie Long."

He was standing near me, and he blushed and said, "Well, I had to tell everybody what I promised Hiram, didn't I? Or they'd think I was crazy traveling with a fifty-five-year-old woman."

Next the Fox appeared. Ellington Foxworth himself. "I know you are taking this trip to satisfy the conditions of the will, but I hope you'll enjoy it," he said with proper lawyer dignity. Was he going on the trip to be sure they obeyed the provisions of the will? No. "I want to wish you all bon voyage," he said.

Lillian materialized at his elbow and laughed. She seemed unsteady on her feet. I thought: *She's been drinking.* I looked at my watch. Just nine o'clock.

Annie Long hurried in at the last minute. She went right over to Brian and apologized for being late. Sure enough, the flight was called almost immediately, and the Fox and I were saying last good-byes.

Now the good luck about all this was that after we waved the plane off and went back to the short-term parking lot, Ellington Foxworth and I were parked only a few cars apart. You might say we were the ridiculous parked near the sublime: his sleek black Cadillac near my old Volvo with the dent in the fender and the bumper sticker that says IT'S AS *BAD* AS YOU THINK, AND THEY *ARE* OUT TO GET YOU. (Ted gave me that bumper sticker. He said it was partly a joke and partly to make me think twice before I got mixed up with crime.) As I opened the door to get into the Volvo, I heard the Fox say "Damn!" very loudly.

It was in that are-you-listening? tone of voice. He wanted me to notice. I got out of my car and walked over to his Cadillac. He had a flat tire. I knew by his scowl that he wasn't about to rumple his pin-striped lawyer suit by changing it. He looked at his watch. "I have an appointment in Asheville in half an hour," he said. That gave him just enough time to get back.

"I can give you a ride," I offered. I was overjoyed to have half an hour to ask a few questions in an informal way.

He glanced at my bumper sticker and raised one eyebrow. "Maybe you need a good lawyer," he said, and grinned, not

111

like a fox but a wolf. Then he walked around and climbed into my car, which was plainly beneath his standards.

He didn't wait for me to speak first. "I understand you are asking people a lot of questions," he said. Then he waited for me to react.

"Yes," I answered. "I want to find out —" I faltered. I wasn't sure what to ask the Fox. He wasn't going to betray confidentiality and tell me all about his client. I could see by his little hint of a derisive smile that he didn't think much of my asking questions.

I backed out of my parking place and drove toward the exit booth. "Marietta wanted me to find out if there was any possibility Wingate was pushed. I'm asking questions for her, since she has to go on this trip and she didn't believe for a minute that her brother would kill himself. She says he was always afraid of heights."

"It's hard to know what's in another human mind," he said. Ah. He was going to take the high road. Fox as philosopher.

I paid the gal in the booth for an hour's parking and noticed the Fox didn't offer to pay it for me. "You've known the whole family for a long time?" I asked.

"Wingate and I went to Carolina to-

112

gether," he said. "And you're right, he was always afraid of heights. He wouldn't go up in the bell tower."

We turned out into the road and headed back toward Asheville. "What do you think happened to him?" I asked.

Long silence. Now we were on I-26 in brisk traffic. "I have no idea what happened," he said. "But that's not really what you want to ask me, is it? You want to ask if anyone had reason to want Wingate dead."

I passed one of those reproduction cars that look like they did in the 1920s. Black and curvy. Like something out of a crime movie. What the Fox was saying would fit right into an old movie. What was he up to?

"Perhaps you wonder if any member of his family would kill Wingate to get a portion of his inheritance," he continued. "Hiram was very eccentric to insist on wording his will that way — providing that half of the inheritance of anyone who died within a year be divided among the others. But why should they risk murder for a small portion of Wingate's inheritance when they're already so well fixed?"

Why, indeed. In front of me an old man in a black felt hat driving a pickup seemed to be going about twelve miles an hour. Several trucks in the other lane kept me from passing. I was so impatient I almost honked my horn. And he was probably deaf. Then I thought: *I'm really impatient with the Fox — that's why the old man annoys me so. The Fox is manipulating this conversation so I won't ask something that he doesn't want me to know. I can feel it. And I'm so dumb I don't know what it is.*

"Did you write Wingate's will?" I asked. A car weaving in and out of traffic cut in front of us, and I had to jam on the brakes. I said, "Damn reckless driver!" I noticed the Fox take out a small black notebook and write down the license plate as the car kept speeding. So the Fox liked to get even?

"I did not write Wingate's will." His tone was disapproving. "Winnie has a friend who is a lawyer. The friend did Wingate's will."

That surprised me. But then, only Winnie and Rich would lose if the will was mishandled, so maybe Wingate figured they could pick the lawyer.

"I think what you really want to ask me," the Fox said, "is where I was the morning Wingate died."

He expected that to rattle me. I kept

calm. "Okay," I said, figuring he wanted me to know, "where were you?"

"I was at home in bed asleep next to my wife till seven a.m. and in the office by eight. I did not have time between seven-thirty and eight to go to Linville Falls two hours away and push Wingate off the over-look, and aside from that I didn't have a motive. Where were you?" He gave me that wolf grin again.

"At home asleep next to my spouse till seven," I said. "Then I wouldn't have time to drive to Linville Falls before Wingate was found dead there. Which proves nothing. If I'd slipped out during the night, my husband Ted might not have noticed. But then, I hardly knew Wingate, so what does it matter?"

The Fox was keeping me from thinking clearly. *Stay centered,* I told myself firmly. A truck whined past.

"You also want to ask me about Hiram," the Fox said. "You want to ask me if I believe, as some members of his family have accused, that Hiram was insane at the end. I do not. Eccentric, yes. Insane no.

"But what I do think," he added, "is that, like any family, this is one where it doesn't pay to get mixed up in the members' problems. They're all strong characters," he said. "Mostly eccentric. With enough money now to have their own way. If I were you, I'd mind my own business."

Beyond this, I couldn't get him to talk about anything more pertinent than the weather and how he hoped this would be a pleasant trip for the family. Maybe he hoped they'd all come back in such a good humor they'd get him to rewrite their wills. We were almost to Asheville, where his office was not far off the main drag.

There was something he'd wanted to be sure I didn't ask, and I hadn't asked it. I was sure of that. He had eyes that didn't show his feelings, and he knew how to put me off. Dern! I moved into the passing lane and honked at the man in front of me. I'm not a natural honker, but it felt good.

CHAPTER
9

THURSDAY AFTERNOON — SUNDAY MORNING

This was no time for me to get some kind of virus, but I got so sick I didn't care. Winter viruses make some sense. When it's cold, I feel like the outdoors is so blustery and the indoors is so cooped up that — what do you expect? Summer viruses seem unfair. Out the window, the sun is shining, the birds are singing, all a waste. Ted brought me lemonade when I could bear to swallow, and reported there was nothing more in the paper about Wingate's death.

Ted sent out a call to various cousins who love Pop to come entertain him, since he was still in residence. I could hear occasional bursts of laughter in the distance. Mostly I slept and wrote down occasional thoughts that came to me, such as the relationship of the Fox to each of the heirs. Explore that. Later.

By Sunday, I was better, restless, and deciding if my knees were strong enough, I'd go to church. The phone rang. The walkabout phone was right near my hand, so I pushed the on button and put it to my ear. "Hello?" I said.

"Oh, Peaches, this is terrible," said Marietta's voice, pulsing with distance. "The killer is here with us!"

Scratch the Fox, I thought with some regret. "What's happened?" I asked. "Are you all right? Where are you?"

"I'm bruised, but I'm not dead," she said. "Somebody made me fall on the steps of the tower in the earl's castle. Yesterday. I'm just pulled together enough to call you up. Oh, Peaches, that tower was just made for somebody to fall down. I felt like Hiram was there laughing at me. Because he sent us there." Long pause. "But I managed to catch the railing as I fell. So I ache, but I'm not dead."

That's just how I'd felt with my virus. "You couldn't see who pushed you?"

"No," said Marietta. "I thought I was the last one up there in this funky old stone tower. I mean, it was noon, and everybody else was saying, 'Come on, let's go have lunch,' and I was peering out of one of the little stone windows at somebody off

118

in a field who looked like they were gathering herbs, and I was wondering what they were picking, and then I started down the stairs and somebody rushed up just past me and pushed me as hard as he could, and — this sounds ridiculous — I was stunned and confused because whoever it was had a paper bag over his head. You know, with holes cut out for eyes. Almost like Halloween. I couldn't believe it." She let out a slightly hysterical laugh.

"But you grabbed the railing?" I asked.

"Yes, there was this cast-iron railing all the way up this strange tower. I think our ancestor was as nutty as Uncle Hiram. The whole so-called castle was ugly, and with lots of small rooms. But thank God for that railing. The rest of the family were down in the main part. I yelled as loud as I could and kicked, and the person pulled away before he could fall and ran back down the stairs."

"But," I said, "you must have seen the clothes and the shape, and people who heard you scream must have seen the attacker running down the stairs."

Now a sigh. "Nobody saw anyone run down, just all of a sudden everybody seemed to be running up. That's what they all said. And all I remember seeing clearly was that stone staircase as I fell, with the iron rail, thank God, that I could grab, and somebody rushing past me and giving me one more shove, but I held on, and I guess when I screamed so loud whoever it was, was scared to stay."

"Was it a man or a woman?"

"I don't know. All the women were wearing pants, and all I saw was a blur and a paper bag. Then when everybody came back because they did hear me scream, the person could have been with them without the paper bag, right?"

"What do the police say?" I asked.

Long silence. "There have been a lot of break-ins in the town here. The police are distracted. There's a nude burglar, like that man in Asheville, but they haven't caught him. One old lady woke up and saw him and had such bad hysterics they had to put her in the hospital. And I wasn't hurt any way you could see till later, when the bruises turned blue. They weren't positive I wasn't just a crazy American who tripped."

"But when they found the paper bag," I said, trying not to be distracted by nude burglars, "then they had to believe you."

Long silence. "Nobody found a paper bag."

And nobody saw the pusher. Odd.

"There was a high wind," she said. "I mean, a really high wind, and they found some little pieces of brown paper here and there but not enough to put together into a paper bag. And I don't think they tried very hard, because they thought I was a crazy American who —"

"Yes," I said dryly, "I get the picture."

"Peaches, you stop that!" Marietta said. "You sound as skeptical as the police! I can hardly walk! I may have to use a cane, and I need you to come on the rest of this trip with us. You're good at nosing out what's going wrong. And I'll feel safer. I have your ticket ordered through the travel agency there. Please pick it up and fly this afternoon to Gatwick. Please come with us on the boat trip back. It's a really elegant cruise. You'll enjoy it and you'll make us all feel better. The rest aren't sure what happened, but it sure makes them feel nervous."

I opened my mouth to object, and then I thought, *Boat trip? Why not?* Suppose Wingate *had* jumped, and even suppose another tourist *had* been scared and ran away when Marietta tripped, suppose I could be no help at all to Marietta, or the kids, or Richard or Winnie and her boy toy? If it was going to cheer them up for me to go along, that was useful, right? I might as well enjoy it. I'd never been on a cruise.

"I don't have a thing to wear," I said. Marietta knew that meant yes.

"There are shops on the ship," she said. "If you need clothes, we'll buy them." Very handy, having money. I might get hooked on it, at least vicariously.

So I set out with the idea that this was going to be an adventure. Maybe a frivolous adventure, maybe a serious one. I felt a surge of energy and packed the most cruiselike clothes I had, which included white shorts and some slacks and a few rather jazzy tops. Also the party dress I got for Cousin Eugenia's wedding reception. I managed to keep that energy going for lunch on the terrace with Pop and Ted. Chicken soup seemed to go down all right, and I was excited.

Ted worried. "But suppose there is a killer who likes to launch people off high places. Suppose he pushes you off the boat."

"You can't swim to New York!" Pop told me. "You must be very careful."

"Who would have reason to push me?" I asked. "Besides, I'll have eyes in the back of my head."

"At least this killer is not into poison," Pop said. "The ants didn't die. You can enjoy the champagne and caviar. I wish I could come, too. I hope you'll know how to behave. This will be more elegant than you're used to, Peaches."

"It will be more elegant than any of us is used to," I pointed out. "Marietta weeds without gloves. Winnie's Alexander the Great never buttons up his shirt, lest you should miss the hair on his chest, and Brian the Lion forgets to comb his hair. We can help each other adjust to elegance."

"If you eat at the captain's table," Pop said, "I would forgo the nicknames. They aren't dignified."

Anyway, I set forth as quickly as I could. Ted drove me to the airport and begged me to be careful. He said he wished he could have figured out some way to come, too, but he had to teach summer school.

Once in the air, I thought: *Am I out of my mind?* But I was looking forward to the trip. It was something new to me.

The flight from Charlotte to London's Gatwick Airport was uneventful except for a small child's incessant crying. He was getting a new tooth, his mother explained to one and all. They all offered cures: most popular was a lump of ice tied in a hand-kerchief to rub against the tooth, and the stewardess kindly brought the ice.

While the kid sucked the ice in blessed silence, I contemplated what I'd learned. Somebody either had or had not killed Wingate and tried to kill Marietta. Some-body had definitely thrown a rock at Marietta near Linville Falls. That made the two others more likely. Annie Long said it was none of my business whether she had been Hiram's lover, which made it likely she was. But Pop had said Annie Long had been sleeping with Wingate. What was true? Or maybe it was all true. Annie and the Fox both said Hiram had lots of women, which could have made Annie mad at him. But nobody suggested Hiram had been killed. The Fox said Hiram died sane, but he was extremely eccentric. He said the whole family was eccentric. Cer-tainly Winnie was eccentric, taking up with a man who'd killed his first wife — in self-defense, she'd said. When pigs fly. Brian had a reason to travel with a woman in her mid-fifties. The Fox said I should not get mixed up in the family's business, espe-cially since they tended to disagree among themselves. But Marietta had invited me. My head whirled, and I was still weak from the flu. I went to sleep and woke up in England.

The less said about Gatwick Airport outside of London and about British security the better, except that I never in my life saw so many people in national costumes — Indians in saris, Arabs in kaffiyehs, Africans in that wonderful printed cotton. Boy, this was really an international airport.

Meanwhile, my "travel count" worked like a charm. That's my system for remembering what I'm carrying on a trip. Instead of trying to remember pocketbook, suitcase, raincoat, and carryall, I remember how many items I have to keep track of: four. Worked like a charm. I didn't even forget my slopover bag, which is where I put everything that should have fit in my suitcase, and didn't quite.

After a short train trip and a taxi ride, I found myself at the Southampton docks, where Marietta stood, looking cheerful and not eccentric at all. She limped slightly, but had no cane.

I hugged her and said, "Thank God you're all right."

She was all right enough not to mind standing there near huge wharf buildings while she told me more about her misadventure.

"I felt so stupid," she said, "not to be able to remember any details of what the person who pushed me looked like, except, of course, for the paper bag. But afterward I asked each member of our group if he or she had seen anybody suspicious hanging around. I asked each one who was with them at the time they heard me scream. Here's a list of who was with whom. Study it when you get a chance. Not now — we need to be boarding."

I stuck the list in my pocketbook for safekeeping, looked around at the huge buildings, and wondered where we were to go. Marietta led me toward a cavernous shed where we were processed through one of many desks, and soon found ourselves in another large room. Here I gave a young woman my credit card, and she imprinted it in the ship's records so that anything I bought aboard ship would be automatically charged to my account. Boy, I thought, they make it easy to spend! My charges would be just for whims — Marietta would pay for the main stuff. Ah, luxury!

Naturally I wanted to take Marietta's list out and look at it, but not enough to risk losing it along the way. Old One-Track Mind here could sign some form with one hand and not know she'd put down the list with the other. Avoid dangerous situations. That's my motto.

Ship's staff in spiffy white uniforms kept pointing us where to go, and finally one led us to our cabins. "I'm sorry," Marietta said, "I couldn't get you a cabin near mine. I got the rest of us cabins close together. But I had to take what they had left on such short notice."

Never mind. I was here. On a cruise! I put my clothes in the closet and noticed I'd forgotten all but one pair of long pants. Dern. And I had a list. I must have been diverted. Well, I had shorts and a skirt. And we folks who forget learn how to manage. We have ingenuity, by gosh!

I thought of Rose, who went to a convention and forgot to take any pants but the ones she had on. And she had to speak not too long after she'd spilled gravy on her pants. So she washed her pants, kneaded the water out in a towel, and dried them the rest of the way with her hair dryer. I'd be like Rose. Except I didn't have a hair dryer.

I noticed there was a TV mounted on the wall. It was playing soothing music and a picture that said WELCOME TO THE *OCEAN QUEEN*. That was interrupted by the news of an upcoming emergency drill. Not yet, but they didn't want us to be surprised.

Shortly after that several tugs edged the ship away from the pier, with several blasts from the ship's deep whistle.

I was tuckered out and sat down to recuperate, pulled out Marietta's list, and studied it. Now I could give it full attention. Richard and Goldie said that when Marietta was pushed, they were talking on the ground floor of the castle. Winnie was in the castle waiting to go to lunch with the others, but she had wandered off to look around. She was alone. The place must have had a lot of rooms. Alexander Flint was exploring the castle, but not with Winnie. Brian the Lion said he had just come down the tower stairs when he heard the scream and started back up. Annie Long said she'd seen him. She said she was at the bottom of the castle stairs, heard the scream, and ran up, too. The others, including Brian, were not positive at what point they saw her. Lillian said she was in the ladies' room — the modern one for tourists, not the pit that served the castle.

Goldie and Richard had solid alibis, unless they were in collusion. Brian had a solid alibi unless Annie gave it to him to alibi herself. The rest had only their own word for where they'd been before everybody crowded up the steps to see what was wrong.

I folded up the list and put it in the zip compartment on top of my suitcase, my important-papers place. So was all the family in danger or just Marietta? How did millions of dollars fit into the picture? Was Pop right that I could be in danger, too?

After my flu and my airline trip, I was exhausted. I lay down on my bed in my clothes and took a nap. Sometimes my most productive thoughts float into my mind as I wake up from a nap. No such luck.

I slept an hour or so and woke up no wiser but ready to case the ship. I looked out of my small round porthole at the ocean and realized I'd been afraid of being seasick. But the ship's motion was so slight I could hardly tell I wasn't on dry land. I remembered those television programs about the first ships that came to America, and how those tiny ships bucked like horses over the waves. A big ship sure was better on the stomach. In fact, I was hungry.

But an alarm began to sound, and I was directed by the PA to find my life preserver in the bottom of my closet under a panel, put it on, and proceed to my lifesaving station. There I figured I'd find all the suspects and possible victims assembled in life preservers. How appropriate.

The preserver was bright orange and went around my neck, like one of those collars on a workhorse, and fastened in front. It came with a whistle to summon help.

Staff members in the passageways directed me to my lifesaving station, which turned out to be in one of the main dining rooms, complete with tables and potted palms. No lifeboat in sight, but there must be an exit to a boat near where they assembled us. The family and fellow travelers Alexander and Annie were congregated in a bunch in their orange life preservers, all talking wildly together. What on earth were they so het up about?

CHAPTER
10

MONDAY, JULY 21

"You didn't get us first-class cabins," Goldie accused her mother. "If we're going to travel on this luxury ship, we ought to have the full experience. We ought to have more than these little ordinary cabins. We ought to travel like our peers." She raised her chin and fingered her heavy gold necklace, which seemed so odd in combination with the bright orange life jacket.

We were in a dining room called the Majestic, I noted. That's where the folks in our group were to assemble if the ship started to sink, which I could hardly imagine on such a large vessel. But I guess the folks on the *Titanic* had the same thought. Anyway, the staff told us what to do in an emergency. I looked at the other people in orange life preservers, the ones who were not the heirs of Uncle Hiram. They all had that well-fed, self-assured look of folks who could afford a voyage like this. I imagined that the two gold necklaces on the woman who appeared to be wearing a red wig were as real as Goldie's, though not nearly as heavy. The woman's wig was quite realistic, but one strand of dark hair had slipped out from under it. Were any of us what we seemed, even the ones without wigs? That's part of what I had to find out about Hiram's heirs.

"Don't be silly, Goldie," Rich said, "these cabins are perfectly comfortable. Every cabin on this ship is luxurious. Besides, we're not paying for this trip, and I for one am grateful." He sounded a little too much like a high-school teacher to get through to golden girl.

"It would be fun to go first class," said Winnie, smiling at Alexander the Great. Obviously she thought he'd want to go whole hog. "Perhaps we could upgrade, maybe get a cabin with its own veranda, and it wouldn't hurt Aunt Marietta's feelings," she said. "After all, she got us all here and worked it out so that we did what was necessary to satisfy the will. That was a big job right there. And of course we're grateful." Hey, Winnie was learning tact.

"I don't give a damn what you do," Marietta said with a frown and a shrug.

"But if we are in any kind of danger, wouldn't we be safer if we stuck together?"

"Unless one of us likes to push people off high places," Lillian said with a slight slur. Several of the other passengers gave her startled glances. She must have a flask in her cabin. She looked first at Alexander the Great and then at Annie Long, who pretended not to notice. I figured she wanted her relatives to be innocent and outsiders to be the menace.

"I thought we'd feel more at home in the staterooms I chose," Marietta said, changing the subject from high places. "We aren't used to being the Rockefellers or Arab sheikhs or Hong Kong millionaire expatriates. We've spent most of our lives being just plain middle class. Do what you please. I like the cabin I'm in."

Meanwhile a ship's officer was telling us how to activate a light on the life jacket so we could be found in the dark. He told us everything to do, right down to blowing our whistles to get attention. Then he thanked us all for coming and dismissed us.

I for one was glad when lunchtime came. Marietta and I set out for the Majestic, and Richard joined us along with Brian and Annie Long. It was not hard to find the dining room because right outside the entrance was a six-foot-high replica of a sailing ship with soaring masts and enough rigging to support a string factory for a year. The plaque said it was the first ship that belonged to the company that brought us the *Ocean Queen*. Beautiful, but I thought: *No radio aboard that ship.* No way to call for help. We were much safer on the *Ocean Queen*, except from the problems we brought with us.

Lillian came and joined us. No sign of Winnie and Alexander or Goldie. They had evidently removed themselves to more rarefied spheres. Our lunch was elegant enough. Two lines of uniformed waiters stood at attention, and the maître d' pointed to one, who stepped out of line and took us to our table. All white and crystal. White linen tablecloths and napkins, and sparkling wine and water glasses. We had the luck to be near a window. Outside, the water shimmered blue to the edge of the world. A waiter took our orders for drinks.

Rich sat on one side of me. He turned to me and said, "It's nice to have you along, Peaches. I haven't seen you much since we were kids and I used to see you at Aunt Marietta's."

Brian nodded to add his welcome. He was across the table from me between Lillian and Annie Long.

"Marietta and I both got so busy we didn't get together much," I said. "At least this has brought us together again."

Lillian raised an eyebrow. "I hear that you've been busy solving murders." She said it in a contemptuous voice as though she thought it was a totally inappropriate thing for me to do. And in a way it was. So I tried to explain as she quickly grasped the glass of wine the waiter brought and took a large gulp.

"Marietta and I were like sisters growing up," I said, reaching out and putting my hand over my old friend's. She sat on the other side of me. Her hand was still callused from weeding and picking and such, and there was also a recent bruise. "Of course, Marietta turned to me like family."

She squeezed my hand, and I thought from the way her mouth quivered that she might burst into tears.

Rich said, "And of course we're pleased to have you along." Rich had manners. Maybe teaching high-school students made him aware how important manners can be.

"So, you want to know everybody's secrets, don't you?" said Lillian. She meant in general, I guess, since I hadn't asked her a question. She sounded angry, as if I had no right to be so nosy. Well, she was young. Wine did not mellow her. I was half inclined to say, Well, I'm not expecting secrets here in such a public place — but I didn't like to shush her and have her clam up.

"Yes," I said, "I'm a curious type."

"Then ask Goldie about the baby that should have been born and wasn't." We all turned to Lil. Brian opened his mouth like a fish, as if he couldn't decide whether to tell her to shut up or was too amazed at the idea of their mother knowing about some baby that should have been born to say a word.

Annie Long said, "Lillian, the steward is waiting for your order."

Lillian was not diverted. The steward hovered uncertainly. "That's all I know," she said. "I once found a note in my mother's desk that said, *'Rosemary: Believe me, I am crying just as you are for the baby who should have been born. I hope the enclosed will help a little bit.'* It was not signed. I was fourteen years old and I was amazed and kind of scared, and that's why I remember every word. You know, of course, that Goldie's real name is Rosemary."

I noticed Marietta was actually quivering with indecision. Wanting any possible clue to come to light, I figured, but not wanting Lillian to make a spectacle of us in public. The others looked amazed but very curious.

Actually, I had almost forgotten Goldie was Rosemary because nobody had called her that since she was a kid.

"So I asked my mother about that note, and she said it was a joke." Lillian made a disbelieving face. "But then she burned the note. I shouldn't tell that on my own mother," she said with a little embarrassed drunken giggle. "But I've always wanted to know. And what was the 'enclosed,' and why would it help?" Then she turned and ordered spinach salad with smoked salmon, pear and raspberry sherbet, and a bottle of white wine.

Revelations were over. Nobody asked further questions about that letter, at least not during lunch.

CHAPTER
11

MONDAY, AFTER LUNCH

Of course, I tried to find out more from Lillian. When we went down to our cabins after lunch, I stood at her open door, talking to her till she had to invite me in. It was a small cabin but, as they say, shipshape, almost exactly like mine. She waved me into a round-backed overstuffed chair and sat down on her bunk with the open porthole behind her. The porthole was too high for me to see the ocean, but the TV, anchored at eye level on the wall next to her, showed the ocean view off the bow of the ship, blue water with sunshine. Exactly as it was in my cabin. Soft music accompanied the view. I wondered whether they had ominous music if we hit a storm.

"Your mother never gave a hint of who sent her that note, or let drop anything else about it?" I asked.

"Never," she said. "Mother would never

even talk about it except that once. All she'd say was that the 'baby' note was an annoying joke." Lillian added, "I hope you won't mind," and took a flask out of her suitcase. "Would you care for a drink to ward off seasickness?" she asked. Well, that was a new excuse. I could tell she expected me to refuse, and I did. She poured an inch of what looked like whiskey out of the flask into a glass and added ice from the bucket that had contained a full champagne bottle — our welcome-aboard present. She must have polished that off earlier. "Cheers," she said, and swallowed the whiskey gratefully.

"Nothing else ever happened that seemed to be related to that note?"

"No." She sighed. "I asked Mother who sent her the note, and she said she couldn't remember, which was ridiculous." Lillian laughed. "My mother can be very mysterious when she wants to be." She trailed out the word "mysterious" till each syllable was like a word. "Well, you know that." She made an ugly face and said, "Enough. Go ask my mother. Solve the mystery. Ama-a-a-aze us. I'd like that." She gave me Goldie's cabin number.

"And just so you'll know," Lillian added, "I was over at the house I'm building when someone pushed my uncle Wingate up at Linville Falls — or didn't, whichever. I'm sure the workers will remember I was there. One of them had just driven a nail right through his hand, and he's suing me for some astronomical amount because it was on my job. That's the trouble with money. People want some." She hiccuped.

"And on Saturday, when Marietta says someone pushed her, I was one of the people down in the castle below the tower. I ran up the tower when she screamed, in case you think I'd kill my own grand-mother. Now, there's nothing more you'll need to ask me." She opened the door for me and stood waiting impatiently for me to leave, so I obliged.

I went right up to Goldie's cabin, but when I got there, no one answered my knock. So where would she be? Out walking on deck? I tried one deck and then another. I saw Annie Long having a con-versation with Alexander the Great near one of the hanging lifeboats. I made a note of that. Outsiders plotting together? Or nonfamily members relieved to have a break from family? I came across Brian talking to one of the ship's officers. He waved. Finally, after getting lost several times in the corridors and stairs and elevators, I went back to Goldie's room to see if she'd returned.

She seemed overjoyed to see me. "I was so lucky this cabin was still available," she said, beaming.

I looked around and figured the cabin was so expensive nobody but Goldie or Bill Gates could afford it. No dinky little porthole here, but generous windows with tieback drapes looking out on a veranda with deck chairs. I went over and looked out on the sparkling water. Live this time, instead of on display on TV. We were much higher up than my cabin. More in command, somehow, of all we surveyed.

I turned back, and noticed that Goldie was ignoring the ocean. She stood near two dresses entirely covered in sequins, which were laid out over the end of the couch nearest the window. One was a sparkling twinkling rose, the other a shimmering green blue. I felt that if I looked at them too long, it would be like looking at an eclipse without smoked glass.

"I have to decide whether to keep these," she said happily. This was obviously a pleasant kind of decision. "They're from that nice dress shop on board." So that's where she'd been. "It's wonderful how this ship has everything," she said. "You know we have to dress for dinner several nights, and I'm not sure my Asheville dresses will be elegant enough."

I ignored this insult to my native city and got to the point. "I had lunch with Lillian," I said.

"Yes," Goldie said, still contemplating the dresses. "I'm worried about her. She's drinking too much, but you've seen that."

"She never did when she was younger?" I asked.

"She was always too busy," Goldie said. "She worked so hard to get everything she wanted. I don't think she knows what to do if she can just order everything she wants and it will arrive. It's like her life has lost its challenge. I don't understand it." She indicated the dresses and the whole cabin with a sweep of her arm. "I even have my own Jacuzzi! And fresh roses over there! This is fun!"

An odd problem, having life too easy, but not the one I'd come to solve.

"When things go wrong for a family," I said, "sometimes the roots are in the past."

"Why do you say that?" she asked. She began to finger her gold necklace nervously, as if I'd hit a nerve. Good.

"Because I've seen firsthand that it's true." Pretty obvious, I thought. "At lunch,

Lillian told me an odd story about her childhood, and I'd like to ask you about it."

I reached in my pocket for the slip of paper where I'd written down what Lillian said was in the note. A pencil is a girl's best friend. No note. A second-best friend is a place where important notes live. Not in the pocketbook jungle. Mine was my breast pocket. It was empty. Moment of panic. It must have showed. Goldie stared at me as if I were a little feebleminded. But wait, I had two breast pockets. I patted the other one. It crinkled. Good.

I pulled out the slip of paper and read: " 'Rosemary: Believe me I am crying just as you are for the baby who should have been born. I hope the enclosed will help a little bit.' "

Goldie went dead white. She walked over to the window and looked out at the ocean, conveniently turning her back to me so I couldn't see her face.

I walked over and stood next to her. "I'm sorry to bring up unpleasant memories," I said.

She turned back to me. "How long ago did Lillian say this was?"

"When she was fourteen. About seven years ago, right? I imagine she thinks you

143

had an abortion, though she didn't say that. She believed that something upsetting had happened because you burned the note."

"I never had an abortion," she snapped. "I never would. All I can tell you is that that note could not possibly have anything to do with what you're trying to find out. You want to know about Wingate's death, right?" She held tightly to the necklace with one hand and clamped that hand in the other one.

"Right now," I said, "I'm trying to find out about that note, because it's obviously upsetting you that I brought it up. I'd like to know the things that have upset this family because I suspect that somehow that may give me a clue to what's happened." Oh, I admit that was thin reasoning. But I was following my hunch that I was onto something. When your memory is flaky, you listen to your hunches. You nurture your hunches, and they grow stronger, God bless them.

Goldie went over and looked in a full-length mirror. Anything to keep from looking into my eyes. She patted her shining curly locks. "There's a salon on board," she said. "I may get my hair touched up."

I gave her the silent treatment. Great for

pulling out confessions and suchlike. She walked over to a long bar and picked up a velvet-lined box. Inside was an ornate gold necklace with rubies, rather Victorian. "If I get the rose dress, it has so many colors in the shimmer that I think this would go with it. What do you think?"

"You do like pretty things," I said dryly. Perhaps my expression showed what I really thought — *You do like to spend money, and more money.*

She made eye contact. "It's just that I can't bear to think about the summer I got that note," she said. "I put it out of my mind so I can go on." She gave a little humorous shrug. "Rubies help."

"What happened that summer?" I asked.

"Nothing you need to know," she said, "or that any living person but me is going to tell. If anything comes up that seems like it could be related to this in any way, I'll tell you about it. I have to be the judge."

She turned back to the necklace. "I don't think the rubies go," she murmured. "I think I'll take them back and get something else. I think I'll get diamonds. They go with everything."

CHAPTER
12

LATER ON MONDAY

I found my way back to our level and knocked on Marietta's cabin door. No answer. She must be out exploring the ship, so I began to do the same. I went through narrow passageways and selected elevators that only went to certain floors, and up carpeted stairs. I followed posted signs to a library and a bookshop, which were closed, but wrote myself a note to stop later to give them a flyer about my book, *How to Survive Without a Memory.* Probably not their sort of thing, but you never know. I put the note in my reminder pocket.

I passed gambling machines that sparkled with light and three well-dressed women and two men, inserting coins and pulling handles with gusto. There were gaming tables of several sorts, and I caught sight of Goldie at one oval table with a wheel. I figured that was roulette. She waved at me. She had on flesh-colored lace. This was not a sequin evening. No diamonds.

Huge plate-glass windows along the side of the ship gave a sweeping view of the dark shining ocean. Passengers sat in comfortable chairs near the windows and talked. Finally I came to a large room full of small tables where drinks and nibbles were being served. There at the edge was Marietta, looking around as if she was trying to decide whether to sit at a table.

"Let's have a drink," I said. "Our first day out, we should try everything." I indicated a table as far away from other drinkers as possible.

Marietta raised an eyebrow. "You want to talk?"

We both sat down, and a server in a spiffy white uniform took our order. After he left, I reminded Marietta of what Lillian had said about the unborn-baby note. Marietta, who never clams up, went stony-faced. "When Lillian is drinking, she'll say anything," she told me. She rushed on to talk about the fat woman she'd seen who could hardly get through her cabin door. "If I eat every day the way I have today, I'll look like that, too!"

I waited quietly for her to stop hiding

behind small talk, and kept eye contact.

Our server arrived to break the tension with a glass of wine for me, a pot of tea for Marietta, and a plate of little sandwiches for both of us. "I've certainly had enough to drink today," she said firmly. I sipped my wine and helped myself to a smoked-salmon sandwich, still waiting for Marietta to react. She made a fuss about pouring and drinking her tea. Setting the cup precisely on the saucer, pouring a little tea to see if it had brewed enough, then a whole cup. Marietta added sugar and slowly stirred, keeping her eyes on her cup. In Asheville, when we want to stonewall, we talk about the weather. But plainly tea worked just as well.

Finally I said, "So I went and talked to Goldie." No glimmer in Marietta's eyes of how she felt about that. "Goldie said the note was related to something so painful in her life that she didn't want to talk about it. She swore that it could have nothing to do with Wingate's death or whoever in the paper bag."

Marietta gave me a surprised glance. I guess she thought I should give more dignity to Paper Bag and say something like "Wingate's death and your difficult narrow escape."

"Goldie said that if there ever seemed to be a connection, she'd let me know, but that she had to be the judge. I don't think it's wise to wait."

Marietta stayed poker-faced and was saved from comment. Our server brought a platter with tiny cucumber-and-egg-salad sandwiches. Two favorites. I took heart. Whatever else happened on this voyage, I was going to be splendidly fed.

"If your daughter Goldie went through something so upsetting, you must have known it. You asked me to come here and try to find out if someone pushed Wingate and tried to kill you, remember? How can I do that if you won't help me?"

Marietta ate a cucumber sandwich deliberately and took a sip of tea. Finally she said, "Goldie will tell you what happened. It may take her time, but she'll do it. And you'll learn more of the nuances from her than you would from me."

Nuances? What sort of complicated situation was this? "I want to know your version, too," I said.

Marietta bit into another sandwich.

"You didn't get me to come on this trip just to eat goodies," I said. "Why are you treating me like this?"

She reached over and put her hand over

mine. "I may be drinking a cup of proper British tea," she said, "but I'm Scots-Irish, as you know. Scots-Irish North Carolina Mountain. When we promise not to tell, we don't tell. And we protect our own." Her eyes were stern.

I was baffled. "But you wanted me to help protect your own!"

"I promised Goldie I'd never talk about what happened that summer. But I'll go to her and explain that you can be trusted, and she needs to tell you everything you ask."

So whatever happened was in the summer. I could see from the stern set of Marietta's jaw that was all I was going to get, so I said, "Thank you."

Perhaps Marietta could see I was still mad. "If you're exploring the past, talk to Rich," she told me. "Not about that note, but about his father. Rich has a good head on his shoulders. There have been things about Wingate I never understood, like why he let his car be repossessed a few years back, or why he seemed so upset the day before Hiram died. And, of course, you're right, whatever is going wrong in this family may have roots in the past."

Then I asked a necessary question: "Just so I can make my chart complete, where were you when Wingate died?"

"I was out in the garden weeding," she said. "I'm afraid the sage and thyme will not give me an alibi."

I looked down at my plate and knew I couldn't eat the last small sandwich. Good grief, was I getting seasick after all? "Marietta," I said, "I think this derned flu is bouncing back. I have to go lie down." That was polite for "I think I'm going to whoops my cookies." I made it to my cabin by the skin of my teeth. Threw up every elegant bite I'd eaten in the little bathroom and lay down exhausted. It is totally unfair when diseases won't stay gone. "You mustn't overdo when you first get up," my mother used to say when I was a kid. It's hard to take that advice. I fell asleep curled up to keep my stomach warm. I was glad Pop wasn't along. He would have been sure that I'd been poisoned.

I was sick all the next day and furious at my body. Hey, I was missing one fifth of the cruise, not to mention everything I might learn concerning who pushed who, or even about the baby. But I followed my mother's long-ago advice, slept most of the day on Tuesday, and didn't even get up in the evening when I was feeling better. The ship had room service and supplied me with lemonade and chicken broth. Marietta came by in the early evening to see how I was feeling.

"What's happening?" I asked.

"Nothing," she said, "except what's supposed to happen. Dance contests and diving contests for kids in the ship's pool. That was fun to watch. I got a massage in the spa. But all of us act nervous. I think we all feel that the other shoe is going to drop. But we don't know when or how."

"I feel okay right now," I said, "but I won't get up and out until morning. I'm going to take it carefully. I'm no good to you with relapses."

"Well, luckily," she said dryly, "the killer seems to be waiting for you before he does anything else."

CHAPTER
13

WEDNESDAY, JULY 23

The next morning I was fine. In fact, I was raring to go, excited to see everything about the ship and determined to find out more about this threatened family. But as I was putting on my red-and-white striped T-shirt to go with my white pants and red sandals, there was a knock on my cabin door. A young man delivering a fax. I thought of the model of the sailing ship. That ship had no way to communicate with land at all. Now I could get a fax from shore in nothing flat. Handy for Pop. He could put in his two bits' worth when I was a thousand miles away. I assumed this was from Pop.

I thanked the young man and hoped he hadn't read the fax, which said, *Crystal sends you a message. Be careful of the drink.*

Whoever read that would certainly think I was a backsliding member of AA. I was annoyed. But what the heck, Pop had been to his psychic and sent me a warning. I'd be careful.

The fax ended: *Hope you are enjoying your cruise. It's hot in Asheville. Pop.*

It is almost never unpleasantly hot in Asheville. Pop was just annoyed not to be along.

At the bottom was a P.S.: *Good luck, and take care of yourself. Love, Ted.*

I smiled and kissed the fax.

At breakfast I took careful small sips of water and tea before I drank the rest. I felt silly in the elegant dining room, with the hovering waiter, to be afraid of — what? A drug? Poison? But it wouldn't hurt me to be careful, though I certainly couldn't give up drinking liquids for the next four days.

I feasted on a fruit cup with strawberries, an herb-and-cheese omelet, and croissants. Then I set forth to explore and see who I'd bump into. I passed the sailing-ship model, of course, and made my way out to the corridor along the side of the *Ocean Queen.* All sorts of shops and amusements opened off that. I found the bookshop again, and it didn't carry my book, alas. Well, I admit an awful lot of their stuff was about ships and sailing. But I gave them my bookmark with the title, ordering number, and three memory tricks, including George Burns's system for never worrying about names: "Just call everybody 'Kid.' " The clerk was distracted by two other customers but said she'd give the bookmark to the manager.

I spotted Rich in the little library next to the bookshop, dark head cocked, examining a wall of books. Somehow I'd been surprised a ship would have a library. How nice. Must make people's bags lighter. A cheerful blond woman with a very precise British accent sat at a desk just inside the door and asked if I wanted anything in particular. I was tempted to say, "Truth serum," but I said I'd just look around.

I needed to talk to Rich. For one thing, I wanted to know more about his father. When a man gets killed, the reason may be as much in himself as in his killer.

Rich heard me speak to the librarian and turned and smiled. Yes, he did look more like Marietta than his father. Some common ancestor had given Rich and his aunt a wiry build and lively glance. You knew by the solid way he stood that he was his own person, though he was only about twenty-five. "I can't seem to find what I'm in the mood for," he said. He raised an eyebrow just as Marietta might have done, as if to say, I know what you want.

"Shall we go for a walk on deck?" he

asked. "I bet you want to pick my brains."

We found our way to the open deck on a higher level and walked along the side of the ship in a pleasant breeze and sunshine. We went to the rail and looked down at the undulating blue water, water straight to the horizon, with tiny bits of golden light at the tip of each blue rise. I was glad the rail was chest-high. And yet, for better or worse, I was absolutely sure in my heart that Rich was not a killer who liked to push people off high places. But killers can be charming, I warned myself firmly.

He guessed my train of thought. "Fortunately," he said, "you'd have to be pretty strong to lift someone up and throw them off this ship."

I nodded and quickly changed the subject. "You must miss your father," I said.

He sighed. "More than I would have thought. We were so different. But . . ." He paused and frowned, then smiled as if he'd found a diamond. "But that helped me define myself." I felt he was working hard to see the positive. And "define" was a nice schoolteacher word. "My father wasn't mean. He was thoughtless sometimes, especially to Winnie. She could get his goat." He shrugged. "She had a talent. But he was generous. Generous and extravagant."

He stared out at the watery horizon, as if his father's generosity stretched to there. His voice went hoarse: "Yes. I miss him."

"Marietta says he was absolutely single-minded about what he went after."

Rich laughed. "Yes, if he was busy with some project, his house got wild, with don't-touch piles all over. Once he walked three miles home from downtown, thinking about some real-estate deal. When he got home, he realized he'd left his car in town." Rich shook his head as if he still couldn't believe it. "I guess that's why his hero was Groucho Marx."

I must have looked surprised.

"Oh, yes," Rich said. "We saw every Groucho Marx movie over and over. My father had videos. Those movies really cheered him up. He had Groucho's picture in a stand-up frame on the top of the bookshelf. He could sing along with Groucho."

I had the feeling Rich might break into song. But I wanted to know about Wingate, not Groucho. "If I understood your father better, I might have some idea why —" I stopped in mid-sentence. A school of porpoises was leaping through the water not too far from the ship, graceful gray shapes. "How wonderful," I said.

Porpoise watchers instantly appeared. I didn't see where they arrived from in their designer shorts and shirts, but there they were. We waited until the gawkers passed us.

Rich leaned against the rail. No laugh lines on his face now. "I try to think who could have possibly wanted to kill my father, because I don't for a minute believe he killed himself," he said sadly. "He was just beginning to enjoy life."

"Why?" I asked. You might say it was obvious. He was a millionaire. An obvious-seeming question often gets a surprising answer.

"I think he was happy because all of a sudden, in the last few weeks of his life, having more and more things wasn't important to him," Rich said in a wondering voice.

"But he had four cars!" The words slipped out before I could stop them.

"Oh, at first he was drunk with so much money! Do you realize it was the first time in his life he was ever out of debt? All the time I was growing up, he kept having to suddenly rush down to the bank to figure what to do about an overdraft. He had to juggle what bills we'd pay and what could go a little longer without something being cut off. There were always two piles on his desk, with a fake gold nugget someone gave him for a joke on the ones to pay and a chunk of granite on the others. The *others* pile was usually the biggest. He earned good money most of the time, but real estate has its ups and downs, and he loved nice things — for us, too. We'd look at television, and I'd demand the hundred-dollar sneakers I saw advertised. I didn't know any better. I was maybe fourteen. And he'd get them. Winnie had to be contrary, of course, and tell him he was contributing to the destruction of the planet with conspicuous waste. But I went along for the ride."

"Until the family car was repossessed?" I guessed.

He flushed. "The Jag. A beautiful car. Hauled off and gone in twenty minutes. I don't even want to think about that. It was so embarrassing. My girlfriend Mina was there and watched. I suddenly woke up and understood my father had a problem. I stopped asking for things. That confused him. I think he felt that if he couldn't give me things, how could we relate? I told him we could. He meant more to me than hundred-dollar sneakers." Tears came into his eyes. "Later, when he had his millions, he said he remembered."

"He could have anything he wanted," I mused. I wondered what that would feel like.

"But after a while he didn't want it," Rich said in wonderment. "I remember how he put it. We were standing by a jewelry store with Rolex watches in the window, and he said, 'You know how it is if you stand in front of a store window and there's something you want and you have fantasies about it and get all hot? Now I look and I know I can have whatever it is anytime, and somehow it's not so alluring. I can live without it.' "

"That made him happy?" We seemed to be getting further and further away from any reason for someone to kill Wingate.

Rich looked up at one of the huge lifeboats that hung at regular intervals above our heads. "To me," he said, "having money is like this ship having lifeboats. I can save myself almost no matter what goes wrong. And I can save other folks, too." I did not point out how the money could be causing murder and attempted murder.

"But to Wingate," he said, "I think the money was first a relief, then exciting, and then after he spent like a drunk man, he was tired of spending, except for what he needed. So he figured he'd have fun giving things to other people," Rich said, "but, you know, sometimes they resented it." His voice rose with amazement.

"Why?" I demanded. At least you wouldn't kill somebody for giving you something. Would you?

"I don't know why," Rich said. "Maybe it upset the equilibrium between friends. One could give and the other didn't have the wherewithal to give back in the same way. It upsets me if somebody is too nice to me. I don't know why.

"Anyway, my father had just contacted several foundations and universities," Rich said. "They loved the offers of money, naturally. And he was so pleased with himself. There was a chance that if he gave enough to the building fund, one university was going to name a building in his honor. He would never have wanted to die and miss something like that."

Two small boys in matching red shorts ran down the deck, giggling, with their mother in hot pursuit. I wondered if they were small enough to get through the three thick wires spaced below the side rail. Is anywhere safe?

"Did he gamble?" I asked.

161

Rich frowned. "I don't think so."

"So who was angry at him?"

"I have a feeling," he said, "my father didn't tell me everything."

For the first time I had a definite hunch that Rich was not being up-front with me. "There's something you're not telling me."

He didn't answer.

"Did he seem worried about anything?"

Rich paused and leaned against the rail again. "He had his ups and downs, of course." He looked away from me. "There's just one thing I did wrong," he said. "I wish I could live over that last day before he died."

A seagull flew by and vanished into the blue. "Why?" I asked.

"He was upset, and I don't know why. He told me he'd been trying to figure out how to make up for a wrong he'd done someone. But nothing he could do would be enough. I knew he did hurt people sometimes. Like the time he was off in the clouds about some deal, and he ran over my dog. He got me another dog, but it wasn't the same. That last day he said, 'What's the matter with me? Why do I do these things?'

"I asked, 'What things do you do? You're always generous.' He didn't answer."

"What do you guess it was?"

Rich shook his head, but he looked down at his feet. I still felt he was hiding something.

"You have your suspicions," I said.

This was certainly a family that kept secrets.

"If I'd stayed, he would have told me," Rich said. "At least he'd have felt better sharing. But I had a date and was going to be late. So I gave him a hug and said we'd talk about it later. Later was too late."

"Where were you when you learned he was dead?" I asked.

"I was in my apartment eating an ordinary breakfast," he said. "Cornflakes. Sometimes I go for a walk before breakfast in the summer when there's no school. So I ate late, and the phone rang." His eyes filled with tears. "It was the sheriff. He said my father was dead. Now I won't ever be sure what upset him so that last day."

I thought: *That's one of the things I'm going to work like sixty to find out.*

CHAPTER
14

WEDNESDAY EVENING

At dinner I sat between Annie Long and Alexander the Great. From Annie I learned that Hiram liked to travel to exotic places like Katmandu when he was younger. Annie made the arrangements, and if he had investments he wanted to look into along the way, she might go along. She'd been working for him for thirty-four years. She seemed perfectly at ease on the *Ocean Queen*. Her gray silk suit was as stylish as Goldie's svelte black with diamonds, but less flamboyant, her dark hair with white streak dramatic as ever. On my other side, Alexander the Great complained that his filet mignon wasn't large enough. I suspected he was bored.

But there was plenty to do on the *Ocean Queen*. After dinner we all went to the Boating Club, a nightclub at the front end of the ship. Many windows around us looked out on the deck. But now in the darkness they were blind eyes. I stepped outside onto the deck. The moon was under a large cloud, but the edges of that dark cloud were outlined in gold. I swear the stars looked brighter than they did on shore. I thought about the overwhelming size of the universe, and how what we see of it is moon close by and stars light-years away. Those stars made me feel how small we are.

But very important to ourselves! I went in and sat with our group, whose members were ensconced at adjoining tables, resplendent in their dinner clothes. We sipped our drinks, and I was especially careful to have nothing but red wine and to taste it carefully. It tasted great. We watched a magician — the Great Whiz Bang. Maybe we did feel there was safety in sticking together as he turned a handkerchief into a live white dove that landed on his shoulder. The spotlight made everything dark except for the enthusiastic young magician, who cracked jokes and amazed us. A pianist accompanied him with flourishes and crescendos. The Great Whiz Bang asked a busty young woman from the audience to stick a fifty-dollar bill into her bra, which wasn't hard because she had on a strapless dress. All eyes were glued to her bra. He pulled the fifty dollars out of the pocket of his own tuxedo pants. I was trying to figure how on earth he could do that one — with a thread attached to the bill? Or was the gal a shill? Then I realized my brain wasn't working right. My thoughts could mesh, but very slowly. I looked down at my drink, the second glass of red wine. I tried a small sip. Yes, it tasted perfectly normal. The magician was bowing to waves of applause. I felt borne on the waves, quite dizzy. I wanted to put my head down on the table.

People got up and were dancing. The music included golden oldies. I hummed to "Smoke Gets in Your Eyes," still quite dizzy. I noticed that people were turning their heads toward the door to the deck. Someone opened the door and let in a scream. It sounded drunken. I should talk. How could I be drunk after one and a half glasses of red wine? I looked up and was startled to see Annie Long being half carried by a bald passenger with a large nose. Rich and the bald man maneuvered her to sit down at the table next to mine. She began to scream again. Obviously drunk. Her voice slurred. "Someone pushed me! Someone tried to kill me!" Everyone stared.

Several waitpeople in their crisp white uniforms rushed over and conferred with Rich and Brian. Lillian had run over and put her arm around Annie, and I could see her lips moving, asking questions. Lillian wasn't all that steady on her own feet. I tried to stand up and go over to join them. I couldn't stand up.

Somebody must have spiked my wine while my attention was on the Great Whiz Bang! What did they put in it? I was alarmed. They'd spiked Annie's wine, too, I thought. She was a woman who wanted control of her life. She wasn't going to get drunk like that without help. *I'm going to be sick*, I thought, but managed not to.

I was aware of Marietta beside me. "What happened?" she asked urgently. "I was in the ladies'."

"I'm drunk," I said. "Somebody spiked my wine. I think somebody spiked Annie's champagne. She says they tried to push her over." I managed to get that out, and then I put my head down. Noises rushed over me. All sorts of talk and then an announcement. Something about being calm, the deck being searched. Nobody out there.

After a while I was aware of Marietta again. "We have to get you to your cabin," she said.

I opened my eyes. The room was whirling. I closed them again. "Somebody did this to me!" I screeched. I realized too late that my voice had risen. Everyone was staring at me. A rather senior-looking person in a white uniform with lots of gold trim came over and conferred with Marietta about getting me quietly out of there. "I haven't been drinking," I said in a slurred voice that came out surprisingly loud, "except a little bit of wine. Somebody did this to me."

White and Gold came over and took a rather bleary statement from me. All I could keep my mind on was the moon on his cheek. Wish on the new moon. It was a scar or birthmark shaped like a new moon. I found myself singing some song about the moon. Good grief! Did I sing that out loud or only think it? His moon was new, but the real moon was full. I wailed, "I didn't watch what I drank!"

Even in my haze I was aware of scornful looks. That wasn't fair! I managed to sit up and sip the hot coffee that appeared in someone's hand, and then managed to get to the ladies' room, with Marietta helping me stand up. There I vomited everything and felt better. With Marietta's help, I got down to my cabin.

"Annie Long," I said.

"Drunk," she said. "Yelling that some-body tried to push her overboard. She said they ran away when she had strength to fight them off and scream. The search team couldn't find a soul, or any sign that anybody had been there near her."

Yeah, yeah, yeah, said the voice in my bleary mind. *And Wingate wasn't pushed, and Marietta wasn't pushed either.* Out loud, I said, "Why Annie Long?"

"I bet she's a secret lush," Marietta said. "But I never saw her act like that before."

"How about me?" I asked angrily, mean-ing didn't she believe someone spiked my drink?

"I never saw you act like that before ei-ther," she said. I was still so dizzy I gave up.

CHAPTER
15

THURSDAY, JULY 24

I woke up at eleven o'clock the next morning feeling that my head needed to be packed in ice and not touched for a week. *Be careful of the drink,* Pop's fax had said. But I *had* been careful. I'm not a connoisseur, but the wine tasted okay. My hanging TV on the cabin wall still showed the ocean ahead of the ship. Dancing blue, as if to announce that this was a lovely day. Oh, yeah?

I thought about "the drink." Some people called the ocean "the drink." That was the trouble with psychic pronouncements. Sometimes you didn't know till after the prediction came true what the words had meant. How could you be sure you hadn't just made what happened fit the words? This was too much for my feeble brain.

Someone was knocking on my door. I felt the knock in my head. I managed to pull on a bathrobe and ask, "Who's there?" I hoped it was Marietta so I could explain about the night before.

A draggy voice said, "Annie Long." Good grief, if she felt as hungover as I did, some wild emergency had been necessary to get her out of bed. I opened the door. Makeup was not enough to hide the puffiness and circles under Annie's eyes. Still, she'd managed to comb that coal-black hair with the dramatic white streak, and dress in a gray knit jogging suit. A black pocketbook hung over her shoulder. She walked in and sat gingerly in my armchair, her back to the small porthole you had to go over and look out to get a glimpse of ocean. That must be why they gave us the television view. I sat on the edge of the bed, feeling rumpled. "Do you have any aspirin?" I asked.

She took out a metal tin from her pocketbook, opened it, and handed me two. I got myself a glass of water and took them before I thought, *Watch what you drink!* Does taking pills count as drinking? But what good would it do her to poison me? Family members got part of the estate of any other family member who died within a year, and neither of us was part of that club.

"Nobody believes me," she said urgently,

171

her green eyes still sharp, if a little blood-shot. "The damn ship's officers have given me the third degree, and I can tell they think I was just drunk. I *was* drunk, but not from the martini I drank on purpose before dinner, the glass of wine with dinner, and the glass of wine I was drinking at the show."

A martini and two glasses of wine would have given me quite a buzz, but I gathered she was saying she could hold that much liquor.

"They need to believe me!" She clenched her hands in a prizefighter's fists. "Whoever pushed Wingate, and I know that happened — he would not have jumped — that same person must have put on a silly paper bag and tried to push Marietta down a set of steps that could have killed her." Annie's voice got louder and faster. "That must be the person who spiked my drink and tried to throw me into the Atlantic Ocean."

"I heard you yell," I said.

"I'd be drowned," she told me, "except I'm stronger than they thought." She stopped and took a deep breath. "That killer is still here!"

I had to stay dead calm or my head would explode. I had to be rational. "So

172

why have you come to see me?"

"Brian says you were drunk, too, and yelled that somebody got you drunk on purpose! Just like me."

Whoever it was had left me with a stinking headache. "But why the two of us?"

She shook her head with a baffled frown. "Yes. Why me? Or you?" Finally she said, "Maybe there was something they didn't want you to see."

"But why didn't we taste something in our drinks?" I asked.

"Pure grain alcohol," she snapped angrily. "I've figured that out. That must be it! It's tasteless and potent. I know because of Purple Jesus."

"Purple Jesus?"

"I went out with some wild medical students when I was young," she said. "They gave me this drink that tasted like grape juice and grapefruit juice. I got blitzed. It was one third of each juice and one third grain alcohol. That stuff is potent. We need to look for a doctor or a pharmacist. That's who can get pure alcohol easiest, because it's used in tinctures and things like that. Somebody has a medical friend."

I held up a stop hand. "First of all," I said, "we need for the family members to believe us. They didn't entirely laugh about that man who wore the paper bag and pushed Marietta. It gave them pause. Do the family members believe somebody tried to push you over?"

"I hope so!" She nodded her head half-heartedly and then winced. "I don't re-member the end of last night very well," she said. "And I've only seen Brian and Marietta this morning. They *say* they be-lieve me, but they act cautious. They told me you were drunk, too. I told them both of us had been set up."

"And you suspect they doubt it," I said. "Have you told lies before that make them doubt you?" I asked. I was not up to tact.

"Only the polite kind," Annie said firmly, "or the kind I told for Hiram. I'd say he wasn't home when he didn't want to see them. That kind of thing." She folded her hands piously. "And I don't care to be told I'm a drunk!" she burst out. "Listen, I know about drunks. My father was a drunk, and he beat me if his team lost. My brother drowned when he was three years old because my father was too drunk to watch him while my mother cleaned motel rooms so we could eat." She sounded sorry for herself. Well, I would have been, too.

"I've worked hard to get away from that," Annie went on, "and I've succeeded!

I went to my high-school reunion last year, and I was the most prosperous person there except for Eddie Jones, who got to be the president of a bank. I am not a drunk!" She clenched her hands into fighter's knots again. I half expected her to punch me.

My head still ached, but curiosity was now in charge. "Tell me exactly what happened last night," I said.

"You remember how we were sitting at those two tables in a row, all having drinks, and I was thinking how this was great." She shrugged, then winced with the pain of shrugging. "There I sat with the filthy rich at the tables around us, and me with my glass of *Ocean Queen* house Merlot. I was watching the show and sipping my drink and all of a sudden I just felt slugged."

"Who was on each side of you?" I asked. I found a pencil and a piece of paper in my pocketbook, which now lived by the head of my bunk. I drew two bar tables in a row. I had been at one table, and she had been at the other. So if someone spiked both our drinks, he had to move around and try not to be noticed. I made an *X* for me, put Marietta on my right, and Goldie on the left. Or was it the other way? I put an *A* for Annie on the far side of the other table.

"Brian was on my left. I'm sort of here as his chaperon, which is foolish," she said. "That Alexander guy was on my right. He never spoke to me all evening. Winnie was the other one at the table."

I filled their names into my diagram and added Rich to my table. "Nobody else joined us or came over and spoke, did they?" I asked.

"Lillian was at a table nearby with some bozo she picked up in the bar. I think I heard her say he was in advertising in New York."

"So when did you go outside?" I asked. I hadn't seen her go. I must already have been drunk at that point.

"The magician was doing his thing, so I figured nobody would notice me if I stepped out on deck. I wanted fresh air to revive me. I could hardly walk. I don't guess I could think clearly either, or I wouldn't have gone out there by myself."

"Somebody noticed you, and you're right, it was crazy to go out there if you thought someone had doctored your wine," I said. "It was their good luck that you went out on deck. Someone knew how to make the most of whatever happened." I made a note to myself. Everything seemed to show that the killer operated like that, not planning everything ahead but seizing the opportunity to strike when it came. Is that what had happened with Wingate?

Annie shivered violently and hugged herself. Behind her head, the TV still showed tranquil blue water. "I risked my life because I didn't expect — well, you didn't expect to have *your* wine doctored either, did you? I figured at first that I'd had a bad reaction to the martini and Merlot because I was tired. By the time I got to my feet and out on deck and realized how bad off I was, I just leaned against the doorway for a few minutes, trying to pull myself together. Then I heard a big splash, like something or someone falling in the water, so I went to look over the rail into the ocean. Yes. That was insane, but I was drunk. Then someone tried to lift me up and over the rail, and I grabbed on for dear life and screamed as loud as I could, and tried to kick back at that person.

"I guess he'd counted on my being so drunk I'd go right over. Splash! But I wasn't. I fooled him." She said that last proudly.

"Did you see the person?" I asked hopefully.

"Not well. It was sudden, and he was in back of me. I fell down on the deck when he ran. He was dressed in black, with something hiding his face. But it's like a dream. I used every bit of my strength to hold on to that rail and scream.

"Someone inside must have heard me and opened the door. That monster began to run right after I started yelling."

"You think it was a man?"

She frowned. "I'm saying 'he.' I have a 'he' feeling, but I don't really know. I guess he ran inside another door and took his mask off and acted innocent."

"Which is a lot like what he did after he tried to push Marietta," I said. "At least we begin to see his method." Which didn't help much. "Was everybody else still sitting at your table when you left?" I asked.

Two frown lines creased between her eyes. "It's hard to remember. People got up from time to time. I'm not sure."

I realized it was the same with me. The few minutes before Annie's scream were very blurry in my mind.

"And why you?" I asked, not really expecting a useful answer.

"They don't like me," she said angrily. "The whole family." She sat bolt upright in her armchair. "They don't want me here. Except for Brian, who doesn't really mind." She leaned back in the chair, stroked the arm, and smiled. "Besides, I know reasons why each one of them would have wanted to kill Wingate! I don't have proof, so I was going to keep mum. But if somebody is going to try to kill me, I'm damn well going to share what I know quick."

I was for that. I reached in the top of my suitcase and pulled out my tape recorder and turned it on. She didn't even blink. "How about Goldie?" I said.

"Goldie was blackmailing Wingate," she said belligerently. "I don't think she said, 'Pay up, or I'll tell.' Nothing like that. But she knew something about him that she could hold over him. Whatever it was made her angry at him.

"I went to Wingate's house to deliver something for Hiram one day about a year ago, and I could hear yelling around the side of the house. I'm no angel; I was curious, so I went closer to try to hear. They were out on the back terrace, I figured. Goldie was yelling, 'No, I won't ever forget what you did to me!' Then I heard a door slam, and she left. So I went back to the front door as soon as she drove off, and Wingate let me in and he looked terrible. He said, 'Oh, God, if I could just relive the past.' So I hoped he'd tell me more. I was still damned curious. I tried to look sympathetic, but he pulled himself together and said, 'Don't mind me, I'm having a bad day.' I could tell it was a hell of a lot more than a bad day."

"But you don't know what it was?"

"No," she said, her voice sharpening, "I'm only the hired help. You have to learn that your sympathy is not worth a whole lot if you're the hired help." But she'd said she was an adviser, a power with Hiram. How odd she called herself the hired help!

"How about Winnie?" I asked.

She laughed bitterly. "Oh, she had good reason, and there's a temper behind that mealy mouth. Her father told her that if she married Alexander, he'd give all his money to charity and not leave her a cent."

"But she had money of her own," I said, "and she believed in living simply. She told me that."

Annie laughed again. "No, she believed in giving to causes that had to do with living simply. That's different. She wanted to be important just like anybody else. She'd be twice as important if she had her father's money. Besides," Annie went on, "money is strange. It's a symbol for other things. Winnie could see that what her father wanted was to take away her power to decide about her life for herself. She's no fool. That made her very angry. I told Wingate that." For a moment her voice quavered. "I guess that would have made me angry, too."

"How do you know all that?" I asked. I could imagine her turning into a fly and stopping on one family wall after another.

Suddenly Annie looked away from me. Green eyes on the neutral rug on the cabin floor. "I had a way of finding out," she said. "I can't tell you how without telling you someone else's secret." That old ploy again.

"I can see why you're afraid that people won't believe you."

Before she could respond, the ship's alarm began to sound. "Life jacket under the closet floor," I said as I put on clothes as fast as I could, and aching head be damned. I put on my orange jacket, and we headed up through the maze of ship stairways to the meeting area in the dining room. Everyone looked nervous because this didn't seem to be a drill. No smell of smoke. I thought of the *Titanic* and how fast it sank after it hit an iceberg. Could we be near icebergs? We milled around among the tables set for lunch with crystal and white linen.

Marietta, Brian, and Rich joined us, giving me covert is-she-all-right-today? glances. Lillian materialized with her advertising man. Neither appeared to be feeling any pain. Lillian said, "I lost my good-luck pebble, so this better not be a big fire!" She looked very young in a pink T-shirt and flowered shorts.

Goldie, Winnie, and Alexander the Great had reasons to kill Wingate, too, Annie had said, but they were off to a drill station in the higher realms. Perhaps up there they served champagne to settle the nerves. Goldie could drink it wearing her life jacket and her diamonds, which she said went with anything. Maybe their lifeboats were equipped with champagne and caviar. Alexander the Great would like that.

Finally an announcement came. A small fire in a cabin was under control. We were thanked for our cooperation.

I turned and saw Annie following Brian. I hurried over as they passed the huge sailing-ship model and said, "Come tell me about Lillian. And give me your life preserver. I'll need to take it back to my cabin where it came from."

She dropped back and let Brian go on ahead, took off her orange jacket, and handed it to me. We stood near one of the glass picture walls on the side of the ship. From our vantage point the waves seemed to be gently lapping, lapping, lapping out toward the end of the world.

"Lillian is superstitious," she said, "and after a few drinks she wants to know the future."

"So?"

"She went to some psychic. Some woman I've heard people talk about. Christie. Some name like that. She reads cards and hands."

"Crystal?" I asked.

She nodded. "That's it!"

I thought what a small world this is. Pop kept going to see this Crystal, and Lillian had gone, too.

"But don't people usually go to psychics to ask if they'll *get* money?" I asked. I read hands because my cousin Fern from California demanded that I learn as an extra tool for solving a murder. People who hear about this are always asking me to look in their hands and see if they're going to get rich. I tell them hands can show if you're the kind of person who would be likely to get rich. If a hand reader was psychic, he might jump on the fact that it would happen on a certain day in a certain way, I guess. I'm not psychic, and I don't think a person's future is frozen.

Annie held out her own long slender hand and stared at it as if it might hold secrets. "They ask about love, too," she said. Her voice was bitter again. "Maybe that's why Lil went. To see if true love was written in her palm." She laughed, as if love was ridiculous. "But what the psychic told Lillian began to come true and really spooked her." Annie looked me straight in the eye. "And made her afraid of Wingate."

An older man with a beautiful young woman strolled by. She looked like a model in her clinging sundress. He held one of her small, plump, tapered hands in his large gnarled one. I thought how I could look at both their hands and figure out their relationship. Her childlike hands already made me guess he was her sugar daddy. But if I were psychic and predicted their future, my chances of being right were about sixty-five percent. That's what the books I'd read said. Sixty-five percent should not be enough to base a murder on. Even ninety percent would not do for murder. I hoped Lillian believed that.

"What did this psychic tell Lillian?" I asked.

"This Crystal told Lillian that a man she

knew would cut the tree that sheltered her, take gold from her pocket, and, unless she was very careful, cause her death. Things happened that made her sure beyond a doubt the man was Wingate."

CHAPTER
16

THURSDAY NOON

"So this Crystal told Lillian that someone would cut down the tree that protected her, take gold from her pocket, and could cause her death. What else?"

"Some *man* would do it," Annie Long emphasized. "Isn't that enough?"

"No," I said. "I'd like to know the context." We were still standing in the long corridor down the side of the ship with plate-glass windows on one side, shops and bars, and a gambling area and such on the other. Big overstuffed chairs could swivel to look out at the water or at the passing crowd.

"The context!" she echoed. She looked me up and down as if I might be crazy. "I can't remember much else about that prediction. Why don't we sit down?"

I was for that, and two pigeon-breasted women had just left the two chairs closest to us. "You'd better go ask Lillian about the context," Annie said. "You see, it all came true. She lived in that little cabin outside of town that she loved so much, and there were woods all up above her, and the animals came down into her yard, and she put out food for them. She also had a crystal-clear spring. Wingate was the agent who sold that piece of land just above her to a man who clear-cut it. Then her spring went dry."

Yes. That would be a shock. Asheville is one of those cities where there are still places half an hour from town where you are in deep country. The people out there love it, but they won't tolerate zoning. I guess it's against their Scots-Irish independent nature. So your neighbor can clear-cut or build a paper mill. No holds barred.

"Lillian thought Wingate was the cause when her spring went dry?"

"The animals in the woods had no place to live. Oh, she was furious."

"So you could take a poetic phrase like 'He will cut down the tree that protects you,' and take that to mean clear-cutting. It could be taken a lot of other ways, too."

Annie Long gave me a disgusted look, brows knit over those cool green eyes. She got up from her chair. "Don't believe me. Go ask Lillian." I'd made her mad. Not a good way to find out what she knew.

"Of course, you're right. What Lillian believed is what mattered," I said. "How about the part about taking gold from Lillian's pocket?"

She hesitated, standing by her chair. "Oh, that had to do with some sort of investment deal. You ask Lillian."

It might not be easy to lure Lillian away from her Mr. Advertising in whichever bar they'd retired to, but of course I'd try.

"But you haven't told me why Brian or Rich might want to kill Wingate," I said.

Before she could answer, an older woman who walked as if her feet hurt plunked down in a chair near us. This was not a conversation that needed to be public. "We'll talk later," Annie said, and strode off toward the restaurant. So I pulled out a notebook and made a chart of all the reasons why people might have wanted to kill Wingate. A list is a wonderful memory device, but a chart has overtones. A chart makes connections. Mine made it clear that Wingate was a much more interesting and complicated person than I would have thought. Much more tempting to push. The rest of the family was far fruitier than I'd realized.

I wrote down everyone's name and found myself including Hiram and his ex-wife, Suzie.

Suzie: Made some sense. She could actually be around, and I wouldn't recognize her. I'd never seen her picture. She might be furious that she never got a cent from Hiram's will, though she could hardly have expected to be included. Maybe she wanted to get even with the heirs, starting with Wingate. But the others would recognize her if she was on the ship. Nevertheless, I made a note to find a picture of Suzie when we got back to the mountains.

Hiram: Dead and buried. All I could blame him for was writing a will that would encourage trouble. Nevertheless, my gut said he was closely involved in what was going wrong. I suddenly recalled how Wingate called Hiram an old skinflint when Hiram wouldn't lend him money.

Marietta: Annie Long hadn't mentioned why Marietta should want to kill her brother. I couldn't think of a reason unless he was prepared to do some dreadful hurt to Goldie or Brian or Lillian, and she lost her temper at him and pushed him. She could fake the bit about Paper Bag pushing her. But if you were faking, wouldn't you

189

pick something that didn't sound so foolish?

Winnie: Was she in a rage at her father for threatening to cut her out of his will if she married Alexander the Great? If so, she'd sure managed to hide it when I talked to her. Perhaps she was a good actress.

Alexander the Great: Had the perfect alibi — in jail when Wingate was pushed. But he had killed his first wife by pushing her off a balcony. He knew that Wingate could stand between him and marrying a lot more money, if Winnie listened to her father.

Rich: Struck me as a levelheaded young man who would never fly off the handle and push his father off a high place to his death. But when I talked to him about Wingate, I had the distinct impression that Rich was hiding something!

Goldie: Had some mysterious connection to Wingate and a baby that was never born. She was frightened when I asked about that. I'd talked to her about the note and about rubies and sequins, and never asked her alibi for the time Wingate died! I sure had to dig deeper there.

Lillian: Goldie's daughter might believe the psychic Crystal, who told her something that she took to mean that Wingate could cause her death. She was also mad because he was the real-estate agent who sold the property above her cabin, which the owner promptly clear-cut. So Annie Long had said.

Brian: Goldie's son seemed too young and too vague to be a killer. But you never know.

One thing I learned from the chart was that I hadn't checked every single alibi. I mustn't get so interested in what made these folks tick that I'd forget to do that!

All of the heirs were possible suspects except the ones who were dead. I needed to know about Wingate, because he had almost certainly been murdered, and I wanted to know why.

As for the cousin who drank herself to death — what was her name? Behind her back they called her Eeyore after the donkey in *Winnie the Pooh.* Oh, yes, she was Poo. Good grief, she could have been murdered, too!

I rushed back to my cabin and called Marietta. She was just about to leave for lunch.

"Wait," I said. "Remember the time in school when Rebecca Holly told Miss Thompson that you'd stolen the questions for the history test, and it was really her?"

"And," Marietta said, "you thought to look in Becky's locker and found the questions rolled up inside her boot. But Miss Thompson hadn't believed I stole the questions anyway, so we didn't snitch — but we got even." She burst out laughing.

"By giving her Ex-Lax and telling her it was candy! Actually, we overdid it. But she was so naive that it was easy."

"So, why are you thinking about Becky?"

"Because you said your cousin Poo was naive and not used to drinking."

"Until she drank herself to death at Wingate's party. Very strange," added Marietta. "They say it's hard to drink yourself to death because most people just throw up — and go on living. But Poo had a weak heart."

"Think about this," I said. "Somebody almost certainly slipped one hundred percent grain alcohol into my wine the other night and got me drunk. Now, suppose I had been drinking a lot of champagne instead of a little red wine? Suppose I wasn't used to pacing myself with liquor?"

"Oh, good Lord!" Marietta cried out. "One more maybe murder! And after Poo tried so hard."

"Tried so hard to do what?" I asked.

Whatever it was hadn't made them like her.

"Poo was never subtle," Marietta said, "and she sure wanted Hiram to leave her money. So she kept dropping by to give him homemade cookies or jam or something good she thought he'd enjoy. Poo was a good cook, and Hiram had a sweet tooth. When she finally inherited fifteen million dollars, we all joked that it was about five hundred dollars per cookie. But it still seems ironic that she died before she got her hands on a single cent of that money."

"The rest of you got part of that fifteen million?"

"Well, yes. Because Poo didn't have any children, the whole amount was divided among the rest of us."

Pregnant silence.

"Certainly you don't think . . ." Marietta began. "We had enough. There's not a one of us who needed Poo's money. We all had our own money that Hiram left us."

A stray thought floated through my mind. Lillian's boyfriend back home was a doctor — and doctors have no trouble getting medical-grade alcohol.

"There are people who never have enough money, no matter what," I said. "So be careful — in case Poo was murdered. Though we haven't proved that. But we do know you were attacked. I'll see you later. I'm not up to a real lunch. I'm going to look for some chicken soup and hope that it's not laced with cyanide."

Fear makes it easier to exaggerate so that the danger seemed a little less real — because the killer was not likely to have a pocketful of cyanide. Besides, I told myself, no one would gain by killing me. But no one would gain by killing Annie Long, either. So what next?

CHAPTER
17

HALF AN HOUR LATER

Exercising my brain had made my head feel better. Toward the stern of the ship there was a cafeteria-cum-bistro type of place called Frankie's, less formal than the dining room where I'd had dinner. Informal sounded good — maybe they'd have some nice hot soup. I bumped into Rich heading for the same place.

"Hi," he said. "Are you finding out anything?" Obviously he saw my bloodshot eyes and was being tactful.

No point in alarming him with my unproven theory about his cousin Poo.

"Can we have lunch?" I asked, and to my surprise he agreed. He should have been off chasing pretty girls or doing whatever else young men do on cruises. It was my good luck that he wasn't.

Frankie's required us to order in a cafeteria line and take our food to a small round table with bent-wood chairs. This seemed to be where the younger passengers were grabbing a quick lunch in their shorts and sun clothes. I found chicken noodle soup and hot tea, and Rich got a ham-and-cheese sandwich with lettuce and pickles and goodness knows what else, a cheerfully fat sandwich with a toothpick bearing a nautical flag on top. We sat down at a small table with a window on the ocean. The ocean was so blue that if I'd painted it that way in a picture, it would have looked exaggerated.

I looked carefully around me. Someone had put extra alcohol in my drink when Annie was attacked, and I hadn't seen a thing. That's one problem with a one-track mind. While you're concentrating on A, you can miss B. I must keep a watch out for B. I crossed my fingers hard to remind myself. Wingate and I, I thought. Marietta said he had a one-track mind, too. But I worked hard to get around mine before catastrophe.

The person who slugged my drink might of course be someone I didn't recognize. Hiram's ex-wife, Suzie, in disguise, say, or someone Hiram hired before he died. If he were really crazy he could have done that: hired a person to get a job as a waiter on the ship and do us in on the voyage. But I felt a little insane myself, thinking of things that far-fetched.

"So, what have you found out?" Rich wore a T-shirt that said I CAN'T REMEMBER YOUR NAME EITHER. Handy if he were going to the activities all over the ship and meeting new people. Friends laughing at his shirt should relax him, but his shoulders were stiff with tension. I must not let the T-shirt divert me, even if I wanted one. Wasn't Rich's what-have-you-found-out? tone a little bit anxious?

I asked him if he knew about Lillian and the psychic. He burst out laughing. He relaxed. "But she couldn't have taken that seriously," he said. Then he considered. "I don't know Lillian very well, even though she's my cousin. She was always busy with her advertising work, and school takes my energy. You have such an opportunity with high-school kids."

"You didn't get to know her when you two were small?" I asked. A woman carrying a tray came very close to my shoulder. I watched her like a hawk. She did not drop anything in my tea.

He shrugged. "When we were kids, I used to see Lil at family get-togethers. We watched the Thanksgiving parade together on TV or something like that, nothing heart-to-heart." He shook his head and grinned. "But she seemed like a practical kid. Always learning something like piano or judo. She seemed to have her head screwed on right."

I sipped my soup. Hot and rich. I love the silky feel of noodles against my tongue. Rich bit into one side of his sandwich, then the other, to keep the fat filling from pushing out one side.

"I never met your cousin Poo," I said. "What was she like?"

"They say speak no ill of the dead, but she was a pain in the ass. Whatever happened in the world, she could make it sound like it was your fault. One of my high-school kids got a scholarship to Harvard, so she said nobody helped *her* get a scholarship, and that's why she didn't have a better job. She had a perfectly good job in a laboratory doing something off by herself. I know her boss, and she said Poo was at her best off by herself. I think we have a droopy gene in this family, and Poo and Winnie got it. That's funny, isn't it? Winnie and Poo, like Winnie the Pooh. Hey, you can use that for a memory aid. But Winnie is beginning to get around her droops."

"I'd like to call Poo's boss when I get home," I said. "I have a hunch it will help to know about every heir, dead or alive."

He looked surprised. "Actually, Poo's boss's name is Mary Wong, and I think I have her number." He pulled his wallet out of his pocket and began to look for the number among various slips of paper. He seemed to be holding his wallet carefully, however. As if there were something in it that I might see if he let it all spread out. I felt my head begin to throb from trying to watch him closely, and also watch every step of passersby. Like that older woman with a big-city black pocketbook, out of place with her navy-blue shorts. What did she carry in it?

"Here's Mary's telephone number," Rich said. Just at that moment there were loud screams of "Help, help!" on the other side of the room. He jumped up awkwardly and ran toward the screams. A natural people-helper, I thought, be they high-school kids or otherwise. Half the people in the room converged in the direction of the screams, rubbernecking.

I stayed put, guarding my soup, and reached over and picked up Rich's wallet. Sneaky Peaches. There was a section of little pockets for cards, with too many cards and bits of paper stuffed in. As fast as I could, I looked through the top few in the row and found an Asheville-Buncombe library card, a YMCA card, a phone number with no name attached. I made a note of it.

I remembered to keep glancing around. I could so easily get absorbed that someone could drug or poison my tea with no trouble at all. I also kept watch for Rich. I *was* searching his wallet! I found a card that entitled him to a free car wash from the Classie Car Wash on Merrimon Avenue, and a credit card. The crowd of rubberneckers moved back slightly from the location of the screams. Rich could be right back. I couldn't possibly look through every pocket in the wallet. Dern. But I had time to flip quickly through the section of clear picture holders.

One of them stopped me. Across the picture was scrawled *Love from Suzie*. There was Hiram's ex-wife, the one the old man was so eager to disinherit, so Marietta said. She smiled at me: blond, about forty-five, with expensive beauty-parlor hair, a come-hither look in her brown eyes, and the brightest possible lipstick. Involved with Rich? I caught my breath. My elbow jostled my soup. I spilled some in my lap. Damn.

Rich caught me gasping.

Fortunately he'd come back bursting with news.

"A man choked, and his wife didn't know the Heimlich maneuver. By the time I got there, a big fat woman who did was clutching him around his chest." Rich sat down and gave an involuntary shiver. "Boy, what a scare. I thought it was something else — like last night. That another one of us had been attacked. If Annie *was* attacked. I'm so confused about this whole thing."

With a little shock I realized I'd been so fixated on the wallet, I hadn't stopped to think the screamer might be one of us.

"Didn't you believe that Annie and I had our drinks slugged last night?" I asked.

He shifted uncomfortably in his chair. "In all of this stuff, even when my father was pushed or fell, I don't know what I believe. Sometimes I'm sure one way, sometimes the other. I'm scared, but I'm confused. Couldn't you have had more to drink last night than you remember?"

Before I could answer, Rich's eye fell on the wallet, still on the table, open to the *Love from Suzie* picture. He glanced up at me, went white, then crimson.

"There's a perfectly good reason why I

have that picture!" he blurted.

"That's a photo of your uncle Hiram's ex-wife, right?"

He nodded.

"Why do you keep it in your wallet?" I asked.

He squirmed. He fiddled with the flag on a toothpick that was all that was left of his sandwich. "Suzie was always nice to me when she was married to Uncle Hiram. She was nice to all us kids." He said that as if he was making an excuse. "She liked the boys better than the girls, but she remembered everybody's birthday. Uncle Hiram never did."

He looked away from me, down at the little flag. "But I have to admit that even after the divorce, she liked to know everything about Hiram and his family. All the gossip. Like how Wingate's car was repossessed the first time. And you know kids. They blurt things out. She knew how to make us her eyes and ears. She's clever."

"And you resented that?" I asked.

"At first I didn't realize," he said. "Not till I was grown. Suzie had a daughter by an earlier marriage, an awfully nice girl who was a friend of Wingate's." Was he trying to divert me?

"Hiram divorced Suzie years ago!" I said. "Why do you carry her picture around with you? You have it right in with your dog."

He gave me a startled look. He squirmed more. "I've had a chance to make a real difference in the lives of high-school kids," he said in a please-understand voice. Not quite begging. "And our school is short on resources. So we try to get extra help where we can. She found that out and she kept giving me materials and underwriting field trips, and once she paid for a special teacher workshop for the whole school." He looked up. "That meant so much. That was before I had Hiram's money, of course. She wasn't in his will, but she did okay at the time of the divorce. And she went on helping me after the divorce."

His eyes went down to his plate again, avoiding mine. "I told her things that I figured couldn't hurt, because I understood she still thought of me as her eyes." He glanced up at me. "This sounds awful, but it didn't hurt anything."

The woman at the next table was bug-eyed. But what could she figure out from our talk? Not much, and I didn't want to interrupt Rich to tell him to keep his voice low.

"But why do you carry her picture around?" I asked again.

He sighed. He hesitated. To perfect a lie

or to get what he said right? "When she gave me the picture, she said, 'This is the size to go in that wallet of yours with the places for pictures.' Oh, she has a sharp eye. She said, 'I want to be in your thoughts, and you know you and your kids are always in mine.'

"So I kept the picture there because I wouldn't want to look through my wallet for something like a number to give her and have her notice that the picture wasn't there."

"Why is the picture still there, now that you don't need her money for the kids?" I asked.

"I was used to it," he said. "I didn't really see it anymore. I forgot it was there."

Did I believe him? I wasn't sure. He didn't seem that absentminded to me. Do we forgetters recognize each other? Maybe we miss the ones who use the best strategies. Or maybe everything he said was a clever lie. But why should he lie? Even if Suzie was his lover. That would be odd, spring and autumn. But not unheard of. Was Suzie mixed up in what was going wrong in the family now?

I finished my soup and realized my head still ached slightly. "I'm going back to my cabin," I said. I looked down at the soup spot on my white pants, the pair I like best and wear most and needed clean. "I hear the ship has a Laundromat," I said. "I think I'll go do a load of wash." A clothes dryer would dry my pants better than a hair dryer, by a lot! Rich said good-bye and walked off down that corridor with the windows on the sea on one side and good-time places on the other. I saw him meet Lillian and Goldie and Marietta coming the other way, saying hello in a surprisingly carefree way. Perhaps they still believed there was safety in sticking together.

Then I did something I never do: I ducked into one of the ship bars and asked for a whiskey sour. Instead of dessert, I told myself as I sipped the sweet-and-sour drink. Why did I feel as if I needed to steady my nerves? I had a second one. It wasn't my nerves. I was angry. Those stinkers believed I was drunk from one and a half glasses of red wine. I wasn't even drunk from two whiskey sours. But I did feel more cheerful. And perhaps less cautious.

CHAPTER
18

1:30 THURSDAY AFTERNOON

I went to my cabin, changed out of my pants, and put the ones stained with soup together with some other odds and ends of laundry into a plastic bag. I found a steward in the passageway who told me how to get to the laundry room. Down, down, down in an elevator, then along a long cream-colored passageway. Odd thought: if heaven and hell were on this ship, I'd be headed down toward hell. Maybe I was psychic.

I turned left past a florist's shop, and there was the laundry. Several people were just leaving with clean shirts on hangers. A black shirt with a white skeleton painted on it flapped on one hanger. Not very appropriate for a cruise. There were banks of washers and dryers and a machine that dispensed laundry detergent. No windows, not even portholes. This was an interior room. I put my wash and the right amount of detergent into one of the machines and sat down to look at the ship's daily newsletter, which someone had left handy on one of the molded plastic chairs.

I read about a Catholic mass, a bridge lecture, a glamour demonstration, and a mixed-doubles table-tennis tournament. Too late. That had all been before lunch. I'd even missed the lunchtime cocktails with Maria Dons at the keyboard in the pub, and a harpist in the Map Room. Just the music of the washer for me. The gaming tables would be open all afternoon. Goldie used the gambling machines. Did Goldie gamble on more than I knew?

A thin woman with elbows that stuck out like a bird's wings came in and went straight over to a washer that had finished its cycle. She had on white shorts and a shirt with birds all over it. One large skinny tropical bird had a posture just like hers. Did she have a sense of humor? Or just not know the effect? She threw all her wet clothes into a rolling basket, took them over to a dryer that was larger than the others, and stuck them in. Then, for some reason, she changed her mind, took them out, put them in a smaller dryer, and turned it on. Thanks to what the cabins cost, the washers and dryers were a perk —

no coins required. "I'll be back in half an hour," the bird lady said, as if I cared. She must have kids with her on this cruise. I'd noticed a small boy's underwear and shirts. "Don't let anyone move this laundry," she ordered. "You can count on my being back in half an hour." After she left, I was alone.

This would be nap time for anyone who took a nap. Also a good time to be out on deck if the weather was still pretty up above. Nobody but me doing laundry. I couldn't hear other life. This was down the hall from the florist's; no other doors nearby. The emptiness, the secludedness of that room was kind of nice, a meditation time. The whiskey sours made me feel mellow. I thought of Ted and wished he were on board. He'd like to sit in a deck chair and read. I forgot to worry.

I went back to the ship's news. I could catch a children's fancy dress parade and passenger talent show in the afternoon. Ah. That's where the skeleton shirt would march. There'd be a dance contest run by Floralinda, who was a contest champion in America and England. She would award prizes. But I never win prizes. A book signing would be in the bookshop. If I'd just had notice, I might have asked them to have a book signing for me! If they had my book. This signing starred Daphne Martin, who'd written a book on healing herbs. Marietta would certainly go to the herb thing.

Were there doses of herbs that mimicked drunkenness? What made me think of that?

In the evening I could go to a "musical" in the aft nightclub. So much to do during the voyage. And so quiet here in the laundry.

So, think useful thoughts. What did I know about the killer? He, or maybe she, was unconventional in method of threat. Also an opportunist. Whatever came to hand would do. Evidently he or she wanted to do away with anyone who had knowledge that might pose a threat. Probably an angry person. Someone who struck partly out of rage at the world? I couldn't believe that Marietta, for instance, really had information that could hurt the killer. But the killer had evidently tried to push Marietta down a long, steep, iron stair in a tall tower. That could have been fatal.

The washer shuddered to a stop. My clothes were clean. I was just moving them into the dryer, about to move the setting from hot-and-heavy to drip-dry, when a deep strange voice behind me said, "Don't bother with the clothes. You get in there yourself."

I whirled around, heart beating hard, and there was someone with a paper bag over his or her head. Holes were cut for the eyes and the mouth. Like the simplest kids' Halloween mask. He belonged in the fancy-dress parade. But maybe he didn't. If it was a he. The voice sounded phony, whoever it was.

A paper bag. I got it with a jolt. The person who pushed Marietta wore a paper bag.

"Hurry up!" Paper Bag was ordering me as if he had a gun to my head. No gun in his hand. He held an ordinary drinking glass of liquid. Was this a joke? Someone who'd heard what happened to Marietta and had a warped sense of humor? No such luck.

"This is powerful acid," the creature said in a deep raspy voice. It held the glass in one gloved hand and a sliver of cloth in the other. It stuck the cloth in the liquid, and the cloth instantly disintegrated. "If I throw this in your face," it said, "your flesh and bones will melt. You'll be blind. You won't have a nose or mouth. If you scream, I'll throw it." My stomach flipped. I backed up. I made myself notice the hand — large for a woman's, small for a man's, and covered in a black glove that obscured everything but the size. The hand held that glass of liquid ready to throw into my eyes. I shivered. None of that. I had to keep my wits about me.

Was this a man or woman? The clothes were all unisex, including the sneakers. The large floppy shirt could hide two bosoms or not.

"Climb into the dryer," the voice demanded. Death by clothes dryer? If I hadn't been so appalled, I'd have laughed. Paper Bag must be a little bit crazy. Crazy people are not afraid of risks. That makes them extra deadly.

But not patient. "Hurry up!" it ordered again. If I tried to run, it stood poised to throw the acid. Why does blindness terrify me so? Somewhere I'd seen a picture of a face destroyed by acid, features gone. But dryers kill, too. My friend Amy's cat jumped in one. Then Amy ran the dryer because she didn't know. The cat was very dead among the dry clothes, and Amy was so sick and upset she hung her clothes on a line forever after. How long would it take a dryer to kill a human being? I shuddered. Maybe I could stall for time till someone came to do laundry. Hey, that woman swore she'd be back in half an hour, and that was a while back. Then at least there'd be more than one of us to fight this thing off. I went over to a small dryer. I didn't want to be steamed to death with my own clothes.

"I won't fit," I said.

"You'll fit, dead or alive," Paper Bag said, and sloshed the acid in the glass. The person picked up a folded lapthrow from the top of a washer in its free hand. "You won't be hard to smother when you don't have a nose." Then it said, "Here. Here's a bigger dryer." Yes. The larger dryer that bird woman had moved her clothes out of. I climbed in as slowly as possible, one foot, then the other, then head and arms. The dryer was still slightly warm from the last use. I moved like a snail. Bird woman said she was coming back. Why didn't she hurry? The fit was still tight, and projections in the dryer stuck into me at odd angles. Paper Bag moved the glass threateningly and said, "Hurry," again. I prayed for people to arrive with dirty clothes.

"You'll be found out," I said. Another threatening slosh. I pulled all of me inside. I should find some clever way to fight back. But how? Paper Bag pushed the dryer door shut with a sickening click. Hey, maybe Paper Bag wouldn't have a quarter! But these machines were free.

Paper Bag pushed a button, and I began to revolve. Cramped as I was, I didn't fly through the air like laundry. I whirled around slowly at first, and hot air rushed around me. I thought, *This can't be happening,* and then *I'll bet this thing is set on hot-and-heavy!*

Maybe Paper Bag was still there and would baste me with acid if I yelled, but I screamed anyway, and I got one fist uncramped enough to pound on the door. The hot air began to heat the metal around me, and also my nose. It dried my throat as I screamed. How much did you have to roast before you passed out? I kept pounding and screaming.

Something hot and wet slapped over my nose. Something left from the load removed. I gasped for breath, then blew out to try to blow it off. I couldn't reach it with my hands pinned to my sides. I couldn't breathe. My chest heaved. I shook my head as it went around the down cycle. The motion of the machine dislodged whatever it was, at least for now. I gulped in fiery air.

Each breath was hotter than the last. My screams became hoarse.

I thought about Ted. I didn't want to die and never see Ted again. My thoughts were hot and disordered. Ted would be left with Pop to look after if Pop didn't go back to Azalea.

I became aware of something moving outside the dryer. Or was it my fevered imagination? I banged harder. I rasped, "Help."

For a moment I was silent, to figure out what I could hear. Nothing. I banged again. Then someone was fooling with the handle on the dryer. Hope surged in me like a volcano erupting. But the door didn't open. I was so hot I felt I was going to explode. So dizzy I was afraid I'd black out. Whoever was still rattling the door. Maybe Paper Bag had come back to tease me.

I was so on fire I couldn't even hope. Then the door swung open, and there, looking in on me, was a small boy, maybe four or five years old. "Mama says not to get in there," he said. "It's for shirts and pants." He sounded disapproving, but his eyes were round with amazement. He wore a white sailor suit like a member of the ship's staff shrunk. Was I hallucinating?

I climbed out as fast as I could, cramped and dizzy as I was. First I just rolled out on the floor, then I managed to get in crawl position, so shaky that I wasn't sure if I could get any farther. Finally I pulled myself up, holding on to the dryer door, and managed to stand up in the wonderful cool air, carefully balanced or I'd collapse.

I heard a piercing voice call, "Hubert! You come here, Hubert!" The small boy grinned. "That's Mama." He came nearer and stared at me. "Do you have candy?" he asked.

I staggered to the chair I'd been sitting in before and fell into it. My legs were rubber.

He stood in front of me and said, "Candy?" again.

I reached in my pocket and found two quarters. "That's all I have," I said. "Watch out, they're hot." I would have given that boy the moon if I'd had it. He accepted the quarters gravely and put them in the pocket of his white shorts. He must be a handful, I thought groggily. Smart, too. He'd watched Mama and knew how to open the dryer door. Thank God. His large blue eyes stayed calm.

"Hi, Mama," he called. "Here."

A fat blond woman, in a too-tight sailor suit to match the child's, came sailing into the room. She ignored me and demanded,

"How many times do I have to tell you to stay with me, Hubert?" Her voice was like the screech of brakes on an out-of-control car.

"I like it here," the kid said. I figured he liked getting her goat. "A great big dog ran after me," he said happily.

She groaned and flushed. "You've got to stop telling lies." He began to sing a little tune to himself.

She frowned and turned her attention to me. She looked me up and down, and her eyes widened. "You're the one who got drunk in the Boating Club," she said with a scornful voice and a pleased smile. "They ought not to allow a lush like you on a fancy ship like this. My husband knows the captain, and I'm going to ask him to see that you're never allowed on this boat again."

Hubert was still singing his song and ignoring me and Mama.

"And now here you are where a little innocent child can find you drunk in the afternoon," she said in triumph. "Your nose is bleeding. You look disgusting."

I started to speak, but my tongue was cardboard. The sound that came out certainly sounded drunk, so I stopped trying.

"And furthermore," she said, "you'd

better put something on that sunburn or you're going to be sick. I suppose you passed out in a deck chair in the sun. For what we pay on these cruises we shouldn't have to put up with people like you."

She grabbed the child's hand in her plump one. She yanked him after her out of the room.

She said sunburn? Of course. I was red from the heat. I realized I was so thirsty my mouth puckered. I pushed myself up on my wobbly feet, went over to a big deep sink, and rinsed out a plastic cup that was probably there to measure soap. I filled it with water and sipped cautiously. I half expected my throat to sizzle. Then I took a long reviving drink. I splashed cold water on my face and arms. Yes, there was blood in the water from my face; I splashed it clean. I sat back down in the chair and waited for my head to clear. I leaned back and actually nodded off.

I came to with a start. I knew I had to get out of this deserted place quickly. Paper Bag could come back to see if I was dead. He or she could finish the job.

CHAPTER
19

IMMEDIATELY AFTERWARD

It was lucky that to get to my cabin I didn't have to go through the congregating places, like the main corridor to Frankie's Bistro, the meeting rooms, and the library. I staggered through long, thin interior passageways. Like going through the ship's intestines, I thought woozily. When an older woman appeared going the opposite way, I tried to look seasick, and hoped my nose wasn't bleeding again. I realized I'd wet my pants. It must have happened in the dryer. Good grief! And I was so woozy I almost didn't care. I was lost.

I found an elevator. Good. But when it stopped, I realized I was on the wrong floor. This could be good luck or bad luck because there, walking toward me, was White and Gold with the moon scar on his cheek. He was the member of the ship's staff who took statements. In a real ship officer's suit.

He walked right up to me and said, "Are you all right?" in an unfriendly voice.

I hoped he wouldn't notice my wet pants. I said I wanted to report a threat to my life. He raised one eyebrow, which I read as unsympathetic. He took me to a small office, and I managed to give my statement standing up. There was a counter, and he and I stood next to it. It wouldn't be fair for me to sit in his green upholstered chair. Though I still felt dizzy, I thought I did a good job of telling him about the laundry-room incident. He took notes.

Then he put down his pen and said, "Ma'am, I just this minute had a complaint about your behavior in the laundry room. You must realize there is alcohol on your breath. May I suggest you think twice before you make a formal complaint. We have only one full day left on the voyage, and if you really believe you are threatened here, I don't think you want to do anything to delay getting off the ship."

I took a deep breath to tell him why he was dead wrong. Then I let the breath out. I was not going to convince this man with the judging eyes and disapproving mouth. Not in my state. But more important, he was right. Above all else, I wanted to leave that ship. I swallowed my pride and asked him which way back to the elevator.

I got off at the right floor. Finally I was in my own cabin, where I could lock the door. I took off my wet pants and put them in the sink with soap and water. I'll bet real detectives never lost their dignity like this. I felt hot and prickly and tender all over, and my head still whirled. My nose hurt, and I held a tissue to it to be sure it wasn't bleeding still. No, it wasn't. A glass sat neatly on the shelf over the basin. I shuddered. A glass exactly like the one Paper Bag had filled with acid. But this glass would hold water! I needed water.

As I downed the second glass, I realized that what I wanted was total immersion. I also wanted to lie down, but that would have to wait. All I had in the small ship's bathroom was a shower.

At least there were no blisters on me — not that I could see. Cold water would feel like a benediction. I took off the rest of my clothes and got in the shower. The water felt so good I almost forgot I was dizzy. Every inch of me enjoyed the cold from the top of my head down.

Finally I got out, grabbed my bathrobe from the back of the bathroom door, and made it to the bed to lie down.

If I lay still, the vertigo subsided. I reached for the phone and called Marietta's cabin. No answer. I'd try again in a minute. The hanging TV still showed a calm and sunny sea in front of the ship. Marietta was probably up on deck enjoying that. I fell asleep and woke up with a start when I dreamed that Paper Bag was in my cabin, standing right near the porthole where Annie Long had stood. I screamed, then woke up enough to see no one was there. Great. Was I going to have nightmares now?

Annie. Some thought about Annie was at the edge of my brain. From the back, Annie looked like Marietta. The situation would make more sense if someone was still trying to kill my friend Marietta. I prayed that wasn't so. I was still so sleepy I wasn't sure why that couldn't be, but I felt it couldn't be. I put it out of my mind.

I sat up and tried to call Marietta again. No answer. I tried Annie. She'd been my co-target in the alcohol thing. Been closer than I to disaster by drowning. No answer. I tried Rich, then Goldie. No member of our group was in his or her cabin. I left Marietta a message to call me. It occurred to me I ought to talk to her about this first, and decide what to do next. I lay back and shut my eyes and tried to think. The next thing I knew, it was the middle of the night. Black as the inside of a whale. I turned on the light and went into the bathroom. I was still a little woozy. I looked at the clock: 2:30. No way I could do anything at that hour. Just before I went back to sleep, I thought of something. Nobody but Rich knew I was going to the laundry room. Did he tell someone, or was I being followed?

I thought of something else: Paper Bag couldn't have brought a gun on board. Our bags were X-rayed. But he could bring bottles labeled witch hazel or toilet water, or whatever. He could bring pure alcohol to spike drinks. He could bring sulfuric or any other kind of acid. He was smart. I hated him for being smart. I fell asleep angry.

I had one more dream about a great banging, maybe a thunderstorm, but it passed.

I woke up with the clock on the table saying ten o'clock and with light through the porthole. Morning. I was wildly hungry. I could sit up without being dizzy. That was a good sign. I stood up. I could do that, too. I was still a little woozy, and my head ached, but not as badly as before. I would get dressed and go look for

Marietta or whoever I could find. We all needed to be on alert. Maybe I'd better try to call folks again before I set out. Why had no one called me back? I looked down at the phone on the table. It was off the hook. Oh, great. I'd been so disoriented the night before I must have knocked it over and not even noticed. I tried Marietta. No luck. And I still felt I should talk to her first, if possible.

I looked for what to put on. Dern. I'd forgotten my clothes in the laundry room. I'd been so desperate to get out of there they'd gone right out of my head. Well, I sure wasn't going back now alone. Unarmed. With maybe someone following me.

So I posted myself a signal to remember the laundry later. Works every time. You put something related to what you want to remember in a ridiculous place. I took a bra and underpants out of my suitcase and hung one over one side of the television set and one over the other side. That should get my attention.

I set forth, walking carefully, in pants that didn't quite match my shirt. My head was a too-full basket of eggs. My brains were about as useful as scrambled eggs, but they were improving. I took the elevator up to the level with the long corridor-cum-lounge at the side of the ship, where some folks were strolling and others sat in big upholstered chairs, looking out at the ocean through the big glass windows and talking. Why sit inside on such a lovely day? None of my folks were. I was so hungry I went off to breakfast at Frankie's, heaping my plate with eggs, rolls, butter, jam, slices of ham and cheese, fruit, and a fruit yogurt. My stomach had not been damaged in the dryer. Not too many people eating at ten o'clock. I took a pot of tea and deliberately sat at the table where I'd sat with Rich. Memory works better if you retrace your steps. Yes. I'd told him I was going to the laundry room. And whoever he told must be Paper Bag! Or maybe *he* was.

After breakfast I walked along, looking in the bookstore and the library. I finally came to the gambling machines along an inside wall. Where had I heard those machines called one-armed bandits? On some TV show about a gambler? A silver handle on one side of each machine pulled down to make pictures of various fruits and things whirl around inside a glass window. I seemed to remember you had to have all the pictures match to win. Even if I'd wanted to gamble, I sure didn't want to watch anything whirl.

But I had no choice. Because there was Goldie furiously pulling down a handle and watching the pictures spin. Assorted fruits came up. She fed in more money and pulled the handle again. She had been to the beauty salon. Her hair was positively neon gold. Her shirt was all printed with maps of the world. Expensive. I was in back of her, looking over her shoulder. The fruits stopped spinning.

"Shit!" she said angrily. "I never win." She fed in more money. I grabbed her arm around about Africa. "Oh, shit!" she said, whirling around, surprised.

I said, "I have to talk to you, or you may lose more than money." This was the gal who had absolutely refused to tell me why she got that letter about the baby who couldn't be born. Which probably meant it was important. But maybe now . . .

She raised one eyebrow, which I noticed was brown, not gold. Her lips were fire-engine red. "You look like hell," she said, and turned back and put more money in the machine.

"Of course I look like hell," I said, standing close in back of her, right behind Canada, so I could speak in her ear. I was almost overwhelmed with hairspray fumes, but I whispered, "Someone tried to kill me and damn near succeeded. You could be next."

That got her attention. She turned and looked me up and down. "You mean — really?" she asked, and I could feel her eyes searching for signs of drunkenness. Damn the person who spiked my drink and got me pegged as a lush!

"I mean, I was almost burned up," I said. That was oversimplified, but I had to get her away from that one-armed bandit.

She sighed. "Come on back to my cabin," she said to me with a longing glance back at the slot machine. "At least I wasn't on a roll."

So I was the lucky beneficiary of her nonwin streak. Thank you, whirling fruits. When we got to her first-class cabin, we'd have privacy and another good view of the endless ocean.

I ought to enjoy that view while I could. Tomorrow we docked in New York. But I knew I was ready to land when the ocean began to seem endless instead of broad and beautiful. Somewhere on the ship was a killer who had already tried to push one of us into that ocean, and fried me in the dryer.

We took an elevator up to Goldie's level.

Higher is fancier. Two Latino-looking men were going our way, and I didn't want anybody to overhear us, so we didn't talk till her cabin door clicked behind us. She stood with her back to her million-dollar view and asked, "Someone tried to kill you how?" Her tone was skeptical.

I went over to her brown velour couch and sat down. "I'm in bad shape," I said. Goldie, with both eyebrows up now, sat down next to me.

I told her carefully, step-by-step, about the dryer, not leaving out the two whiskey sours ahead of time and the woman in the sailor suit who was sure I was drunk afterward, or Moon Scar, who smelled my breath. She squirmed and kept staring at me as if to decide if I was sober now.

"Ask Marietta," I said. "She'll tell you I don't drink too much. I never have. Somebody did slip something in my wine the other night, even if the ship's officers won't believe it."

On a small bar to her left, one rose stood in a silvery vase. Ah, the perks of traveling first class. Why should she believe a peasant like me?

"Look, Goldie," I said, "there's no way to know when Paper Bag, whoever he is, will do something else. God knows he's unpredictable. Or *she* is." And, I thought, God willing, Paper Bag is not Goldie.

She got up and paced back and forth, frowning. I was happy to keep sitting, even if I got a crick in my neck from looking up.

"Listen," I said, "if I were going to make something up, I'd make it sensible, wouldn't I? Not totally off-the-wall. I honestly don't tell lies, except sometimes to be tactful if I forgot something important." I reconsidered the off-the-wall bit. "Is there any member of your family who's known for doing crazy, unpredictable things?"

That stopped Goldie's pacing. "Oh, sometimes," she said, but with a shrug. "On certain subjects. Like, don't get Rich talking about conspiracies, all the way back to who killed President Kennedy. He collects conspiracies. He thinks there is some underground group trying to control the world, and things are all linked together. He can sound like a nut. But he doesn't *do* anything except read conspiracy books."

She laughed, but I noticed she twisted her hands together nervously. "And don't get Marietta started on the postal service and how somebody is stealing her mail." She was wound up now.

"Lillian believes in living life fast because she thinks that, way back in the

1500s, Nostradamus predicted the end of the world before long, and his other predictions have been right and so the end of the world must be coming soon."

No wonder Lillian drank.

"But otherwise," Goldie said, "my family is very sensible, unless you count Winnie having no sense of humor. You don't kill people because you have no sense of humor, do you?" She paced over to the window and stared down at the water, obviously not expecting an answer. Then she whirled back and stood right in front of me, feet apart, looking down at me. "So you think one of us is a killer?" She plunked down beside me, staring me in the face.

"It's possible," I said calmly, "but I don't think anything yet. I'm trying to find out more. Why does Marietta think someone is stealing her mail?" I needed to keep her answering questions. Marietta's mail was easier to pin down than the end of the world.

Goldie fingered her gold charm bracelets. One charm was a tiny greenback. "Marietta wrote some letter, and it never arrived. So she's sure it was stolen from her mailbox. Or from the mailbox of the person she sent it to."

"And who did she send the letter to?"

"She wouldn't say," Goldie mumbled.

I wanted to yell, Oh, for God's sake! Not more of that crap — but I held on to myself and answered dryly: "I suppose she said it was a secret that involved someone else, so she couldn't tell."

Goldie jumped up, put a hand on each hip, and tried to stare me down. "You're making fun of me, aren't you? Because I said that about the letter Lillian saw. That's what you came to find out about, isn't it? You want to scare me so I'll tell you." Goldie was not dumb. She plunked back down on the couch and turned directly toward me.

I looked her straight in the eye. "You ought to be scared," I said. "If a small boy hadn't run away from his mother into the laundry room, I might be dead. Whirled senseless and burned to death. What makes you think something just as bizarre couldn't happen to you?"

She shivered involuntarily and chewed her bottom lip. I hoped I'd gotten through to her. She'd turned as pale as the cream-colored walls around us. She took a deep breath. "Okay," she said, "I'll tell you about the baby letter." She'd become rigid. "It will make you think I killed Wingate."

She spit the words at me, with a scornful flash of her eyes. "But I didn't. So what good is this going to do?" She choked back a sob and clenched her hands in her lap. She chewed her lip so hard I was afraid it would bleed. This was going to be heavy stuff.

"That letter about the baby may be a clue to who killed Wingate and tried to hurt the rest of us," I said as soothingly as I could. "A puzzle piece may be nothing by itself, but it could be the key to the whole picture."

Goldie shot me a dirty look. "I don't see how. And you have to swear you'll keep this secret unless it turns out to be related to murder. And it won't."

I promised.

"It had to do with Hiram's damned money," she muttered.

"Not so *damned* now," I said dryly. "Did you buy the ruby necklace?" That just popped out. Maybe I was jealous. Though, in another way, I was glad not to be any more a part of the family can of worms than I was.

She burst into tears. I reached over and put my hand on hers. "His money has been hurtful to you," I said, trying to get her back on the track after my thoughtless words.

"I used to know what I wanted," she sobbed. "Not just rubies or diamonds. Diamonds are instead of."

She reached over to a small table by the couch, grabbed a tissue, and blew her nose.

"Diamonds are instead of marrying Verner Ray Jones. That's all I wanted to do, from my first year in high school. He lived on the next farm, both of us off at the end of the road at the top of the mountain." Goldie had stopped sobbing, focused on her story. She'd left this great ship in the middle of the ocean and was back in the mountains.

I looked around at the silk drapes, the window onto the balcony with the deck chairs, and the deep pile rug. I had to work hard to think in terms of a mountain farm.

"We got kidded about being end-of-the-world kids." A wry smile twisted her mouth. "Verner was so great. Whatever he told me was fun to hear, even about worms or compost or diseases. And it didn't matter what his father was like." She stopped and sobbed once, as if somehow it did matter. Then she went on: "Verner's father said God was all love and would forgive absolutely anything if you just asked. His father would listen to people. So sometimes people came and talked to him when they felt bad, as if he was a preacher. But Verner's father had to farm because he wasn't a preacher. You'd go by and see him out picking tomatoes, and somebody was telling him their troubles and helping pick."

"Handy," I said, and she must have seen in my eyes that I thought we were off the subject.

"You need to know that," she said. "Verner's mother was dead, and he helped his father farm and everything. But he wanted to be a nurse or a doctor. He was smart."

Yes. Verner the fast *learner*. Who had a career on the front *burner*.

"I knew what I wanted even when I was fifteen," Goldie said. "All I wanted was to marry Verner. I loved him. I still do. If he just hadn't been so strong. If he hadn't been so strong that he rode his bicycle up the mountain — not just down but up. If he just hadn't done that."

By now I understood that all these irrelevant-seeming details were heading somewhere, somewhere dark and unhappy and connected to Hiram's money and Wingate's death. Just as the endless-seeming ocean connected to the shore.

That ocean was taking on a leaden gray color with flecks of white. We were going to have a storm.

"You see, Uncle Wingate had a damn one-track mind. I don't care if Wingate's dead. He was a bastard when it came to that." Goldie began to cry again. In back of her, a seagull flew past the window.

"A one-track mind?" I asked, trying not to look guilty myself, since alas, I have one. "What was so terrible about that?" What on earth could a one-track mind have to do with the letter about the baby?

"Uncle Wingate wanted to buy this piece of property. He'd heard a highway was going near it. The owner, who needed money, would sell cheap. Only Wingate didn't have any money. He never had any money. He wanted Hiram to invest."

"When was that?" I asked.

"Back when Verner and I were juniors. We were in Madison High, and Verner was the smartest boy in the class. He really was. Back then, Uncle Wingate did everything he could to butter up Hiram. Wingate took him places in his car, and he drove too fast. Uncle Hiram liked that. He was always in a hurry. I think it made him feel important."

She stopped and held her hands over her

mouth as if she couldn't bear what she was going to say next, but all she finally said was, "Hiram heard that maybe herbs could help his arthritis. Someone sent him an herb newsletter from a place called Pecan Springs, Texas. Hiram wanted to talk to Mother, and he wanted to see our herbs where they were growing, since he'd never been to our place."

I wondered what on earth that could have to do with the baby, but she was so intense, I didn't ask.

"Wingate's whole mind was on that property and on getting Hiram to put up money for that land, so he didn't worry about anything else. He just brought Hiram up on our mountain fast around the curves." She took a deep breath with a sob in the middle and then pressed on.

"My Verner was riding his bike up the mountain. Just at that moment. If he'd only waited ten minutes. If he'd just come back sooner. And Wingate swerved around a curve in a narrow place."

Now she stopped for a few sobs, though she tried to swallow them. "He didn't hit Verner. Verner was too quick. He turned out of the way, but he skidded in the dead leaves by the road. He skidded off the edge. He went off a high place with these awful rocks down below.

"I heard the horn blow like the end of the world and a squeal of brakes and ran to see what was wrong, but all I saw was Wingate's car standing still. After a minute or two Wingate jumped out and came running to look over the edge like something scared him to death, and I looked, too, over the edge, and there was Verner on the rocks, all limp and still. And down beyond, his bike — all bent from the fall. I guess I was screaming, and we scrambled down. But when we got there, Verner was dead. I couldn't even tell him good-bye. He was dead."

"But Wingate and Hiram weren't hurt?"

"They weren't even scratched," she said bitterly. "I could see that Wingate spent several minutes calming Hiram, before he even came to see if Verner was dead. He didn't want Hiram to be shocked out of the mood to invest." Her voice shook with rage.

"But Wingate knew Verner went off the edge?"

"He said he wasn't sure what happened till we found him." Goldie shrugged.

"What did the sheriff say?" I could smell Hiram buying off the sheriff.

Goldie looked startled, "Oh, the sheriff

didn't come. Verner's father came. He'd been out picking kale and saw it all and heard me scream. He came with a kale leaf in his hand, so fast he forgot to put it down. But when he saw that Verner was absolutely dead, with no breath and no pulse, he said it must be God's will. He said that everything that happened was God's will." Her words were slow with amazement.

"Wingate was yelling it was his fault. He was pretty shook-up. So Verner's father went right to him and put his arms around him and forgave him. Just like that. I didn't forgive Wingate. I never will. But Verner's father begged me not to tell what happened — to protect Wingate from more pain, he said. He was a silly fanatic. Poor old man. But what good would it do if I talked about how Verner died? I didn't talk about anything. I didn't go to school. I was sick." Goldie became silent as if the story were over. She slumped on the couch and traced circles on the back with her index finger.

I waited a long time while she drew circles, then stared into space. Finally I asked, "What did that have to do with the baby?" She turned her eyes toward me dully, as if she couldn't collect her thoughts, as if she'd used up all her strength. I pulled out the slip of paper with the wording of the note about the baby on it. I read it out loud. " 'Rosemary: Believe me, I am crying just as you are for the baby who should have been born. I hope the enclosed will help a little bit.' "

Goldie screamed, "Oooooh!" so loudly I was afraid someone would come investigate. "The bastard," she said, sitting up straight. "The bastard had the nerve to persuade Hiram to send me away to boarding school." I figured the bastard was Wingate. "I had a kind of breakdown. They told Mother I needed a change, and I couldn't just go on refusing to leave my room and refusing to talk to anybody. Although Wingate made it pretty clear he was grateful that I didn't talk about what happened." Goldie shook her blond curls as if she couldn't believe all this. "Ma said I needed to be someplace that didn't remind me of Verner all the time, and that Verner would want me to go. He believed in reaching out and trying new things. And that's true. He did. His father came, and he encouraged me to go. So I went.

"But first I wrote a letter to Wingate. I told him that all I'd wanted in life was to marry Verner and have a baby like him. I guess that's old-fashioned, but that's what I wanted. I said it didn't matter where I was, in school or out of school, I'd always know I'd lost the thing I wanted most. Nothing could make up for that. Wingate called me up and said he understood how I felt and he was sorry, but he hoped I'd try to go on with my life anyway. Then he sent me that note and a check for five hundred dollars marked 'for school clothes.'

"I was so angry I almost burned the check and then I thought, Well, damn it, I'll never have Verner so I might as well have pretty things 'instead of.' I did it like thumbing my nose. I looked as good as any of those rich kids at that school, and I dyed my hair and I became this me. And I try not to think about what happened before, except when you make me." Goldie's eyes flashed anger again.

"You never forgave Wingate."

"He was part of what I didn't think about, but, no, I never forgave him. Would you? Because of him, Verner cracked his skull, and I never had a chance to say good-bye. When I did marry, my husband left me."

"So the way Wingate died was rather appropriate," I said. "He fell off a high place just like Verner."

She jumped up and clenched her fists. "I

knew you'd say that. But I didn't do it. I swear to God I didn't do it. Why, I even got so I was friends with Wingate in a way. By not ever thinking about what happened. By being the new me. I was friends with everybody. Why not? I'm a good-time girl, right? I married a good-time man, we had two kids, and were almost happy for a while. Then he got bored and went off with a younger good-time girl. Now I have diamonds and new clothes, and somebody will probably marry me for my money. I can have a choice of gold diggers, can't I? I can have a wonderful life.

"You say someone could kill me, Peaches. Maybe they could. And maybe part of me is dead already."

I got up, went over to her, and gave her a hug. I didn't know what else to do. I hoped I wasn't hugging a killer. She didn't feel like a killer. More like a sick child, stuck in the past.

I waited till she calmed down. We both sat back down on the couch, then I changed the subject. "When Annie and I were drunk," I said, "when someone spiked our drinks and tried to push her overboard, there was an officer with a moon-shaped scar on his face who took statements from us all. Remember him?"

She nodded and relaxed. Folded her hands in her lap. We were talking about my problems now.

"I bumped into that man when I was lost on the way back from the laundry room," I said. "I tried to give him a statement about what happened there, how someone tried to kill me."

Goldie nodded. Maybe she had accepted what I said as true. About time.

"But Moon Scar didn't believe me," I told her. "That woman who accused me of being drunk in the laundry room got to him first. He said I was dumb to make a complaint because that might delay our getting off this ship. And I decided he was right. I don't want to do anything to delay our getting out of here."

"Yes!" Goldie cried out. "Please don't! I thought I liked it here. But now I hate it. I want to go home. I'm glad that man didn't believe you. I'll tell Lillian and Brian what happened so they'll be careful. You tell the rest. Tomorrow we'll be safe on land. I can't wait!"

We still had the afternoon, the evening, and breakfast to get through alive. Also a storm. The sky was now battleship gray. Appropriate. More white foam on the waves. I could feel the big ship rock.

CHAPTER
20

LUNCHTIME

It was essential for me to find the others in our group, especially Marietta. Goldie had distracted me. For a while I'd been so absorbed in her story that I'd almost forgotten we were in bizarre danger from an improviser with imagination.

Moon Scar had refused to believe my life had been threatened and made me decide that getting off the ship as fast as possible was our best hope. But any member of our group might be at risk. I needed to confer firsthand to see what they felt we should do next. Why did I feel like a scout deliberately leading a troop into landslide country? *Be sensible*, I told myself. I had merely blundered, or been enticed, into a bunch of millionaires. They could all afford to hire bodyguards if they wanted to. But I was the one who knew the latest twist of danger.

I went down to the Majestic dining room

and looked around carefully. Not one of the group was enjoying a gourmet lunch. Where were the family members hiding? I wouldn't have minded hiding, myself, but actually, staying in public places with lots of people was probably the safest bet. I went off to Frankie's to see if some of our group could be having a fast simple snack. I was in luck. There sat Brian with a double cheeseburger in front of him and a sexy-looking gal on each side. The blonde's mouth was too large, though interesting in a wry, sensual way. The brunette's eyes popped slightly, but in a boy-am-I-interested gaze. Both gals were done up to the nines and absolutely focused on Brian. He looked overcome with pleasure. Floating on hormones. Very teenage. He could hardly coordinate as he took a sip of his soft drink. His red mop was as unruly as if he'd just been through a storm. He gave me an inane grin and said, "Hi."

"Have you seen your grandmother?" I asked, slowly and clearly, to be sure it got through his fog.

He shook his head no. No point in trying to get through to him now. I walked off and then turned back to look. The three at his table were shaking with laughter, but somehow it seemed a little forced. I thought he wore glasses. Did I not remember right?

Yes, I was sure he did — thick ones, too. I laughed to myself. He left them off for vanity. I hoped he wouldn't bump into the furniture when he stood up. The girls leaned forward, hopeful and competitive. Brian leaned back, supercharged and — yes, I thought — unsure. Brian would not be pulled together enough to be Paper Bag, I told myself, though the chances were that one of our group was. Unless some person we didn't even know or suspect was following us. Equally horrible thought.

I headed back to the dining room because maybe the others were just late eaters. I thought about Brian as I walked along the window corridor. Suppose you suddenly learned when you were a teen that you were a millionaire? With possibilities as endless as the ocean. Money for anything. I mean, it's enough of an adjustment to deal with sex. Would a mother like Goldie be any help to a kid like that? What kind of trouble could he get into with all that money all of a sudden? Maybe he was high on drugs, as well as sex and money. Could Brian's state of mind be related in some convoluted way to Wingate's death? I was beginning to feel that whatever went wrong was due to boxes within boxes, to strange twists and turns. Under my feet, even the ship was less stable. I could faintly feel the swells.

Back at the Majestic, the maître d', in his sparkling white-and-gold uniform, bowed as if he were overjoyed to see me again. I was pleased to see Marietta and Rich at a table near a palmetto. None of the rest of Marietta's folks in sight. Lillian was probably off with her new friend. I hoped he was big and strong and protective. Goldie and Winnie and Alexander the Great must be eating in higher realms, I told myself. Did killers use a different weapon up there? That left Annie Long unaccounted for. No sign of her in the Majestic. But Annie was already on alert, I figured, because she knew firsthand that the attack on her was not hallucination or fraud. A waiter escorted me to the table where Marietta and Rich were just ordering. Lots of empty places. I sat next to Marietta. I realized I was starving and ordered a truffle omelet and green salad with Roquefort dressing and iced tea. I like omelets. I'd heard that truffles cost about thirty-five dollars each and were dug up by pigs. I'd never tasted a truffle, and this was my chance. *Live life. Don't think about danger,* I told myself. And what could I say to

Marietta with the waiter hovering?

We weren't near the window this time — just as well, now that the sea was ugly gray — but we did have our own palmetto nearby and the usual white tablecloth and a pink carnation in a small vase. From the florist by the laundry room, no doubt. I shuddered.

"Something is wrong, isn't it?" Marietta asked. "What is it? I got your message to call, but your phone must have been off the hook. I knocked at the door, and there was no answer."

"I dreamed of thunder," I said. "I bet that was you, and I was just too knocked out to wake all the way up. I have something to tell you when we can be alone." I pantomimed writing a note. The tall thin woman at the next table had begun to stare at us when Marietta asked me what was wrong. I did not intend to tell her. I searched in my shoulder bag, but I didn't have a pencil. Dern. I'd left it somewhere.

Marietta frowned. "Winnie and her beautiful man are coming down for lunch. We arranged it. She wants me to meet some new friend."

"I need to tell her about this, too," I said. I could see Marietta almost exploding with curiosity. She pulled a pencil and paper out of her pocketbook and wrote: *You need to talk to us concerning what?*

I wrote: *Someone threatened me, but I don't want to talk about it here and maybe spread rumors. Let's eat. Then come to my cabin.*

Next thing, Winnie arrived hand in hand with Alexander the Great, and with Goldie in tow. Also a New Age-looking young man with a ponytail. He had soulful blue eyes and a determined mouth. His clothes were all signed by the maker in out-front embroidery, and here he was on a cruise, so I assumed he was a super-rich New-Ager. He was going to delay us, which annoyed me.

Goldie eyed him like a good boyfriend prospect. We'd have more than one agenda at this table.

"This is Bob Waters from California," Winnie said importantly. "He puts together deals that make the world a better place."

I might need to remember him for some reason. So I pictured him out in that rough water, fallen overboard. He'd *bob*bed up and down in the *water*, about to drown. That was dramatic enough to keep his name in mind.

I noticed his hands, quite long, with knots at the finger joints. The palms were covered with many lines. People with a philosophic bent often have hands like that, people who want to know what's in back of what's obvious. I hoped that wouldn't mean he'd tell us more about today's deal, whatever it was, than we wanted to know.

Winnie, Alex, Goldie, and Bob ordered. Thank goodness for the brisk service. Marietta announced that she was sorry to say she and Rich had to eat fairly quickly, so she canceled their dessert. Winnie looked annoyed, but Alexander the Great, who had sat down next to me, gave me a wink.

"You have a wonderful opportunity," Bob told Marietta and Rich. He had a deep voice that sang with enthusiasm. "You can help buy a paper mill that can be converted to use kenaf fiber instead of trees." He said that triumphantly. Winnie glowed with approval. Marietta and Rich seemed interested.

"There is already a small mill that makes that paper for people who care enough about saving trees to pay extra," he said. His voice said that was all the best people. "Farmers raise kenaf just for that purpose. But any paper made on a small scale is more expensive and has trouble competing in the mainstream market. This is a very large mill —"

I could see this was well out of my league. I could not help buy a paper mill, especially when Bob mentioned something about twenty million dollars. I noticed Alexander the Great yawned. Goldie batted her eyelashes at Bob. She seemed to like his earnestness. No hint in her manner of what we'd said to each other.

I turned to Alexander on my right. "How's your upgraded cabin?" I asked.

"Quite comfortable," he said, as offhand as if first class were his natural due.

"Are you enjoying all the activities?" I asked, trying to get the conversation around to where he and Winnie had been at about one forty-five on Thursday when I was forced into the dryer. He couldn't be Paper Bag. Nothing would have disguised that chest span. But Winnie was just possible. Or perhaps they'd been to the florist, for example, and seen something.

Our food arrived and interrupted me, with lamb chops for Alex on my left, smoked-salmon salad for Marietta on my right, and my truffle omelet. So, okay, I can always worm out information better when I'm well fed. The omelet had what looked like dark bits of mushroom sprinkled on it. Not enough truffle to have strained the pig. It was good, but not, I decided, that much better than mushrooms, maybe because there wasn't enough to get the full thrill of the taste.

Alexander ate with gusto. He did enjoy Winnie's money, I'll say that. I kept asking about activities, but all I was finally able to extract was that Alex and Winnie had been in their cabin early Thursday afternoon. He winked at me again to imply what they'd been doing. The wink seemed to be the most used "word" in his entire vocabulary.

"And so, you can help to curb the lumber interests that want to raid our national forests," Bob was saying, with Winnie smiling at him like his proud mother. Marietta finished her salad with smoked salmon, and Rich polished off his East Indian curry. Winnie had hardly touched her platter with caviar and stuffed eggs and other choice bits. But Marietta turned to her briskly and said, "We have enjoyed learning about this opportunity from Bob, and thank you for introducing us. Now we need to have a meeting of our group.

"Thank you," she said to Bob in a that's-the-end-of-that tone of voice. "We'll get in touch with you if we need to know more."

"I'd like to learn more!" Goldie trilled.

But Marietta took Winnie and Goldie by the arm and all but dragged them to my cabin, which was the closest one. We had the good luck to meet Brian and his two gals on the way. Marietta told the three of them that Brian was required for family business. When she takes charge, she takes charge. Marietta even pressed Brian's girls into service. She asked them to look for Brian's sister, Lillian, and tell her she should come to a family meeting in Cabin 333 right away. Thank goodness they'd given me that number. Any fool could remember three threes, even me.

We proceeded in convoy. I opened my cabin door, and Alexander and Winnie went in first, then Rich and Marietta, now clasping Brian's hand as if he might get lost.

"Now, *that's* an interesting place to keep your underwear," Marietta said. The others gawked. I rushed to undrape the television set.

"That's temporary found art," I said, and that sounded even worse — my bra is serviceable, not arty, not even lacy. "I mean, it's a memory device. You hang something symbolic in a place where you can't help noticing it." I grabbed my underwear. "And these were to remind me I have laundry in the Laundromat, which is what I want to talk to you about." I stuck my underwear in a drawer — a real no-no for the absentminded. Never put anything where you can't see it in a temporary room, unless you put it in your suitcase. But I was rattled.

Alexander and Brian laughed. Winnie giggled and eyed me as if I'd lost my mind.

Marietta said, "No, this is serious. Somebody tried to kill Peaches in the laundry room."

That got everyone's attention. They settled in to listen. Marietta sat in an armchair. Brian and Rich and Goldie sat at attention on the bed. Winnie and Alexander stood over near the porthole, holding hands. They rocked slightly with the motion of the ship. On this big expensive ship, how much of a storm would it take to be dangerous?

I stood with my back to the bureau, facing them all, and told them about the person, be it man or woman, with a paper bag over the head, who'd threatened to blind me with acid and forced me into the dryer.

Marietta stood up. "It was the same

person who pushed me!" she cried out. "It must have been!" She looked from one face to another with fear in her eyes. We all eyed each other.

Marietta sat back down, frowning with distress, and picked at a small spot on her skirt. Next to her, Brian was wide-eyed under his chaotic mop of red hair. Winnie had let go of Alex's hand and was shredding a tissue between her hands and watching me carefully as if she still hoped this whole story might be an act on my part, but she said, "So if somebody tried to kill Marietta and then Annie Long and now you, we know beyond a doubt there is a killer. So my father was definitely pushed."

Alexander put his great muscled arm around her. "I told you so, baby."

Marietta stared at each of us one by one. "But if this person is mad at our family, why did he attack Peaches and Annie?" she asked. "It makes sense for him to push me, but why them?" Nobody answered. Maybe we ought to warn Brian's gals that associating with this family was not safe.

There was a knock on the door. Marietta opened it, and speak of the devil, there the gals stood, staring at us all, rampantly curious, with Lillian in tow. Marietta thanked them profusely, pulled in her grand-daughter, and shut the door in their eager faces. She sat Lillian, who was not too steady on her feet, down in the chair and moved herself to the bed. I repeated my story.

"Was there anything to distinguish Paper Bag's hands?" Rich asked.

"Gloves," I said. "They were black."

"And you've told whoever you tell on a ship about this?" he demanded in a school-teacher voice. "I mean, it's not police or a sheriff, but there's someone."

I explained how I'd tried. "But listen," I said, "I was drunk the night Annie was at-tacked. You all remember, somebody spiked my wine. The staff of this ship al-ready thinks I'm a lush. They think I make trouble. So, after that woman reported that I was staggering drunk in the laundry room, do you think we can convince the officers on this ship that someone tried to kill me by forcing me into a clothes dryer? There was no witness except for a kid who likes to make things up."

Lillian began to laugh. Marietta shushed her.

"But if that happened, there must be proof!" Winnie cried out. "Something to show this paper-bag person was there."

I noticed she still said "if."

"Maybe" I said, "but acid can be poured overboard. A paper bag can be torn up and blown away by the wind, as one evidently was after Marietta was pushed in the tower. A sea breeze would grab a paper bag fast."

"What have we got to lose if you report what happened, even if no one believes you?" Rich asked.

"Time," I said. "We're due to land in New York in the morning. If we put pressure on the authorities on board, they may go through the motions of investigating, even if they don't believe me. That may delay our getting off this ship. I'm prejudiced. I want to get out of here to my nice familiar mountains where I know the dangerous places."

Rich said, "There must be evidence right here on board that would show us who the killer is. There must be some official here on board who could search all our cabins, and that should be done!"

A knock on the cabin door silenced us. I went to the door and opened to Annie Long. "Oh," she said, surprised to see us all, "I was looking for Peaches. I found laundry with her name tapes on it in the laundry room." Good. Maybe you think name tapes are just for summer camp, but they sure do help us absentmindeds. Now I wouldn't have to go back to that infernal laundry. She'd even folded my things, bless her. I quickly put the clothes in the closet on my suitcase and went back to my place, leaning against the bureau.

Annie hesitated near the entrance to the cabin as if she might suddenly leave.

But of course we had to tell her what was happening. "Damn!" she said, combing back her widow's peak with her fingers. "Why did this person try to kill me and Peaches? We didn't inherit all that money. I was only Hiram's damned housekeeper. Why us?"

Just what Marietta had wanted to know, and a good question.

"How did this person know where you were, Peaches?" Winnie asked suspiciously, glancing from one face to another.

So I asked Rich if he'd told anybody where I was going.

"I don't think so," he said. "Why would I?" Could Paper Bag be Rich?

"Evidently someone shadowed you," Marietta said, "waiting for a chance."

"It must be a woman," Alexander said with a smile. "She used alcohol, almost like a poison, and then a clothes dryer. A

256

man's mind wouldn't work that way."

"You'd be off the hook — if it was a woman," Lillian said sharply. "I say it was a man." She started to stand up, but sat back down unsteadily. "A man would know . . ." She paused, collecting her thoughts. ". . . a clothes dryer . . . would throw people off." Her voice slurred. Lillian was getting drunk earlier and earlier in the day, it seemed to me. "A man tried to kill Annie and Peaches." She nodded to herself. "So when he kills the real one he's aiming at . . . no one will think it's him." She glared at Winnie. "Watch out!"

This was getting out of hand. Marietta stood up. "If we accuse each other without evidence," she said, "we can't work together to protect ourselves. Now, I say we need to do two things. Most important, we should get home as fast as we can."

Alexander and Goldie cheered. Annie Long said, "Amen." I thought, *Right on!* Rich frowned. Lillian hiccupped.

"Second of all, we need to be sure there is no incriminating evidence in anyone's cabin."

Marietta was so right, but how could she persuade them all to let us search?

"But at this point none of us entirely trusts the others." She challenged them

257

with her eyes. Nobody disagreed.

"So we need teams of two to do the searching, in order for one to keep an eye on the other, and two teams so that one team can search the cabins of the other team members."

Rich nodded. "I would accept that."

The others nodded one by one, even Annie Long over near the door and Alexander the Great by the porthole. So if the killer was one of us, he thought his cabin was clueless.

After much discussion we set up two teams, each with two people who seemed to have absolutely no reason to be in collusion with the other. Rich and me on one, Marietta and Winnie on the other. The other people had reluctantly put their trust in us.

I don't know what Marietta and Winnie learned, except they found no paper bags or acid in anyone's cabin, and nothing else incriminating. I learned that sniffing expensive perfume and aftershave — to be sure that none of it is acid or grain alcohol or whatever — eventually turns my stomach, that Winnie stepped out of her underwear and left it on the floor in her fancy first-class cabin, but Alexander was so neat it was hard, at a glance, to tell he existed. I learned that Lillian had enough bottles around to carry every kind of dangerous liquid, but they all smelled of plain old Scotch whisky. Rich found an empty aftershave bottle in Brian's suitcase, which seemed to smell of aftershave as it should, but I did wonder why he brought the large size.

We reconvened to my cabin. "So we vote not to discuss what happened, except among ourselves," Marietta said. "Tomorrow we'll go back to our mountains." Lillian looked wistful. Brian sighed. The rest of us cheered. I'm not sure why we were so encouraged. So far, only one person had actually been killed, and that was in the mountains.

But everyone seemed cooperative. I seized the moment.

"While you're here," I said, "we can do one more thing to sort out what has happened." I found a yellow legal pad in my suitcase and marked a page for each person into a chart. Then I asked if each one would write in where he'd been at the time of Wingate's death, Annie's struggle not to be thrown overboard, and my stint in the dryer. "I already have Marietta's chart of where you were when she was pushed," I said. "So unless you think of anything new about that, you don't have to put in that near catastrophe." Amazingly, no one balked. Any effort to find out what threatened them appeared to be welcome now. Each of them seemed pleased to find something they could do that might help, or maybe something that would make it look like they wanted to help. Nobody even said I should stay out of this. By now they were good and scared, Goldie nervously twisting her diamond necklace, Rich frowning, Winnie holding tight again to Alexander the Great, Brian large-eyed, Lillian taking a flask out of her pocketbook and drinking straight from it.

I asked Brian if he'd stay and talk to me a little while. I wanted to ask him about the big empty bottle in his suitcase. He sighed. The gals were waiting. Marietta told him firmly he should stay.

I asked the others if they'd check their phones for messages. I might want to ask questions about the charts. Not one of them told me to go sit on a tack.

Then Marietta made her suggestion. "This is our last night on board," she said. "There'll be a musical show tonight. We got in trouble at the magic show because we didn't look after each other. I'd like to suggest that tonight we have a buddy system. Each person has a buddy he's in charge of watching, and we stick together and we all watch for anything strange that could happen to any one of us."

Everyone agreed. Fear drew them together, even though I noticed them giving each other little furtive glances. Was Paper Bag one of us?

CHAPTER
21

LATER FRIDAY AFTERNOON

Nobody was left in my cabin but Brian the Lion and me. He was in the armchair. I sat on the cot. I suppose at this point I should have been nervous about being alone with any one person. But I couldn't believe that Brian was a threat. I looked down at my chart. Under *Wingate: Friday, July 11, Fell to his death about nine a.m.* Brian's entry said, *Collecting wild mushrooms with Annie Long.* Now, there was an unusual alibi!

I looked up at Brian with his wild mane of red hair and his dreamy eyes. He sat with his back to the hanging TV. The TV showed high waves, silver crests. The music was interrupted by an announcement: our arrival in New York would be delayed an hour. We were losing time because of the storm. Brian smiled. "I don't care if we never get there!" he said. I figured his girlfriends were more important to him than any fears about his life. In fact, he might be too young to believe in death as really possible.

"Tell me what happened when someone pushed Marietta," I said.

Brian stretched back in the chair, then forward. He had an India-rubber body that seemed boneless. He could twist and turn in any direction. He laced his fingers together behind his head.

"We were at this stone tower," he said. "Part of this second-rate castle. Not as good as the ones you see on TV. But the tower was tall, and we went up and looked out of these little stone windows. You could see a long way. That was nice. Marietta had stayed until last. She said she was watching somebody picking herbs in a meadow. She wondered what kind."

Yes, I thought. Paper Bag waited until he had her alone. Did he keep that bag folded up in his pocket, waiting for a chance to kill?

"I went back down the stairs," Brian said, "to the others, who were in this stone hall in this old castle, and I heard this wild scream, and we all ran back up the stairs. There was Marietta saying somebody pushed her, but she looked all right, except hysterical, and nobody was there except us.

It was all scary and confusing."

"You didn't see anybody with a paper bag?"

He shook his head. "But at first we were all trying to figure out what Marietta was talking about, and when we looked for a paper bag, there wasn't one." So someone in that confused crowd was probably the killer.

"Were there windows in the tower?" I asked.

"These little stone windows."

So maybe Paper Bag tore his bag up and dropped it out of a window.

"Nobody acted suspicious?"

"Everybody was acting funny," he said, "but not one more than any other."

"Who would remember seeing you at the bottom of the stairs?"

"I don't know," he said. "It was all so fast and so confusing."

That was not much help. Perhaps he'd do better with Annie Long.

"And on this ship, when Annie said someone tried to push her overboard, what did you see?"

"I was up dancing with this red-haired girl," he explained. "She said we matched. I don't remember her name. I heard Annie yelling that someone tried to kill her, but she sounded drunk. I wondered if it was really true."

"And who was still sitting at the table?"

"You were, weren't you?" Brian asked. "But we all moved around so much. I'm not sure."

"On Thursday, early in the afternoon, when someone whirled me in a dryer, where were you — and did you see anything suspicious?"

He flushed, embarrassed. "I was taking a nap," he said. "The sea air gets to me. I get up early and walk on the deck, and I get sleepy in the afternoon."

All of that sounded reasonable. Now for the mushrooms the day Wingate died.

"How did you happen to go early in the morning to gather mushrooms and take Annie Long with you?" I asked, trying not to sound flabbergasted. "That wasn't the kind of trip Hiram required you to take her on, was it?"

"I took her kind of by mistake," he said. "But she was good at finding mushrooms! See, I went by to see her the night before, to deliver her tickets for the trip. The travel agent sent them to me along with mine for some reason, and she asked me in for a drink. That seemed cool."

Evidently Brian's raging hormones made

him like women of all ages.

"I told her how I have this friend in the Western North Carolina Wild Mushroom Club and we go out and pick mushrooms to eat. It's a cool thing to do. He likes to go early in the morning, which is a great time in the woods. You know, the woods smell good early in the morning." Brian wiggled one foot up and down, up and down. His shoulders moved this way and that.

"And, see, when Annie heard I was going in the morning, she asked if she could come. Her mother collected mushrooms. She said it always made her feel so good to do that again, like she did as a kid. And she'd been feeling kind of blue. So I said, 'Why not?' "

"Your friend came, too?" I asked.

"No, he called in the morning and told me he couldn't go. But I said we'd go. That would still be cool. In the morning I went by, and Annie gave me waffles. She makes good waffles."

"So you and Annie went out in the woods and gathered mushrooms, and you stayed together?"

"Pretty much," he said. "This is a good time for oyster mushrooms, chanterelles, and lacterius." He gave that happy goofy smile I'd seen him give to the pretty girls.

"Once I got lost, but not for long. I'm pretty good in the woods."

"Where do you pick mushrooms?" I asked.

He shrugged one shoulder, then the other, then hunched them together, then back. "There are so many good places," he said with enthusiasm. "Any trail off the Blue Ridge Parkway. Coon Tree or Pisgah Forest, or you can even go closer to Asheville to Lake Powhatan. Turkey Pen Gap is a good place to pick, and we went there."

That was no help to me. "Where is Turkey Pen Gap?" If he said near Linville Falls, what then?

"Less than an hour away," he said vaguely, massaging the arms of the chair. "I always let Tom drive when we go out. Annie drove. She can tell you exactly where."

I wished for Ted, who has a wonderful sense of geography. Then I perked up. I'd see Ted the next night. Hallelujah!

"I didn't even hear that Wingate was dead till we got home after lunch," Brian said. "Annie found the news on her answering machine. That was a shock." So he'd gone back in to Annie's after they picked the mushrooms.

"How did Annie take it?"

"She burst into tears. She really liked Wingate. I think he was nicer to her than the rest of the family was. My mother and my grandma treated Annie like a servant. Wingate didn't do that. He was cool."

"Why did you bring a large bottle of aftershave on a short trip like this?" I asked. That was the question I'd meant to ask all along. He did a double take.

"Oh," he said. "Oh, I guess that does look odd. When I went to pack at the last minute, it was all I had. And on this trip I wanted to be, well, you know, cool. Wingate gave me that aftershave stuff, a fancy kind and a big bottle, Christmas before last. To celebrate my being grown up, he said. Only I got here and discovered it was really all gone, just a splash at the bottom. I don't know why I didn't throw away the bottle."

I got up from the bunk. That was all I could think of to ask at the moment. The empty bottle bit sounded just like Brian. He wiggled up out of the chair and said, "Is that it?"

"Yes," I said, "unless you can think of something else that could help us find the person who killed Wingate and did all those other nasty things." That was an understatement! He shook his head no.

He paused as he went out the door. "You know," he said, "us kids kind of liked old Wingate. We didn't see him much, but on Christmas Eve he always brought us some great thing. One time he brought me this super skateboard, and once he brought Lillian this dollhouse with little chairs and tables and all that. He was Santa Claus but he was real."

"What did your mother think of that?" I asked, wondering about Goldie and her bitterness.

"She said a funny thing once. She said we might as well enjoy those things. And that seemed strange, because why wouldn't we enjoy great presents like that?"

As he started to close the door behind him, I said what I felt we all had to do: "Remember to be careful, Brian."

What a family, I thought. *Two members are as likely to forget as I am!* Then I thought, *No. More likely.* Because they don't use strategy to get around it. I made a note to give them copies of my book.

CHAPTER
22

THREE O'CLOCK

When I'd packed for this trip I'd forgotten my pants but remembered I might need Scotch tape. A Swiss-cheese memory works like that. I taped my charts to the wall so I could see at a glance who did what when, or at least who *said* they did what when.

A chart is a godsend if you find it easy to forget one detail while you track down another. Even a group of charts helps, with a place for everything, all in order. When I got home I'd assemble all my charts into a big one on poster board. That's best for complicated situations. A dozen or so new multimillionaires who may be either victims or killers makes for a very, very complicated situation.

I looked at Goldie's chart. Under *Wingate's fall, Friday, July 11, about 9 a.m.,* she'd written that she'd slept late and was just getting dressed to go shopping at

Constance Boutique — an "in" shop in downtown Asheville, particularly good for willowy women like Goldie.

When Marietta screamed down the castle stairs, Goldie said she'd been talking to Rich on the lower level. That might give them both an alibi. When Annie Long was attacked, Goldie said she was at the table with the family, watching the Great Whiz Bang. I wished my memory of who was there wasn't so fuzzy. She said that while I was in the dryer, she was shopping in the ship's boutique. I'd drop by the boutique and see if anyone remembered.

Lillian said she was sleeping late when Wingate was pushed. Like mother, like daughter? When Marietta screamed, Lillian said she was in the castle loo. And in parentheses, she wrote *the modern one, not that dreadful medieval pit.* During Annie Long's struggle, Lillian said she was with George Allington III. That must be the man I saw her dancing with. I did vaguely remember that. The chart said that while I was roasting in the dryer, she was taking a walk on deck alone.

And how about my friend Marietta? I certainly didn't think she was a killer, but the rule is "Suspect everybody." Lots of holes in her alibis. When Wingate fell, she said she was at home, weeding her herb garden. During the Annie Long episode, she was in the ladies' room near the Boating Club. During my ordeal, she was first in the bookshop, then in the library, then reading in the sitting area nearby. I might be able to check that.

Rich said he was going for a walk before breakfast, then eating cornflakes about the time his father died. No alibi. When Marietta screamed, Rich had said, he was talking to Goldie in the castle. I looked back at Goldie's chart. Good. If they were lying, their lies were synchronized. During the Annie Long episode, he was at the table with the family. While I whirled, he was in the spa.

I was just thinking I'd have to hurry to find out who was in the bookstore or spa or boutique when there was a knock at my door. I hoped it was someone who had remembered something crucial and came back to tell me. I opened the door carefully. It could be Paper Bag — though, of course, I wouldn't recognize him without his mask.

It was the young man who brought faxes, with another one in hand. *Oh, for heaven's sake, stop it, Pop,* I thought to myself. *We'll be home tomorrow.*

Crystal says it took many people to kill Wingate, Pop's fax read, *and some of them loved him.* That didn't seem to make sense. The fax continued, *Crystal says watch out for Hiram.* That didn't seem to make any sense at all. Could Hiram rise from his grave? I liked Ted's note: *Take care of yourself. I'll see you soon. XXX.*

"Do you want to send an answer?" the young man asked hopefully.

I said, "No, never mind, it's just from my crazy father, and I'll see him tomorrow." That was not loyal, but it made me feel a little less crazy myself.

I turned back to my charts, but the fax stuck in my mind. How could it take many people to kill Wingate? I thought of the old classic mystery where a number of the suspects stabbed the victim, but, luckily for most of them, by the time they did it, he was already dead. Was I remembering that right? Anyway, Wingate wasn't stabbed, and to push a man off a cliff several times was about as unlikely as you could get. Was this a conspiracy? Or was Pop's Crystal simply wrong this time? She'd been right that I should have been careful of the drink. On the other hand, if I'd been pushed into the ocean, I'd have thought the same thing.

I looked at Winnie's chart. Certainly someone could vouch for the fact that she'd been in the hospital waiting room at the time her father was killed, but I'd have to check. She'd been very cool about his death. I'd also have to check who was with her in the castle when Marietta was pushed. She'd said merely *with the others, waiting to go to lunch*. I should have known whether she was really with us at the table in the Boating Club when Annie rushed in to say that someone tried to throw her overboard, but I'd been too drunk. And was Alexander's lascivious wink a smoke screen, or was she really in his arms in her cabin while I was in the dryer?

I studied the two non-family members last. Alexander said he was in jail when Wingate was killed. An excellent alibi. So good you might almost imagine it was arranged. But how could you arrange to get picked up for driving under the influence? He said he was exploring the castle when Marietta was pushed. Why was he off by himself and not with Winnie? I did think I remembered him at the table when Annie Long burst into the club saying someone tried to kill her. But I wasn't positive. And was he lying about being in the cabin with Winnie during my encounter with Paper

Bag? I'd have recognized his chest span if he'd been Paper Bag. But maybe Winnie was the one who needed an alibi.

I turned to the last chart. Annie Long had been picking wild mushrooms with Brian the Lion when Wingate was pushed. They'd both said they'd been at Turkey Pen Gap, which they said is an hour or so away from Linville Falls. And besides, if Annie killed Wingate, why would someone try to throw her overboard? Was she making that up? Or was she part of a conspiracy, and someone was afraid she'd give away the game?

I hated this conspiracy idea. If there was some sort of conspiracy, then almost every alibi was suspect.

But back to Annie. She said she'd been at the bottom of the castle stairs and rushed up with everyone else when Marietta screamed. She'd been lying in a deck chair by the swimming pool on the rear deck getting a real sunburn while I was getting red in the dryer. All perfectly possible.

I sighed and wished the charts showed something more definitive. I might be able to check some of these alibis out, like whether Rich was really in the spa when I was being steamed alive. But some alibis would be hard to pin down, like who was really at the bottom of the stairs to the tower, and who was higher up pushing Marietta. I gathered it was quite a tall, hard-to-climb tower. That would give Paper Bag time to tear his bag up, throw it out a window, and then pretend to be one of the people running up the stairs. If several people were lying to protect each other, what then?

I'd check out the spa, the library, and the bookstore to see if anyone who worked there could back up alibis. I had to go sign some paperwork related to reentering the good old USA, but I'd have time to check alibis after that. Then it would be time to pull myself together for our last big night on board, with a gala final dinner and the musical show. With our buddy system and by staying in public places and sticking together, I hoped we'd all be okay.

On the other hand, we'd all been together when the Great Whiz Bang's act diverted us from the attack on Annie, and from the spiking of our drinks.

At least, according to our cabin checkers (including me!), none of us had a substance that could be used as a weapon in his cabin now. No bottle of grain alcohol. No sulfuric acid. I prayed we'd be safe till we reached land.

CHAPTER
23

FRIDAY, LAST NIGHT ON BOARD

Somewhere on this big ship was a person I wouldn't recognize if they arrived at my cabin with a bunch of flowers, wouldn't know to fear if they found some excuse to get me alone — a person who had tried to kill me and had apparently tried to kill Marietta and Annie Long, who had almost certainly killed Wingate. Someone wily and possibly insane.

I hurried down the long narrow corridor from my cabin. It was empty, just to scare me. I took the elevator up to the deck with the shops. What if Paper Bag was the mild-looking man in sunglasses who got in the elevator halfway up? No sign that he was. I arrived at the boutique safe and sound. The shop was designed to tempt me with cases of jewelry and racks of pretty clothes, all in a small space, but carefully arranged.

The elegant clerk wore a designer cruise

set with anchors embroidered on the front in red, white, and blue, as well as gold anchor earrings and about four rings on each hand. If someone had been stabbed, I might have suspected her bloodred fingernails. Her ice-blue eyes took me in from head to toe and probably found me lacking. She said she remembered Goldie by the beautiful necklace she'd bought, not to mention several cocktail dresses and some fancy underwear. "A woman with wonderful taste!" she said. "What can I show you?" She gestured toward a rack of shimmering dresses. I did not want to shimmer, even if I could afford to. I asked if she could remember whether Goldie had been in on Tuesday. I said she took a drug that gave her memory lapses, and I was helping her figure out where she'd left a book she was reading. The clerk shrugged, less interested in me, suspicious of my nosy question. No. She couldn't remember.

On to the bookshop, where I said I was trying to help a friend who'd lost a book. I described Marietta. The clerk thought she could recall a dark-haired woman who came in and looked at a book on herbal medicine and then didn't buy it. She wasn't sure when. She didn't think that woman had another book with her. The librarian was equally vague. Marietta lacked backup.

In the spa, I let the pretty young woman at the desk think that I was Rich's mother. I said he'd left his allergy medicine somewhere, and I was helping him find out when and where. I don't usually tell such outrageous lies, but after all, I was leaving the ship the next day. She wanted to know if Rich was the one with the wonderful tattoo of the dragon on his right arm. They had all talked about it. *Ocean Queen* clients were not likely to have such wild tattoos. If he was the one, he came in at about one-thirty on Tuesday. She looked at her appointment book. Yes, that was him. They'd keep an eye out for his medication.

Anything really out of the ordinary can turn out to be a clue, even if it seems unconnected. Why on earth would a high-school English teacher be tattooed with a dragon?

Actually, I discovered I was going to have a good chance to ask him that myself. I got back to my cabin safely to find a message from Marietta. Rich was going to be my partner in the buddy system she'd worked out for the evening. I sure hoped it would keep us safe on our last night aboard. If we could just make sure that no one killed one of us, this could be a splendid evening. I might never take a cruise this luxurious again. I was going to enjoy it or die trying. Wrong expression. I remembered an old joke: *Apart from that, Mrs. Lincoln, did you enjoy the play?*

I did enjoy dinner with Rich and Marietta and Goldie and Lillian and her boyfriend, not to mention Brian and Annie. Winnie and Alexander were in a loftier dining room. I had lobster Newburg and ordered baked Alaska for dessert. The waiter treated us like royalty. We all looked incredibly elegant. Even me. I wore green silk and a necklace crafted from small rough crystal spears. It was made by a famous mountain craftsman, and I acquired it while my first husband and I ran a craft shop. Fell in love with it and had to have it. Here was its chance to shine.

Marietta had on black lace and what looked like emeralds. Goldie wore a gold dress and antique jet jewelry. Rich wore a dinner jacket, and so did Lillian's advertising man. Lillian glowed in red satin, and even though her earrings didn't match — one gold hoop, one silver star — she looked smashing. She was also a little smashed. I tasted my Chardonnay carefully. No hint of an off flavor. I watched

280

myself. No symptom of too much alcohol.

I noticed Annie Long, resplendent in purple satin, was sipping her wine very carefully, too.

I almost laughed as I thought how Annie grew up on a farm, and Marietta usually had dirt under her nails from weeding herbs, and just a year ago Lillian might have been the one waiting on the table, and here we were, done up like fashion plates. Pop would have been impressed.

But I had better be canny as well as elegant. I brought up the subject of tattoos as I savored my lobster. I said I understood they were now back in vogue.

"There used to be a song," Marietta said, teasing her salmon with her fork, "about a tattooed lady, about various body parts and what tattoos were where." She looked up from her salmon with hollandaise sauce. "I think the battle of Waterloo was on her back, and somewhere was a view of Niagara, and ships on her hips."

Rich choked on a bite but saved himself with a cough. I noticed his face became strained. Over ships on a lady's hips?

"Hey. I remember that!" said Lillian's advertising man. "An admiral looked at those ships on her hips and took command of the fleet." He winked broadly at Lillian.

"I heard the man who wrote the words sing that song on *Larry King Live*."

Lillian winked back.

Rich kept a poker face. He fidgeted. He did not join in the conversation. Why would the very idea of a tattoo get to him like that?

"I can't imagine getting tattooed myself," I said. "Have any of you ever done it?"

But Marietta was still stuck on the "Tattooed Lady." "I think Groucho Marx sang that song in *A Day at the Circus*, and the Kingston Trio sang something about a tattooed lady. Back in the sixties. About a Union Jack on her back, and a view of Sydney over her kidney." She burst out laughing. Hey, this was getting international, but not useful. How could I get it back on track? Rich was so pale I thought he might faint, and I needed to know why. Goldie was frowning and fidgeting as she drank her whiskey. Was it her second or third? What was her problem?

"That song was in *The Philadelphia Story*," Marietta mused, "and Katharine Hepburn's little sister played the piano and sang it."

Lillian shrugged. "Thanks for all this boring talk about movies from the Dark

Ages. This is our last night on board."
Then she did me a favor. She turned to
Rich. "*He* has a tattoo and he doesn't want
you to know it," she crowed. "Because
Wingate and Rich got drunk, and old
Righteous here slipped." She wagged a
finger at Rich. "Wingate muffed some deal
or something." She frowned and seemed
confused, then recovered. "And a kid you
tried to help overdosed or something like
that — right, Rich?"

"Do you have to bring that up?" Rich exploded. "It's not a joke!" He put his fork
down and seemed so upset he might just
leave the table.

Lillian was not to be stopped, and I
didn't try. "So Wingate and Rich got
drunk together — and if you are very good,
Rich might show you the tattoo he got for
good luck." She began to shake unsteadily
with laughter.

"You must have felt terrible," I said quietly to Rich, "to lose a student like that."

"It was right before Hiram died!" Lillian
screeched. "And obviously the dragon did
bring Rich luck, because now he's filthy-
rich Rich." Heads turned to stare at her.

Rich spat, "You mind your own business,
Lillian."

Goldie threw her arm around Lillian

and whispered something in her ear, which silenced her at least for the moment. Lillian's boyfriend watched us all like we were a prizewinning play.

My, my! This tattoo thing was something to explore. Could just a dragon tattoo make Rich get so upset? Or was there more? And what drove Lillian to stay pickled? Marietta said it was because she no longer had anything to strive for. Because she had everything she had thought she wanted. But I had the feeling it was more than that.

The waiter arrived with my dessert. The flames from the baked Alaska reflected in the dark windows on our left. Very pyrotechnic! No ocean in sight in the black night. Just us diners, reflected back on ourselves. I needed to find out about the darkness in us.

CHAPTER
24

LATER THAT EVENING

We had lingered over dinner until we had just enough time to get to the musical in a large room near the stern, a cross between a theater and a bar. Ripples of cheerful conversation. The ship hardly rocked beneath my feet; the weather had calmed. We walked toward a low stage with lots of tables and chairs around it. Waiters were serving drinks. A small orchestra on one side of the stage played show tunes.

Rich and I were the last of our group to arrive, and the table with the others was jam-packed. They had saved us two seats at a small table next to theirs, not too far from the stage. Good. Maybe Marietta had even engineered that so I could be alone with Rich, or so Rich didn't have to put up with Lillian.

The lights were low, which I didn't care for. Low light could be a killer's friend.

Spotlights on the stage announced that the show was beginning as Rich ordered a daiquiri and I stayed extra-safe with diet cola. This was mostly a costume-and-body show. A well-turned young woman in a Siamese-looking headdress that came to a point, and just enough bits of silk to cover essentials, came out and sang "Getting to Know You" from *The King and I*. More spotlights, and out came sexy dancing girls in the same sort of costume but less headdress. They danced with nice Siamese-looking hand gestures. With hardly the skip of a heartbeat they changed into T-shirts and jeans and sang a bit from *West Side Story* with young men and girls both dancing. This was going to be a revue. Good. We didn't have to keep track of a plot.

So what should I ask Rich, quick while the table on the other side of us was empty? And our folks were singing along with the floor show, forgetting their worries, I guessed.

Onstage, a rather sinister-looking young man sang "Mack the Knife." Wicked Mack killed lots of people, for money, wasn't it? I found myself thinking of Hiram. In fact, I realized with a start that he'd been at the edge of my mind ever since I wondered if Poo was killed. Whose death brought the most money to the most people? Hiram's, of course. Then anyone who seemed likely to find out he was murdered would be in danger, right? Now, that made sense.

Suddenly I heard myself say, "Rich, do you think that maybe your uncle Hiram was killed, in some hard-to-detect way?"

Rich choked on his drink. He put his glass down. "Hiram!" he sputtered. "Good God, no! What makes you think that?"

"I don't think that," I said. "It's just that it would make everything else make sense." But I did notice that Rich was deeply upset. A muscle in his jaw kept working as we listened to the next song.

"There's something you're not telling me," I said.

He didn't answer and was quiet and moody for several minutes. Then he took a deep breath, turned to me, and said, "There is something I didn't tell you, because I didn't think it mattered, and I guess I was ashamed of it."

Ah. I smiled encouragingly. "Anything can turn out to matter."

"I was at my father's house." Now he seemed at ease with what he was going to say. He leaned close to my ear, and I was thankful for the music that would keep others from overhearing our conversation.

"This was shortly before Uncle Hiram died. My father would get busy with some project and ignore everything else. His house looked like it had been trashed by vandals."

"Could it have been?" I asked.

He laughed. "No, he just left everything wherever it fell. After a week or so that gets bad. And I couldn't stand to look at it, so while I waited for him one day when we were going to have lunch together, I began to sort things and put them back in place. I noticed he had a stack of mail he hadn't even opened and several messages on his answering machine that he hadn't bothered to listen to. I was annoyed with him because he'd gotten in trouble that way, not paying bills or answering messages.

"So I pushed the button and played his messages. I shouldn't have done it, but I did. And one of them was from a woman. She said something like, 'Please call me, dearest. I know we have to be careful, but I miss you every moment.' "

"Did you recognize the voice?"

"Oh, no!" he said. I felt that Rich was lying and hating to do it, all at once.

"You couldn't even guess who?"

"Not at all."

The lights came on to a young woman

singing a sad love song. "And after you heard this message on your father's answering machine," I asked, "what happened next?"

"I was embarrassed because I shouldn't have listened to my father's messages," Rich said in a rush. "So I didn't mention it when he came back in the room." He put that like a challenge or an excuse.

"A few days later, my father showed up at my place drunk. That wasn't like him," Rich said sadly.

"And you thought those things were connected?" I asked. "But why?"

"He said, 'Rich, stay away from women. They can ruin your life.' "

"What did he mean by that?"

Rich looked down at his feet. "I don't know."

"Did you ask him about the phone message?" I demanded.

"Yes, I did. And he absolutely refused to say who left it — even drunk as he was, he wouldn't let it slip. Like it was some big deal. Unfortunately he found a bottle of whiskey in my cupboard and then he got really drunk, so it scared me.

"I finally got him to go out for a drive and get some air. With me driving, of course. We drove around awhile, and he seemed better, but of course I felt dreadful because I understood that this was some-thing simply horrendous, or so he thought, and he wouldn't tell me what it was." The young singers had pitched into a rousing chorus of "There's a Great Day Coming Mañana." Bad choice.

"And we drove past this tattoo place on Merrimon Avenue, and he said to drive around the block again. So I did, and he said 'Stop.' Then he said, 'Dragons bring good luck.' I guess he was still drunk, be-cause he was so serious and so determined. He said if I had a dragon tattoo, we'd have good luck. I felt so upset and couldn't think of anything else to do to make things better. So I agreed."

"Now wait," I said. "You couldn't make your father tell you why he was upset, so you got a dragon tattoo to make him feel better?"

That was wilder than anything I could make up. "I don't believe it," I said.

"Yes. Yes, I did. I even let him tell the girl which dragon to use. There were pic-tures of tattoos to choose from all over the wall. I guess my dragon is my silly thing I did for my father."

"That's not at all what Lillian said," I pointed out.

"Lillian found out we went and that my father was drunk, but she never knew why. She made up a reason to please herself."

Could Rich be making this up? But why?

"I try to think of that dragon as a symbol of good luck, because my father wanted it to be that. But then he was killed. That's not good luck."

"You did this just before Hiram died, right? Wingate was killed about ten months after Hiram died," I said. "So at least you might say you had good luck for ten months."

Rich took an extra-long swig of his daiquiri. "I bet that woman who left the message could tell us what was really wrong," he said. "I was so stupid! While I was getting that tattoo, my father went back out to the car and probably drank from a bottle he had there, because when he came back he was even drunker, and he smelled like mint — and I realized he'd stolen my bottle of crème de menthe. Boy, he must have been desperate! He began to repeat that I absolutely must not believe any rumors I heard about him. I tried to shush him up, because the tattoo girl looked so interested. She was just about finished, and I prayed I could get him out of there quick. But before I could, he gave me this straight-in-the-eye look and said, 'I'll tell you whose voice that was, and then you can't believe the rumor.' "

I stopped breathing. I waited.

Rich rubbed his face all over. He shook his head as if he couldn't believe what he was saying. "Father said some name I never heard of, and then he got sick all over the floor, right there in the tattoo room, and I was so embarrassed and upset that the name went right out of my head. I helped the girl clean up the mess. It was the least I could do. I got him home to sleep it off."

"You didn't ask later?" That's what I would have done.

"When he was sober, he wouldn't tell me, and after Hiram died, it didn't seem to matter, because all of a sudden he was cheerful again, and we were all so busy figuring what to do with all that money." He said that just as the orchestra played a crescendo. Lights went off again. This must have been intermission, because when the lights came back on, the stage was empty.

I had the feeling that Rich was terribly relieved to have finished his spiel. He ordered another daiquiri and a cola for me.

But I wasn't about to let him off the hook. "I see why you were upset back then," I said. "But why did you turn white as a sheet when the subject of the 'Tattooed Lady' came up tonight?"

He went pale again. "All right," he said angrily, "I'll tell you." He paused. He braced himself. "Because whoever I heard on the answering machine also said five more words: 'I have something for Groucho.' Tonight when I began to think about Groucho Marx, who sang that song about the tattooed lady — and believe me, I heard it hundreds of times — suddenly I realized exactly what those answering-machine words meant. How could I not have understood before? I didn't want to know, that's why! Or I would have asked my father."

I sipped my drink and let him reach the point where he could make himself tell it all.

"You see," he said, "Groucho was a family favorite, and my father kept a framed picture of him in the living room in one of those stand-up frames. To remind him to laugh, I guess, when things went wrong. It was one of those frames that comes apart if you turn a little lever, and if he had money around the house, he hid it in the back of that frame. Whoever called was saying that she had money for him. Enough to hide. What else could those words mean? She must have known my father well to know about the Groucho frame. I know my father was honest — at least I've always thought so. But what could he have been mixed up in? That scared me silly."

I let him sip his drink for several minutes.

"But you must know what women he knew well," I said.

"He could get intense with a woman pretty quick," Rich answered, "but then it never lasted. I don't think he wanted to commit himself to anything after my mother left him. There were women who were just friends, but not the type to get him into trouble.

"It frightens me to realize there must be a lot about my father that I don't know, and maybe that's why we're all in danger. In danger from someone who's cooped up with us on this ship." He downed the last of his daiquiri. "Thank God we get off this ship in the morning."

CHAPTER
25

STILL LATER THAT EVENING

I followed Marietta as the crowd dribbled out of the theater. Waiters were removing glasses, and the stage was dark. "We need to talk," I said as I walked up in back of her — or at least what I thought was her. When she turned around, I saw it was Annie Long. Actually holding hands with Brian. He probably needed the guidance. No glasses again. Vanity, vanity.

I found the real Marietta and asked her to come down to my cabin to talk.

"Does Brian wear contacts?" I asked. "He seems kind of rocky without his glasses."

"He can't wear contacts," Marietta said. "Some sort of allergy. I think he gets around by pure instinct, because he won't wear glasses when he's trying to impress a girl."

I stopped dead, right in front of the sailing-ship model with a mile of rigging. "Is there anyone else around who can't see?"

Marietta gave me an odd look. "What are you getting at?"

"We'll talk below," I said. "I don't like what I'm thinking."

So she came to my cabin, sat down in an armchair, and said, "Well, so far we're all alive!"

I sat on the bunk and shrugged. "So far. Has it occurred to you that someone meant to throw *you* overboard? You, not Annie Long? You know, from the back you do look alike."

"Me? That's ridiculous," Marietta said. But I noticed she hugged herself as if she were cold.

"It would be pretty far-fetched," I said, "for someone to spike the wrong glass and then push the wrong person — but not impossible for a killer who couldn't half see. And that would explain why Annie's attacker gave up. Because he suddenly discovered he had the wrong woman."

Marietta got up from the chair, came over, and hugged me. "Peaches, you are my favorite person in the whole world, my favorite original thinker. But sometimes you go beyond the edge of what's possible. Brian is vague and he's silly about his glasses — but he isn't a killer."

I hoped she was right. So I changed the subject.

I told Marietta how Rich was afraid his father was mixed up in something secret, maybe even something crooked. I glanced at my notes. Because Rich listened to Wingate's answering machine and heard romantic words about *Please call me, dearest — but I know we have to be careful* and also some very odd words about Groucho Marx.

"Sounds like he was romancing someone's wife," Marietta suggested dryly.

"But," I said, "the message said 'I have something for Groucho,' which made Rich think somebody was sending a hidden code to Wingate about money — because he always hid his money in the frame of a picture of Groucho Marx."

Marietta raised an eyebrow. "Don't you think that's a little fantastic?"

"You're too loyal to believe bad things about your kin, Marietta," I said, "but somebody had a reason to kill Wingate. And what about Rich's idea that his father was into something shady?"

Now Marietta looked me straight in the eye and shook her head violently. "I don't believe it! Wingate was careless, extravagant, a skirt chaser, but I don't believe he was dishonest — except for white lies to cover up goofs. Wingate was absolutely infuriating, but he was also kind of a darling."

At least he'd snowed Marietta.

"We've always been honest with each other, Marietta," I said, "so I'm going to tell you something I can't get out of my mind. There'd be a motive for someone to kill Hiram if one of the heirs had to have money right away — if they felt they couldn't wait for nature to take its course. Then the others might be killed to cover that up. Was anyone that broke?"

"I hope not," she said fervently.

"The doctor said Hiram died of natural causes. Could the doctor have been wrong?"

Marietta's eyes went round with horror. "Look," she said, "we have enough trouble. I hope to God you don't find more."

CHAPTER
26

NEW YORK, SATURDAY MORNING

First thing in the morning I got another fax. It said, *Crystal says be careful of what's underneath your clothes.* Then, of course, there was a note from Ted: *Pop insists this is important. I am so glad you'll be home soon! Love.*

I thought, *What's underneath my clothes? I'm underneath my clothes. Nude! But maybe this meant underwear.*

Thank goodness Ted isn't inclined to be a jealous and suspicious type. I mean, I'm not a kid, but there are philanderers who prefer older women. In fact, I remember reading once that there was a "house" in Paris where all the girls were grandmothers, in order to cater to that taste. I felt younger just thinking about that. If a philanderer had come along, I might have winked at him. A wink couldn't hurt.

Could this message be some kind of pun like "the drink"? Did I think this Crystal was psychic because "the drink" warning came true in a way? Or was she just cryptic enough so whatever happened could fit her predictions? She hadn't unearthed the killer yet, which made me cynical.

Of course I had on underpants, the red polka-dotted ones that Ted gave me as a joke, and panty hose, and the rest of the necessary. Most of my clothes were packed and ready for the ship's staff to move off the ship to the customs area.

I figured I'd think better after breakfast. One last delicious breakfast: I picked cinnamon buns and croissants with sweet butter and wild strawberry jam. I sat with Marietta and the usual suspects. We didn't talk much.

I paid one last visit to my cabin and then started down the hall to disembark. A hard-looking, overdressed woman, whose hair looked like a red wig, followed me. *It's Paper Bag in disguise,* said my wild imagination. *It's a tourist leaving the ship,* said my practical side. Just as I got to the elevator, *underwear* stopped me right in my tracks. I'd forgotten my underwear.

I never put clothes in a drawer in a temporary place. That's rule one for the absentminded. Keep stuff safe in your suitcase. Never ever put it where you can't see it. Never even put a black pocketbook on a black rug, or a white shirt on a white sheet. It'll vanish. But when I'd swept my underwear off the TV, I was so embarrassed I stuck it right in the drawer. Out of sight, out of mind. It must still be there. Travel Count doesn't help a bit with things that should be *inside* bags. I turned around and went back to the cabin.

The key was in the door. I'd been so eager to get out of there, I'd left the key. Oh, brother! Suppose the killer was inside? But that was silly — with me gone, why should he be? I opened the door and peered inside. Nobody in sight. But the closet doors and the bathroom door were shut. Hadn't I left them open? I screwed up my nerve and looked in the nearer closet, now entirely empty except for hangers. I shut the door with a metallic snap, and looked in the farther closet. That was empty, too. I began to feel less nervous and turned back to the cabin. I glanced at the clock on the bedside table to see how late it was. I was due to meet Marietta on deck at ten. I had fifteen minutes. Most folks were probably already on deck to watch the docking.

This would be my last look at the cabin. All the family suspects had been assembled in this small cream-colored space. Was there someone else I didn't even know about who was following us? Maybe Hiram wasn't really dead, but only insane. He'd had another body buried in his place.

But I needed to be practical. I went over to the bureau against the far wall of the cabin and pulled open the drawer. There were my underpants and bra, not looking dangerous at all, until I noticed something else. In the corner of the drawer was a bottle of clear liquid. A cylindrical bottle with a black top and a label. What kind of secret booby trap? I looked all around me, heart beating. But nobody materialized. Did somebody intend to frame me? Make it look as if I were the one who brought bottles of alcohol and sulfuric acid on board? It was just chance they found the key in the door. But Paper Bag seized the chance. Took whatever opportunity came, to kill or at least make trouble. That seemed to be his or her style. I started to search the room for clues.

Suddenly my stomach turned over. I caught my breath. I realized I'd forgotten to look in the bathroom! I went over to the door, frightened. I looked around for a weapon. All I found was a coat hanger. I opened the door into the hall so I could get out fast. Then I opened the door to the bathroom about an inch, ready to slam it shut if someone was inside.

I didn't see anyone. I clicked on the light. The frosted door to the shower burst open, and Lillian jumped out with a knife raised in her hand.

I didn't believe it. Lillian? She was just a kid. Just twenty-one, and her brains were pickled half the time. Could she plan murders?

Fortunately my body ignored my mind and absolutely believed the danger. I lunged, and my hand reached out and caught her wrist. Amazing what you can do if you're scared enough! We wrestled for control of the knife, almost like arm wrestling when I was a kid but much more deadly. She smelled of alcohol, and her coordination wasn't good. Well, it was good for me! I got her down on the floor in the little hallway outside the bathroom, with me holding down the hand that held the knife.

Neither of us had screamed. I'd been entirely focused on control of the knife. Now she yelled, "Help!" and footsteps ran toward the open door.

Alexander the Great burst into the cabin. Was he in on this? He was definitely too strong for me. I was about to scream for help myself when Marietta came into the cabin and shut the door behind her. "Shut up!" she ordered us all.

"Grandma, she's the killer!" Lillian squealed.

"Then why," I asked, "is the knife in your hand?" It still was, although I had her wrist pinned down.

Could Marietta be part of some conspiracy? Could I be that wrong about my old friend?

"But it's only a table knife!" said Alexander the Great.

We all stared at the knife. Marietta reached down and took it from Lillian, and I released my grip on her. She sat up.

"It was all I had when the phone rang," Lillian said defensively. "A room-service knife."

"What does the phone have to do with you and the knife?" I demanded angrily. "And why did you attack me?"

We both stood up, and Marietta said, "Come into the cabin where there's more room." We were packed tight in the hallway.

So we moved to the cabin, and Lillian plunked herself on the bunk. The rest of us stood. Her eyes went from me to Alexander the Great, to Marietta, and back to me. She frowned. "I got this phone call," she said, "just as I was leaving my cabin. This hoarse voice said there was evidence in your cabin, in the bureau drawer, that you were the killer," she said to me, "and you were gone and the door was unlocked."

"And you were just looped enough to grab a table knife and come and see!" Marietta glared at Lillian. "Honestly, Lillian, you've got to get help! I don't know what would have happened if I hadn't been worried because Peaches didn't meet me on deck."

"And why is Alexander here?" I asked. He was admiring himself in the mirror over the bureau. "Did he get a phone call?"

"I grabbed Alexander for a buddy when I came down to find out what was wrong," Marietta said, and I had to admit that if she'd needed muscle, Alexander had it.

Listen, I told myself, *keep your eye on the doughnut and not on the hole.* Lillian's room-service knife was probably the hole.

"There is something in the drawer!" I said. "I forgot to pack some underwear and I came back to get it, and there's a bottle of clear liquid in the drawer." I was tired of putting my underwear on public display, but what could I do?

They all came over and peered into the drawer.

"It was an attempted frame-up," I said defensively as I pointed to the bottle.

Lillian leaned over and stared. She reached out. I said, "Don't touch!"

She looked confused. "But what's in it?" If she was deliberately acting innocent, she was doing a good job.

"I don't know," I said. I sat down on the bunk. My heart rate was back to normal, but I felt tuckered out. "What should we do? I don't know whether to just take my stuff and leave this bottle here, and get off this derned ship where they think I'm a drunk as fast as possible, or bring that bottle along and find out what's in it. It's the right color for alcohol, not sulfuric acid."

"Of course you'll bring the bottle," Marietta said. "The cleanup crew would throw it out. We need to find out what it is. And we need to get off this ship without delay."

I knew we shouldn't disturb evidence. If the bottle was alcohol, the crew would merely raise their eyebrows. I picked up the bottle carefully, using my underpants to avoid putting fingerprints over any that might already be there, though I was sure Paper Bag was too smart to leave fingerprints. I looked at the bottle more closely. The label said WITCH HAZEL. I said, "Good camouflage."

"Open it quick," Lillian demanded. Marietta nodded agreement.

Protecting the top with cloth, I gently opened the bottle. Carefully, so as not to burn my nose with acid fumes, or whatever, I sniffed.

"Witch hazel!" I cried out. I got them to sniff, too. We stared at each other, amazed. So why the phone call to Lillian?

I laughed. "Paper Bag wanted us to make more fools of ourselves again with the ship's staff." The other two sniffed and nodded. Lillian still eyed me suspiciously as if I had arranged this just in order to confuse her.

"What did the person on the phone sound like?" I asked her as I slipped my underwear and the bottle of witch hazel into a plastic bag that Marietta brought forth from the trash basket in the bathroom.

"Hoarse," Lillian said, "and phony."

"Whoever it is," I said, "the aim is to keep us off balance, to make us paranoid, to make us feel foolish, like I do when my underwear gets into the act. This person has contempt for us. I don't like this person one bit." I was still not positive that Lillian had told the truth about why she was in my cabin. I still felt off balance.

We all headed back toward the deck to watch the docking. At least, it was great to see land, to see the skyscrapers of New York, to see the happy greeters waving from the dock below. They were there for their relatives and friends, not for us. But they made me feel welcomed anyway. I thought, *Thank God we are leaving this ship!* And I'd soon be home.

Pop would be overjoyed to learn that Crystal's message was on target. He'd wanted to be mixed up in finding out who killed Wingate, who had pushed Marietta, and he had, in a small way, warned me what to watch out for. Now he'd be impossible.

But I had one last job to do before we dispersed. I wandered around and asked each of our group a question as we waited for the signal to debark. "Where were you from nine-thirty till now?" All but Lillian said they'd been up on deck watching the ship dock. That didn't prove anything. But when I asked them who else had been up on deck, every single person was seen by several others. So who made the phone call to Lillian? If there *was* a phone call. And who put the bottle in my drawer?

CHAPTER
27

SATURDAY AND SUNDAY

Marietta, Goldie, Rich, and I shared a taxi to La Guardia Airport. Marietta paid, which was lucky because the tab was so high I expected the meter to explode.

We flew to Charlotte, Marietta still treating me to the trip in first class, which meant I had my wine in a real wineglass and a menu with my meal.

We had a long holdover but finally landed in Asheville after the short flight from Charlotte. I pulled my wheelie bag in back of me like Mary's Little Lamb, overjoyed to be home — but there was no Ted to meet me. An airline official held up a placard with my name on it. When I rushed over to find out what was wrong, Mr. Signholder had a message from Ted that he couldn't get to the airport. Could I get a ride home with one of my friends or take the shuttle to the Radisson Hotel?

"Yes," I said, "I'm sure I can get a ride."

Winnie was in hearing distance, and she volunteered. She and Alexander were going to spend the night at the Radisson in Asheville. Their house was being painted in their absence, and the job wasn't finished. I said, "Thanks."

That was a plus. Perhaps en route I could learn more about the rumor Rich thought was related to Wingate's death. How very odd if his death was actually caused by a rumor.

I called Ted to tell him I had a ride, and it was so wonderful to hear his voice. He explained he hadn't been able to start the car. Some technical reason went in one ear and out the other. The sitter was off in Pop's white Cadillac getting Pop some Cherry Garcia ice cream. "Pop says he deserves to have the best if everybody else goes off on cruises." Yes, Pop was going to be impossible.

I gave Marietta a hug good-bye, and we agreed to go jointly first thing in the morning to the sheriffs in Buncombe County, where we lived, and Watauga County, where Wingate was killed. Perhaps we should have gone to see at least one of the sheriffs right then, but by now it was nine-thirty at night. We were both exhausted and homesick.

So off I went with Alexander and Winnie in her Volvo, Alexander gallantly insisting I sit with Winnie in the front seat. She was driving. Volvos, she said, are the only cars to have because they last practically forever.

Even in the black night I could feel I was in the mountains. The air smelled crisp. I-26 snaked along, with taillights outlining the curves.

"Do you feel close to knowing who killed Wingate?" Alexander asked from in back of me.

I twisted in the seat. "At least now we assume that somebody did," I said.

"It was always strange to me," Winnie said, "that the people who didn't love my father hated him."

I turned back to her. "Who?" I asked.

"Oh, ex-girlfriends. And the ex-boyfriends of ex-girlfriends."

"That's pretty general," I said.

"I never bothered to keep up."

Still some hostility, I thought. "Were you angry at him?"

"Frequently," she said.

"Rich said there was some sort of rumor that upset Wingate just before Hiram died," I said. "Do you know what that was?"

Immediately Winnie's face closed. She went tense all over, making a great effort to pull herself together — to cover something that hurt. I could feel the strain. "If you are looking for rumors," she said, "try Hiram's ex-wife, Suzie. She knows every rumor in the state." She gave me a forced smile. "But how will you know which are true?"

"Wingate had a weakness for women," I said. "Or so I understand." Winnie didn't deny it. "Were there rumors about that?"

"You think this had to do with why he was killed?" she asked. "You think it had to do with jealousy?" Her hand was clutching the steering wheel as if it might run away.

"What do you know about jealousy that you don't want to tell me?" I asked.

"Nothing," she said, and I had the oddest feeling that this was both true and false.

Winnie turned off Route 19-23 at the Woodfin exit and drove down twisty Lakeshore Drive, headlights picking out the trees in the yards by the road and the mailboxes on posts. We turned off down my road toward my house, my wonderful square-cut-log house. It looked more beautiful to me than the most luxurious cruise ship there ever was.

"Won't you come in?" I said to be polite.

"Yes," she said. "I'd like to use your bathroom."

Winnie and Alexander came in, to Pop's delight.

"So who do you think killed Wingate?" Pop asked immediately, leaning back in his wheelchair.

"I wish it was a tramp who tried to steal his wallet or someone else we don't know," Winnie said, standing near his wheelchair.

Pop raised an eyebrow. "Most people know their killers." He made that sound darkly ominous. Perhaps that's why Winnie and Alexander left so fast.

Immediately Ted and Pop wanted to know everything. We went into the kitchen and sat around the table and had coffee. That's where we tend to brainstorm.

"I tried to call you Tuesday morning, Ted," I said, "but I couldn't get you. I wasn't sure of the time difference. Then on Wednesday morning I was in such bad shape I just tried to get through the day. Besides, I knew I'd be home in a couple of days to tell you everything myself. I figured you might find some of what happened less scary if you could see me standing here in good shape."

"So you hid things from us!" Pop cried

314

out. "I told Ted there was more going on than we knew!"

"That bit about the drink was right, Pop," I told him. "Somebody spiked my drink on Monday night. They did it so I wouldn't be clear about what was happening." I told them about the magic show and Annie Long's screams, and how the staff of the ship couldn't find any miscreant so they figured Annie was just drunk and delusional, and then they saw that I was drunk, too. "And perhaps the killer wanted to discredit me with the staff," I said. "That worked."

"A fiendishly clever killer," Pop said with relish.

Then I told them about my misadventure in the dryer, and about the woman who accused me of being drunk again when I was woozy from the heat. Ted was shocked that the ship's officer would believe the other woman and not me. A loyal husband is a fine thing. "And what else have you been hiding?" Pop demanded.

"My underwear," I said. "That fax you sent about Crystal and how she said to be careful for my underpinnings jogged my mind as I was leaving the ship. So I went back to get my underpants from the bureau drawer. I'd left the cabin unlocked.

And somebody had gone in there and left a bottle of liquid in the drawer to scare me."

Pop beamed. "So Crystal helped!"

"But why," Ted wanted to know, "would a bottle of liquid scare you if no one was there to throw it at you or put it in your drink?"

"Because," I said, "we figured that the alcohol to spike my drink, and the sulfuric acid to scare me into getting into the dryer, must have come on the ship in bottles. Because the security X ray wouldn't pick them up as anything unusual in someone's suitcase. So the killer, whoever he was, would have bottles of dangerous liquid. When I saw that bottle I thought maybe someone was trying to frame me. Whoever it was called Lillian and told her to go look in my bureau drawer. And Lillian, who was feeling no pain as usual, came down to my cabin and looked, if we can believe her. She said she only threatened me with the knife because she thought I was the killer. She was pretty looped and ready to believe anything."

"And what was in the bottle?" Pop demanded. I could see he was hoping for something dramatic like Ebola virus in a growing culture, or some liquid with deadly poisonous fumes.

"Witch hazel," I said. "I could tell by the smell. But tomorrow I'll give it to the sheriff. He can get the State Bureau of Investigation or somebody to test it for sure."

Pop made a face. "Witch hazel! Why go to the sheriff with that?"

"Marietta and I are going to the sheriffs and tell them how she was pushed and Annie was almost thrown overboard and I was forced into a dryer. We want them to know that somebody is still attempting murder, and it must be the one who killed Wingate. Who else would it be? Unless we've been plagued by Wingate's ghost! Which I don't believe for a minute. Ghosts don't bother to put paper bags over their heads."

I yawned and realized I was about to fall asleep sitting up. This had been a long day and a long week. Pop yawned, too, and tried to hide it.

"That's the important part," I said. "I'll tell you the rest at breakfast."

CHAPTER
28

NEXT MORNING

Pop was up by six-thirty, and I was amazed that Ted and I woke up early, too. Partly it was hearing the music of the birds out the window. Partly I was anxious to hear what Ted would make of the tattoo story and the alibi charts. The morning was lovely, with a light overcast, and all the trees shimmered green and fresh from rain the night before. Our house is across the street from undeveloped woods, which is nice.

I wiped last night's rain off the glass-topped table on the terrace, and we had breakfast there. Not truffle omelets, but cornflakes and strawberries.

During breakfast, I told them about the dragon tattoo, about the message on the answering machine about some woman who missed Wingate and had to be very careful, and also about Groucho Marx.

"Groucho Marx was a damn ugly man,"

Pop said, "and furthermore, he's dead. So why did this woman leave a message about Groucho Marx?"

"Wingate had a picture of Groucho Marx in a stand-up frame, and Rich says that's where his father hid money, back when he didn't have a lot," I explained. "Rich thinks the message had to do with somebody giving Wingate money, some woman who said she missed him."

"Hot diggedy," Pop chortled. "He was a kept man."

"I doubt that," I said, "because back when he got this phone message, back before he inherited money, Rich says Wingate changed girlfriends a lot. Kept men don't get to do that."

Ted is great at summaries: "So Wingate got a message that Rich played, and Rich says he didn't recognize the voice but he believes that message is related to some rumor Wingate talked about when he was in a terrible state and got drunk. So Rich thinks that the woman who left the message may have the key to what upset Wingate. Wingate mentioned her name in the tattoo parlor, but Rich doesn't remember it. He also thinks his father may have been mixed up in some shady financial scheme involving this lady."

"You must be out of breath after all that," said Pop.

"But I'm also not positive Rich is telling the whole truth," I added, "and I think Winnie is hiding something, too."

"If I were you," Ted said, "except for going to the sheriffs with Marietta, I'd flake out for today. It's Sunday. Go to church, recharge your brains, call anyone who might have heard a rumor."

"Then on Monday," I said, "I'll go to the tattoo parlor. Goodness knows what I can find out after nearly a year, but women did tend to remember Wingate. Maybe I'll be lucky the tattooer was a female." I crossed my fingers.

"I love crimes that involve mysterious women," Pop said. "But you need more than that to solve murders."

"I made a chart, just like you always do," I told Ted, "with everybody's alibi for every attempted murder."

I went into the house and got it. We all pored over it.

"What it amounts to," Ted said, "is that nobody has a really watertight alibi except Alexander for when Wingate was killed."

"I like the one about picking wild mushrooms," Pop said. "My cousin Beulah used to pick mushrooms, and she thought she knew the good ones and cooked some for her whole family. They all died on Easter. All but her husband, who wouldn't eat mushrooms. Which proves you ought not to eat what you don't like."

The walkabout phone rang. I picked it up. It was Marietta. "Rich and I decided that the sheriffs would be more impressed if family members came to ask them to re-open Wingate's case. So Rich and I will go. We'll tell them about you, and I'm sure they'll ask you to come in and tell them what happened to you. But for now you don't need to come."

I was as bad as Pop. I felt left out. But that left me free to do what I liked.

I asked what Pop had heard from Azalea, his wandering wife who was off seeing a doctor who promised to make her ten years younger.

"She sounds good on the phone," Pop said. That was a hopeful sign. They were still in touch. "I can't say she sounds any younger. She still wants me to come and be 'youthanized' with her. I'll think about it."

I went for a walk with Ted, took a nap, and by bedtime I had recuperated from my vacation. I was ready for whatever the next day might bring — or so I thought.

CHAPTER
29

LATE MONDAY MORNING

The tattoo parlor wasn't far, just down Merrimon Avenue, and our house is only a little way off Merrimon. I drove past Grace Episcopal Church, high on the left, with its gray stone walls and bright red door, past shopping centers and finally the modern, flat-roofed post office, also on the left. Rich had said the tattoo place was called Sky Writers, and it was right near Weaver Boulevard, which leads to the college. It took me two passes to find the small sign and find my way down a side drive to a door surrounded by raised flower beds blazing with marigolds and zinnias. I figured flowers were a good omen.

I knocked and tried the door. Unlocked. I went into a corridor with one whole wall covered with tattoo pictures, from quaint cartoons to pretty flowers to grinning skulls, and yes, including several dragons.

A small sitting room, which seemed to be the reception area, was on the other side of the hall. The room pulled me in. The walls were covered with poppies as large as serving platters, painted in rose and purple. A pretty young woman with dark hair and a ring in one nostril sat on a chartreuse couch with lamps at each end. The lamps had leopard-spotted shades with rose-colored ball fringe around the bottom.

"Hello," she said. "You're in luck. We're not busy right now."

A young woman with purple hair, green bangs, six rings in each ear, and a ring in her nostril nodded in agreement. "We're usually booked pretty solid." She sat in a platform rocker across from the couch.

"I have an appointment just coming in," said a third young woman with long blond hair and about two inches of black roots showing on top. She looked me up and down. "I doubt if you want body piercing."

I noticed a sign on the wall with body-piercing prices. Nipples were fifteen dollars. I said I could do without being pierced.

Two young men came in the door, and Miss Body Pierce went off with them down the corridor. Purple Hair said she'd be back and vanished.

I introduced myself and sat on the couch next to the young woman with dark hair. "Who painted your poppies?" I asked.

"I did," she said. "I'm an artist. I also custom-design tattoos." She had a gentle artist's voice. I noticed the two large bookshelves that covered one wall were full of art books and books on Oriental myths, Eastern philosophy, and suchlike.

I felt more at home. I know artists.

"I have a friend who is in trouble," I said. "Someone killed his father, and someone has tried to kill his cousin."

"Good grief," she said. "He must have terrible karma."

"He came here for a tattoo about six months ago," I said. "You did a dragon on his arm. His father was alive then and came with him. His father was drunk."

She gasped. "Oh, my God, I remember. They were both so attractive. Well, at least at first. And you know, we're regulated. We can't do a tattoo on someone who's drunk. But the one who wanted the tattoo was sober. And the father, if that's who that was, was a quiet, sad drunk — at least at first. Very good-looking. He made me feel like I ought to take care of him. I had a lull in business, so I could do the tattoo right then. They picked a standard dragon off the wall, so I didn't have to draw up a design. It only took me a couple of hours."

I felt encouraged. It was just barely possible she might remember what they said that night. *You're crazy*, the negative part of me said. *She never will.* The positive part said, *You never know till you ask.*

"I believe they were talking about a woman who left a message on the older man's answering machine," I said. "Or maybe about a rumor." That sounded so ordinary. Who would remember that for six months? This tattoo gal was used to the bizarre and the romantic.

"Oh, it was all so strange," she said. "I write short stories, too. So I notice things like that — you know, things I could use."

Boy, she was really busy, with tattoos and writing, too.

"How was it strange?" I asked.

"When they came in, the older man was drunk, but kind of quiet, like I said. But then he went back out, I guess to his car, and when he came back he was really in bad shape. And he said to the young man something like, 'That rumor was a lot of bullshit.' And something about changes someone might make — and I remember because the poor man was almost in tears about those changes, and the young man got all upset and said, 'Dad, shut up.' "

Oh, brother!

"And you're pretty sure you remember that right after all this time?" I said amazed.

"I keep a journal," she confided, "of things that I can use in stories. I wrote that in my journal. It was so dramatic." She went over to the bookcase and pulled out a loose-leaf notebook. She brought it back to the couch and leafed through it. Strange little drawings in pen and ink were on nearly every page. She noticed me staring. "I keep tattoo ideas in here, too."

She stopped at a page with a trunk, locked with a huge padlock. How appropriate. "Here it is," she said. "Yes, what I said is about right.

"The older man said, 'It wasn't her. Never her. That was a rumor. I'll tell you the name so you'll know it wasn't her.' Of course I was dying of curiosity, and here's why I really remember. It was a friend of mine. He even used her newest nickname: Bubbles Dean. She had taken to chewing bubble gum after her divorce. I meant to ask Bubbles about that man, but then she went to Puerto Rico for two weeks on vacation, and I got busy and forgot. I ought to ask her now."

"How can I reach her?" I asked.

"Her real name is Mary Lou Dean. Why, she works at the consignment shop just up the street, Clothes Encounters. And I'm sorry to hear that poor man was killed. He said I was a wood nymph." She smiled dreamily.

I wrote down *Mary Lou Dean* and *Clothes Encounters*.

Before I could ask more, a boy came in who looked about twenty and had his hair in dreadlocks. A girl in a miniskirt hung on his arm. He asked about a custom-designed tattoo, and of course that was Miss Tattoo's first priority. I thanked her and departed as I heard him say he wanted to give it to the girl for her birthday. Maybe a rosebud on the inside of her thigh.

I think I am getting old. I have no desire for a rosebud on the inside of my thigh.

CHAPTER
30

SHORTLY AFTERWARD

Clothes Encounters had summer suits in the big plate-glass windows. Quite stylish. One with a floral jacket and solid cream pants looked great, but too small for me. I wish I didn't always ask myself if the last owner gained weight or died. But then, perhaps like Goldie and Lillian, the last folks could replace their clothes on a whim.

Inside, a young woman in tennis whites and a green sweatband sat behind a glass counter with jewelry that blinked in the light. A cash register was by her elbow. Behind her, more jewelry hung on a Peg-Board; earrings like clear green glass marbles with silver wire coiled around them caught my eye. There was a nice pair made of old coins, a pair with plastic roses, and much more. Necklaces hung in big loops, from sensible fake pearls to third-world souvenirs, to cheerful foolishness.

That's what I have to do, I thought. *Sort out the sensible things I learn about Wingate and his relatives from the foolishness that doesn't count. The junk.* But how could I know which foolishness didn't count? I mean, if Groucho Marx's picture turned out to be a clue to murder, what next?

"Hi," I said, "I'm Peaches Dann. Are you Mary Lou Dean?"

She shook her brown curls. "No," she answered, and called out, "Mary Lou! Someone is looking for you."

A cheerful, slightly chubby young woman, maybe twenty-five or thirty, in a blue-and-green stained-glass-patterned caftan popped out of a back room that said PARTY CLOTHES over the door. A price tag hung from her sleeve. Evidently she modeled the stock. She wasn't chewing bubble gum.

I drew her to one side behind a rack marked 60% OFF and said, "I need your help."

"Whatever I can do," she said. "Personally I'm beyond all help." I could see by her big smile that she expected me to laugh. I obliged. Then I got serious. "I have a friend whose brother was killed," I said. "She's asked me to ask a few questions." That seemed to be a good opener. Shock treatment.

"My goodness," she said, and clutched at a brown leather belt that hung from a rack as if to steady herself. "I hope I have some answers. Who is your friend?"

"Marietta Scott Anderson."

"Oh, I used to know her, before I was married. Before I was divorced. I've led a full life!" Before she became Bubbles, I thought. Now, there was a name that was easy to remember!

"Did you know Marietta's brother, Wingate Scott?" I asked.

"Sure, I knew old Wingate. He was fun. We were even related in a way."

As one who is related in a way to half the people in western North Carolina, at least according to Pop, I didn't pay too much attention to that last. Besides, I was distracted by the tears in her eyes.

"He gave me these earrings," she said. "Real gold!" She reached up and touched both earrings. They were hoops in the form of kissing dolphins. "I felt so bad when I heard he was dead." Her voice wavered. "They said he fell." Suddenly she did a double take. "Oh, God, you mean it's him? You mean somebody killed him?"

"His sister thinks so."

"But why? And who?"

"That's what his sister wants to find out,

330

and I'm trying to help. What his sister does know is that Wingate certainly would never have killed himself."

"No," said Bubbles, "I'm glad she thinks that."

"You and Wingate were good friends?" I asked.

"We got together," she said, dabbing her eyes with the back of her hand, "when I had time. I go to UNCA and do this on the side." She waved at the racks of clothes. "This is fun." She swallowed a sob.

Everyone to her own idea of fun, I thought, but if you liked to dress in all sorts of wild clothes, here was your chance.

I noticed a T-shirt that someone had decorated with a gold replica of the electric chair. That must have been a joke!

"We went out a lot about a year ago. We had a hoot," she said with a satisfied grin. The grin melted away. "But I made a mistake. I wanted to get serious. I know he was older and all that, but he made me feel so great. Getting serious spooked him, and he took off." She shrugged as if life was like that. Then she frowned. "And someone killed him?"

"Did you ever leave a message on his answering machine?" I asked.

"Oh, sure," she said. "We left silly messages, back and forth." Fleeting smile again. "I'd say, 'The early bird catches the worm, but the second mouse gets the cheese, so it's okay to come late if you like cheese better than worms.' That wouldn't mean anything to you, but we had in-jokes, and some of them I actually remember because they pleased me."

"Did you ever leave Wingate a message about Groucho Marx's picture?"

"I could have," she said. "This was a year ago. Before he got to be a rich man. We joked about all sorts of things."

"Would you have said" — I pulled out my notes — " 'Please call me, dearest. I know we have to be careful, but I miss you every moment'?"

"Only if it was some kind of joke," she said, frowning. "He reacted very badly to mush. But I could have been razzing him about that. This was a long time ago," she said sadly.

"Was there anything about him that seemed strange or suspicious?" I asked.

"Wingate? He had mood swings. But I have to admit he didn't really confide in me about anything like that. He said I was his sunshine. I hope he wasn't murdered. I really liked Wingate. He was a charmer." Tears again. "Excuse me," she said suddenly, "I have to go to the ladies'." Bubbles ran off — to have a good cry, I suspected.

Tennis Whites reappeared, just in time to take over before I left. "Can I help you?" she said.

I wished she could. I knew that women seemed to love Wingate and that somebody hated him enough to kill him. But I needed to know more.

CHAPTER
31

A FEW MINUTES LATER

I walked back to my car, sat down in the driver's seat, then turned on the motor and the air-conditioning. It was drippy hot outside — unusually hot for Asheville. The mannequins from the Clothes Encounters window looked down on me, oblivious of the heat. They were doing their job well, making someone's castoffs look arresting, especially the one in the purple pant suit and the yellow straw hat with the pink rose in the band. I felt I was doing badly.

To tell the truth, the more I found out, the less I felt I knew. What else was it the tattoo girl had said? That Wingate was afraid of some kind of change, that he was terribly upset about somebody making a change. What change could leave him so distraught and feeling in need of luck in the form of a tattooed dragon?

The dragon in this family was Hiram.

The dragon with the treasure. Whose will — good Lord, suppose Wingate had thought Hiram might change his will? I caught my breath. If Wingate were afraid he'd be done out of fifteen million dollars, no wonder he got drunk!

If this were a grade-B movie, Hiram would have been killed, not Wingate. One of those odd memories that drifts into my mind did just that now: what did Willie Sutton say when he was asked why he robbed banks? "Because," he said, "that's where the money is." Hiram was where the money was. Until the will.

I started to back my car around. My car phone rang. Ah, technology. It was Marietta. I stopped the car. I don't like to talk on the phone and drive if I can park and give it my whole attention, especially when I'm already thunderstruck.

"We've been to see the Buncombe County sheriff, and he's mad at us," Marietta said. "He says how do we expect him to deal with something that happened in England and something that happened in the middle of the ocean. He says we were damn fools not to report what happened to the captain!"

"We did report it," I said impatiently.

"He says we weren't forceful enough. Anyway, he says there's not much he can do till something happens here. But the Watauga sheriff may do better. We're going there this afternoon. I'm at Rich's place for now." She gave me his number. I wrote it down.

A woman in a white nurse's uniform and cap walked past me into Clothes Encounters.

"Marietta," I said, "tell me about Hiram's doctor. What was he like?"

"Old," she said. "Wingate begged Hiram to get a younger doctor, because even with glasses Dr. Humphrey didn't see too well. But Hiram wouldn't do it. Why do you want to know?"

"Tell me about Dr. Humphrey first."

"Last year, Dr. Humphrey had a stroke, a mild one, but Annie and Wingate talked Hiram into getting a second opinion. The second doctor said it didn't matter. Hiram's body was so full of cancer he'd never get well, so he might as well have the doctor who made him happy. So he still had Dr. Humphrey."

I had to admit that made sense.

"But suppose," I said, "that Hiram was killed, and the doctor had expected him to die, so he didn't look into the cause too closely?"

Marietta laughed. "But even if we were all natural-born killers, who would bother? He was going to die soon anyway."

"Suppose he was killed so that he wouldn't change his will?"

"Oh, come on!"

I told her what Wingate had said in the tattoo parlor.

"Now look," she said, "you've let yourself be carried away. Even if that girl remembers right, we don't know who was maybe going to change what."

"What else could have upset Wingate that much?"

There was a long silence. Then: "Are you suggesting," Marietta demanded, "that Wingate killed Uncle Hiram? That's ridiculous! Then who killed Wingate?"

"Perhaps Wingate didn't do it," I said. "Perhaps other people were going to be affected by the change, and Wingate knew about it. I haven't stopped trying to find out more. The tattoo-parlor gal knew the name Wingate gave for the person who left the message on his machine who was somehow connected to the rumor —"

"Which was somehow connected to Wingate's death," she said. "This is all pretty *somehow*. What is the girl's name?"

"Mary Lou Dean," I said.

337

"Oh!" She let out a yelp. "Oh, I can't believe this!"

"It didn't sound that amazing to me," I said, wishing it had.

"I guess you don't know!" she said. "Mary Lou Dean is Suzie's daughter."

"Suzie?" I said. "Suzie who?"

"The one who divorced Hiram! She was married to another man before she married Hiram. She had a daughter. A nice girl, but drifting. I heard she was into drugs for a while. And then divorced."

"Suzie is the one that Hiram hated?"

"Yes. In the end. He thought she was a gold digger. I kind of liked Suzie myself."

Rich carried her picture around in his wallet, although he was young and this Suzie was old enough to be Mary Lou Dean's mother. Now, how did Suzie's daughter Mary Lou fit into this mess? Why didn't Rich recognize her name? Maybe he didn't know her new nickname was Bubbles.

I told Marietta I'd talk to her later, hung up, turned off the engine, and headed back into Clothes Encounters. I found Mary Lou in the back room pricing blouses. Her eyes were still a little red, but she was deliberately calm. She held up a blouse with an Elvis head and shoulders on the back.

"This could be a collector's item!" she said. "That's what's fun about working here. I get first choice when stuff comes in."

"You are Hiram's ex-wife's daughter," I said, getting right to the point.

"Yes," she agreed. "Which made me Wingate's ex-stepniece. This blouse would be nice for you," she continued, as if trying to divert me. "Just your size." She held up a blouse with a tigerskin design. "Washable," she added, looking at the tag. "On sale because it's more of a winter blouse." It was nice, but I was not here for blouses.

"Your mother was very angry with Hiram," I said.

"No," she said. "*He* was very angry with *her*. My mother is just back from Italy with an Italian boyfriend. She is not angry with anybody."

"She lives here in Asheville?"

She nodded.

Asheville is getting very sophisticated. Twenty years ago an Italian boyfriend would have been an all-out scandal. Now he might rate a raised eyebrow, at least in the circles where I imagined Suzie moved.

"Where were you when Wingate died, Mary Lou?" I asked, switching back to my original quest. I keep forgetting to ask this

339

question because it upsets folks, but I need to know.

"You don't have to answer questions, Mary Lou," said a familiar voice behind me. I turned, and there was Ellington Foxworth, glaring at me. He had on his lawyer suit and white shirt. What was he doing in a women's consignment shop?

"I know this young lady," he said. "What do you want to ask her?"

"I know she's Suzie's daughter," I said. "The Suzie that Hiram divorced. I'd like to tell you all about what I want to know from her and why. May I come talk to you?" This might be my main chance with the Fox.

I was in luck. To my surprise, he said, "All right, as soon as I buy some jewelry. This is my wife's anniversary." Not his, too? What a chauvinist.

Mary Lou, meanwhile, had vanished among the maternity clothes.

I could hardly believe that the Fox, who was stuffier than a stuffed owl, bought his wife presents in a consignment shop. I watched with amazement as he asked to see "the pieces you called me about."

Tennis Whites brought out a necklace that looked like a hammered-brass new moon with round blobs of green glass fastened on it, all affixed to a chain with a clasp. He held it up and admired it. The whole thing looked like a Gypsy had made it over a campfire fifty years ago with tin snips and a bellows and maybe a file to round the edges. Yet the thing had flair and style.

"Oh, Marsha will like that!" he said. "That's quite an original. Do you know where it came from?"

"No," she said. "Someone's aunt who travels picked that up and sent it to her niece. The niece thinks it's hideous."

"But you have an eye," the Fox said. "That's just the thing for my wife's anniversary present. We're celebrating tonight."

"I have another piece of primitive jewelry," she said. She dangled a string of beads with copper arms and legs and hearts sticking out at all angles. Not valentine hearts, but rough replicas of the organ itself. Yuck.

"Oh, she'll like that!" he said. "To add to her primitive collection."

I pictured the couple going to a formal reception with Mrs. Fox wearing hearts to counter the jokes about lawyers not having hearts.

Whereupon the Fox paid forty-five dollars for both necklaces. Talk about a cheap date.

If it turned out that he was being bled dry by a blackmailer, that would explain it. On the other hand, maybe he was just stingy.

Meanwhile Mary Lou Bubbles Dean, who had come out from behind clothes racks, was watching me and looking troubled.

I gave her a good-bye wave and called, "I'll be back for the tiger shirt and maybe those coin earrings." I made my exit with the Fox, who said he'd lead me to his office.

A solid Victorian house not too far off Merrimon turned out to be it. This particular house was long on stained glass and short on gingerbread. The door, with a dove carrying a letter in colored glass on the large upper pane, opened into a hallway with a big oak desk, a hefty but stylish receptionist, and a graceful winding stairway to the second floor. We stayed on the first floor and went into a room off the hall. We sat down at a mahogany table in front of a fireplace with a carved golden wood mantel. No fire, of course, this being July.

Why was the Fox giving me his time? With the will settled, it wasn't his job, was it? Suppose he actually was being blackmailed. Suppose I was close to finding out why. What would he do then?

"All right," he said, "Rich called me this morning. He told me about three attempted murders. I believe one attempt was against your life. So he and Marietta went to see the sheriff. About time to get real help. Don't you realize it's dangerous for you to be poking around like this?"

Well, yes, I did. "Why do you think a killer would be prevented from trying again to kill me, anyway, if he thinks I know something?" I asked, and was immediately sorry I'd put that into words.

He tapped a pencil on the table impatiently. "Has it occurred to you that you're addicted to danger? Perhaps you should get help." I stared him down, hoping he was wrong. He demanded, "Why are you questioning Mary Lou Dean?"

I explained about the tattoo and the message on the answering machine, and the mention of a rumor, and how Wingate had said that something that upset him very much would be changed because of that rumor. The Fox did not look impressed.

I told him that Wingate said Mary Lou left the message. And all the time, I wondered, *Should I be telling him this?* But I wanted to see how he'd react. The answer was: He didn't react so you'd notice. Old Stuffed Owl had a consummate poker face. How could I think of him as both an owl and a fox? Well, there is a certain resemblance between the two.

"That's a lot of foolishness," Foxworth snapped as soon as I finished my account.

"Hiram was going to get you to change his will," I said. "Wingate was upset about that."

The Fox burst out laughing. "Just to show you how wrong you can be," he said, "I *did* change Hiram's will. He called me to come do it the very morning of the day he died." He leaned toward me, across the table, as if he might like to push me backward.

I was careful not to lean backward. "Hiram was well enough to call you?"

"Feeble but determined. And it's none of your business how I changed that will," he said firmly, "but the result was that Wingate got more, not less. So let that be a lesson to you not to let your imagination go overboard. Now, that's all I'm going to tell you." I could see by the rigid line of his mouth that he wasn't likely to change his mind.

"Just tell me one other thing," I said.

"Did Hiram mention that anybody else was coming to see him that morning?"

He looked quite annoyed that I hadn't followed his advice and bowed out. Then he laughed. "He said someone was going to bring him chicken soup. Now what can you make of that?" His eyebrows said I was a fool.

He stood up. "Good-bye, and let me give you some free advice. Go home and be careful."

As it turned out, that was excellent advice, but I wasn't able to take it, even when I wanted to.

CHAPTER
32

EARLY AFTERNOON

I drove a little way up Merrimon Avenue, went into Wendy's, and had the salad bar because I was starving. If someone was following me, either I didn't know them or they were a master of disguise. Then I went back to Clothes Encounters. I saw Mary Lou outside, got out of the car, and started to suggest we go back inside the store. The sun was fierce, but she took hold of my arm and held me in place.

"Listen," she said, "the day before Wingate fell or was pushed or whatever, he called me up — as he did from time to time — and he seemed to be joking, but maybe he wasn't." Mary Lou squinted with the sun in her eyes, but she held us both in the hot sun. "He laughed that great laugh and he told me that sometimes what he said was bullshit. I laughed, too, and said yes, he could make anyone think they were great when obviously they weren't all *that* great."

She smiled. "He could do that. And then he said he'd learned his lesson, that he wasn't going to be like that anymore. I said I'd believe that when I saw it. He said that the next day he was going to tell somebody the truth — and that, if he lived through that, he was going to ask me to marry him."

"Why did you think that was a joke?"

"Oh, Wingate had told me a hundred times he was out of the marrying business. But suppose it wasn't a joke? I would have said yes. If it wasn't a joke, then maybe he did tell somebody the truth and died because of it."

I put my arm around Mary Lou, and she cried on my shoulder.

CHAPTER
33

MONDAY AFTERNOON

I began to feel as if I almost knew who killed Wingate, as if I had the answer just at the edge of my mind, just beyond my reach. As I sat in the car, I watched a small girl across the street struggle with a giant ice-cream cone. It was almost too much for her to handle. Was this too much for me to handle? Was I addicted to danger? I shut my eyes, trying to concentrate. Nothing came.

I needed to bat this around with somebody who knew all Hiram's heirs well, who knew who Wingate might tell a surprising truth to, and whether that was dangerous, and how. That might help. I started to call Marietta on the car phone and discuss the new twists. But people can tap into car phones. That's how Prince Charles was caught talking to his lady friend. Perhaps I shouldn't have said as much on a car phone as I already had.

I drove down Merrimon Avenue and found a pay phone at the Texaco station. Actually there were two phones, one on each side of the corner of the building. Not much phone booth, just a minimal box above my head. If a fat lady got under that box in the rain, she could keep her hair dry, and that's about all. I put in thirty-five cents and dialed Marietta's number. No answer. A kid about seven or eight came along and began to use the other phone. The cars shifting gears on the hill in front of the station almost drowned him out. Not quite. "I have three dollars," I heard him say. "So what have you got?"

Money has power for good and for evil. Did the truth that Wingate was going to tell have to do with money? Did it have to do somehow with Hiram's will? I stood right there by my phone and thought hard about the will. How could it be changed so that Wingate got more than he did before, but that all the heirs got the same amount? Had he received less than the others in the earlier draft? But why, if he threatened to disinherit Wingate, would Hiram have changed his will to leave him more? That didn't make sense.

A line of ants was marching near my right foot, carrying crumbs from a bit of cookie someone dropped. Something in the back of my mind said, *Think about ants*. That seemed ridiculous.

I tried Marietta again. I've been known to dial wrong. This time she answered: "I just got here. Hi!"

The kid with three dollars walked off. I looked around the corner. Nobody near enough to hear. Good.

I told her what Suzie's daughter said about Wingate's last phone call. I told her what the Fox said about Hiram's will, and then I said, "We have to remember that people do kill to prevent wills from being changed."

There was a stunned silence at the other end of the line. Then she said in a shocked voice, "Are you *still* suggesting that Wingate killed Hiram" — a long pause, with cars roaring by — "but that Wingate got there too late, after the will was changed? Besides, he didn't need to have killed Hiram after all."

Before I could think of an answer, she said, "That's pretty far-fetched. And then why would someone kill Wingate?"

I was stymied.

Marietta went on: "I did ask you to help and I know you will, but you've got some crazy ideas."

Okay. I'd upset her.

"I mean, who would ever think that Brian could be the killer?"

I had all but forgotten I'd suggested that. "But he turned out to have an alibi," I said. "He was first in Asheville eating waffles with Annie Long, and then off an hour away from Linville Falls, where they were picking mushrooms."

"Besides, he's much too vague," Marietta said. "He'd leave his wallet at the scene. He'd leave his fingerprints on the body. He'd leave a note saying he didn't do it. And he's just a kid."

Billy the Kid was a kid, too, and guilty enough to hang. I didn't say that out loud. A boy about Brian's age came out of the door near the phone booth with a box of clean laundry. By gosh, there was a Laundromat in this end of the gas-station building. He had the same sort of happy lost look as Brian. No, I didn't think Brian was the killer.

"Why, he's so vague," Marietta said, "that once I expected him at my farm for lunch at noon, and when he got there at one-thirty, he said his watch had stopped. I asked him if he didn't notice it said the same thing for an hour and a half."

"And he said . . . ?"

"He said his mind was on something else." Her voice became triumphant. "He could never get away with murder!"

Vague and picking wild mushrooms. Boy, I wouldn't want to eat what *he* picked. Some of those things can be deadly.

I peeked around the corner again. Still nobody in earshot. *Mushrooms,* said the back of my mind. *Remember that.* I found myself looking again at the ants.

"Who drove to Turkey Pen Gap?" I wondered out loud. Brian had told me, but I couldn't remember.

"Well, it certainly wouldn't have been Brian. He could get lost in his own backyard. Brian has absolutely no sense of geography."

I thought of Brian being steered between two pretty girls on the *Ocean Queen.* Maybe they weren't distracting him with raging hormones and making him vaguer. Maybe they were looking after him so he didn't stay lost.

"Suppose Brian just *thought* he was in Turkey Pen Gap," I said, beginning to get excited. "He said he got lost in the woods for a little while and sat down and wrote a poem. Suppose they were actually near Linville Falls. Suppose he was lost for longer than a little while. Then Annie could have killed Wingate."

"Yes," Marietta cried happily, "yes! To Brian, noon is the same as one-thirty. I bet Annie did it!" She sounded overjoyed. "My boys will be off the hook. Brian and Wingate would never ever kill. You'll see! You're on the right track! Now I have to go. We'll talk later."

A boy in wire-rim glasses and a red T-shirt came out of the Laundromat, eating an apple. He threw the core as hard as he could toward a big ivy-covered tree in back of the station. The core exploded. Like my theories up to now. But maybe this one was right!

I stood in thought. Somehow I couldn't help watching those ants. Like the ones Pop used to test the gingko potion to see if it was poisonous. *Remember mushrooms.* Annie Long knew about mushrooms, so she knew the poison ones. Death caps! Suppose she went out to pick those the day Hiram died, and the Fox came early — which lawyers virtually never do, so she wouldn't have expected it — and he revised the will while Annie picked the mushrooms. What poetic justice! Because suppose Annie was the one who feared she'd be cut out of the will and didn't know she hadn't been — and neither had Wingate.

An interesting theory. I figured I'd bat it around with my logical husband. I looked through my pocketbook for thirty-five cents to call home. Dern. Was I out of change? But my pocketbook has hidden depths. I searched again, concentrating on feeling in every crevice. I shook papers that might have change stuck in their folds. Finally I found a quarter and two nickels. I dialed. No answer. That was odd. Pop and the sitter should have been there even if Ted was out. They could be out for ice cream again. I left a message for Ted on the answering machine: "Ted, I may know who did it. You're my favorite brain-stormer, and I hope you'll be there to bat this around. I'll tell you what's up when I get there shortly."

I have to admit I forgot to keep my voice down and I hadn't seen anyone come up behind me. I noticed when I felt something hard poke the middle of my back and a voice whispered in my ear, "This is a gun. Get in your car."

My stomach jumped in my mouth, and I was quite sure the Fox was wrong about one thing. I did not enjoy danger.

CHAPTER
34

IMMEDIATELY AFTERWARD

I looked around for the kid with the apple core or someone with a basket of laundry, someone who might notice if I mouthed *help*. Nobody in sight except a man in the distance putting gas in his car and ignoring me.

"Get in from the passenger side and slide over. That way I can keep the gun on you," Annie Long said. Those green eyes were imperious, her mouth hard. With one side turned away from her, I slipped my wallet out of my shoulder-hanging purse and into my pocket, where I could get hold of it more easily. Identification. Maybe I could drop the wallet somewhere useful. Thank goodness I'd forgotten to zip my purse.

It did not cheer me to think that I was right about Annie Long.

"You killed Wingate and tried to kill me," I blurted.

"I did not kill Wingate," she said. "I'm going to show you who did."

"Who?" I demanded.

"I'm not going to tell you. I'm going to show you," she said. "Shut up and drive." So maybe she was a vigilante, not a killer. But her manner was too dark, too wild, for that. Her dark hair straggled as if she'd forgotten to comb it. She was all tense angles, and one eye twitched at odd moments. She seemed as tense as I was. I started the car, and it occurred to me that if I backed into that blue car parked near the front of the gas station, I'd be stopped.

"Watch where you're going," she said, and poked the gun in my side. "Turn right," she said as I headed out onto Merrimon Avenue. I prayed someone I knew would be passing by, would see me with Annie. We passed Clothes Encounters. I wished someone would come out and wave. Annie guided me or maybe goaded me through back streets onto US 19-23. There was much less chance of seeing a friend on the highway.

"Who killed Hiram?" I demanded, hoping to shock her into admission.

"Shut up," she repeated. Was she part of a conspiracy or what?

I drove. Now and then I tried a question.

"Why did you try to kill me? I didn't know anything." No answer except, "You do now."

With so many cars on the interstate, couldn't just one be a friend of mine? Preferably a psychic friend?

"You put a paper bag over your head and tried to push Marietta off a stairway. You tried to roast me in a dryer." I was scared but I was also angry.

She laughed. "Wingate always said I had imagination. Hiram always said I could plan ahead better than anyone else he knew, and then improvise on the spur of the moment when I had to." She sighed. "But everything went wrong. I meant to show them all that I was as good as they were!" she said. "But they ganged up."

"You left Wingate a message on his answering machine," I guessed.

"That nosy Rich walked right in his house and played it. If that damn Rich hadn't been so nosy, or that damn Wingate hadn't been so sexy, or if I hadn't been so worn down . . ."

Someone beeped a horn at me. I wasn't driving my best. I was distracted.

"Do you know what it's like to look after an old man like that? Always demanding, always complaining. I began to feel so old and dried out," she said. "So tired inside. Wingate made me feel alive again, and nothing we did hurt Hiram. He never had to know."

"But he found out because of a rumor."

"Oh, Wingate called it a rumor about the message on the machine, when he swore to Rich that wasn't my voice. He swore Rich had just jumped to that conclusion. And Rich believed him. That's what Wingate told me. The rumor was two damn women who couldn't keep from blabbing what they heard, and got more money because they did me in." Her eyes stayed furious, and the one that was out of control winked harder. Her tension meter.

We left Asheville on the expressway, and Annie directed me to turn onto I-40 East where the road divided.

Now she was so angry she choked on her words. "First Rich told his sister Winnie that his father was sleeping with me, that the message proved it."

"Didn't Rich tell Winnie that was wrong after Wingate told his lie?"

"It was too late. Winnie'd shot her mouth off. She told Goldie. Goldie was a sexy babe, and Winnie was a droop. I bet smartmouth Winnie told her just to impress her with how much she knew."

I shivered to think of all the coincidences that had led to murder and to my danger. "Goldie told Hiram?"

"She wanted to borrow money — what else? — and she came when he was sick and angry at the world and he said no. Goldie kept begging, and he was angry. He knew she didn't like Wingate. So he said, 'The only person I'd lend money to is Wingate. The only one I trust is Wingate.' Goldie went into a rage and told him."

"Did Wingate know?"

"You'd damn well better believe it. Hiram called him up and told him he was cutting us both out of his will. Wingate told him it was all a mistake. That wasn't my voice. At least he lied for me, and also to save his own ass. Hiram didn't believe him."

"So you improvised a way to kill Hiram," I said. "You went out to pick poison mushrooms, and he managed to get Foxworth to change the will while you were gone."

"The old bastard didn't even let on he'd done it," Annie groaned. "He must have promised Foxworth a bundle to drop everything and come right then. But don't get encouraged — they'll never find poison in Hiram's body. When I came back he was so frail, and you know he had cancer in his lungs. He'd failed even in the last hours. I could see that all I had to do was hold a pillow over his face for half a minute. So I did. Those damn mushrooms cost me fifteen million dollars. While I picked them, Hiram changed his will. Then I didn't even need them." Her face was ridged with hate and anger lines. She looked old.

I thought of the Fox saying that the change in the will gave Wingate more. Yes, I thought, because Hiram wouldn't deny his own blood. Because he believed that men could play the field and a woman mustn't. Especially a woman that he'd bought and paid for. So Wingate got his inheritance plus a share of Annie's portion.

The Fox! The Fox had mentioned chicken soup — that someone was going to bring Hiram chicken soup. "But Poo came to bring some soup," I said, "because Hiram was too sick to eat cookies."

She looked startled. "How on earth did you know that?"

"What did she see?" I asked. "What made you have to kill her? Very clever to have done it with alcohol so she'd appear to have drunk herself to death."

"I was lucky," she said. "Some people throw it up before it's lethal. Of course, it helped that she had a weak heart. I made it my business to know things like that."

"But what did Poo see?"

"She came right in the kitchen and she saw the mushrooms. Destroying angels, with their white bulbous root. I don't think she knew what they were. But she'd know if she ever saw a picture later. All the deadly amanita mushrooms have that root."

"Now Poo and Hiram and Wingate are all dead," I said.

A look of anguish crossed her face. That didn't make sense. But she was smiling again in nothing flat. She smoothed her dark hair back with one hand. Young again. The white streak was like a bolt of lightning.

"You were all terrified," she said in a boasting voice. "All the ones I had to be so damn polite to all those years. And the meddler. That's you."

"You even threw a rock at Marietta and me when she took me to the place where you — or somebody — murdered Wingate."

"I warned you," she said. "You don't take warnings, do you? Shut up and drive." That was her refrain.

The vistas from the Blue Ridge Parkway were as lovely as always. Green mountains, near and far, bright in July sunshine. My fear made colors brighter. This could be the last time I'd see the wildflowers, the occasional waterfall on the nearby mountainside, the far blues and greens, or the soaring sky.

We passed scenic overlooks with people parked and soaking up the peaceful view. Little did they know the lack of peace in our car. The air was thick with my fear and Annie's tension. Did she suspect she'd be caught? Her nervous eye was twitching faster.

My car phone was near to hand. If only I could call for help. But by the time I dialed, she could shoot. I looked at the car clock. Four-thirty. At least there'd be plenty of tourists around for a while. The weather report had said it was due to rain, which would have chased them away to indoor fun. So much for weather reports. The sun continued to make the mountains emerald green.

I noticed Annie did not have on her seat belt. I prayed for a ranger to stop us for that. No ranger appeared. If I went as fast as I could and then jammed on the brakes, would that throw Annie against the front window? But it wasn't likely to knock her out, and she'd still have the gun.

"Where are we going?" I asked. I was

afraid the answer would be Linville Falls, the place where Wingate was murdered.

She kept her mouth clamped tight.

"Why did you hate the family so much?" I asked.

"Listen," she said, "I don't need you to interrogate me. If you keep your mouth shut, you could live a little longer."

Desperately I searched my mind for ways to escape. If I drove over the edge of the parkway where some drops were long and some were shorter, she was more likely to be knocked out than I in my seat belt. If I did it in view of tourists, they'd call for help. But that was an extreme measure. We could both be killed. I'd try to think of something else.

I found myself thinking of Ted. I shouldn't have tried to help Marietta. Maybe I *was* addicted to danger. No. I didn't think so. I was addicted to being helpful, and in this case I could end up being very unhelpful to Ted, who was the one I cared about most. If I died I'd leave poor Ted to look after my outrageous father. And poor Pop — he had such a feeling for blood relatives that he wanted one of those to keep an eye on him, namely me. And I wanted to live!

For comfort, I summoned up Ted: his peaceful face when I woke up and he was still asleep, his wonderful warm laugh, his hair stuck out at funny odd angles when he ran his fingers through it trying to figure something out. I visualized the sudden glint of wisdom in his eyes when a puzzle fit.

Okay, I thought. *Forget everything else. Survive.* But how?

We seemed to drive forever. Ted would get home and find my message and wonder where I was, since I'd said I was coming right home. But he'd have no idea where to look for me. No way to fit this puzzle together. A few raindrops spattered on the windshield, then a few more. Then the promised rain came. Not hard, but steady. The road turned from gray blue to almost black. Good-bye, tourists. If I drove over the edge, no one would know.

After a long time, when my hands were cramped from holding extra tight to the steering wheel — which I do when I'm uptight — we turned in to a parking lot. The one at Linville Falls. Even in the wet gray light I recognized the flagpole and the weathered welcome shed. I turned cold. Was she going to reenact what she did to Wingate? I'd die knowing just what happened.

But she said she was going to show me

who killed Wingate. Not *what* but *who.* I was scared, but wildly curious. Who else was in on this?

"Get out!" she ordered. "Slip over, out my side of the car, so I can keep the gun on you." I did what she said. She wore a shoulder bag that hung to about the same level as her hand. She slipped the pistol and her hand into the open purse, out of sight but ready to shoot. "Walk in front of me," she ordered.

A car was just driving off, splattering a puddle. One or two cars still stood in the lot. I prayed some people were hiking in the rain.

No mud in the parking lot. It was paved. But there'd be mud on the paths, I told myself. Maybe I could push her and she'd slip in the mud.

We walked through the welcome building, me in front. Someone was in the gift shop at one side. I slipped my wallet out of my pocket. Maybe if someone found it, they'd call to see who left it and reach Ted. A long, long shot. But he'd know there was something fishy since I'd said I would come home and then showed up in this place. Long shots are better than none. But how could I drop it without Annie seeing me? I pretended to trip. I let the wallet skitter across the floor toward the gift shop door. Annie was so angry she missed that. She jabbed me hard with the gun. "Stop trying to call attention to yourself. I can kill you and that woman, too. I wouldn't hesitate." She snapped that as she pulled me up.

The woman ran out of the gift shop and asked, "Are you all right?"

"I'm fine," I said, and winked at her. She gaped as if she thought I was a little crazy. Luckily, or unluckily, I hadn't twisted or pulled anything. I could still walk fine. So I had to.

Followed by Annie, I crossed the river on the walking bridge. Rain pinged on the dark water. Beyond the bridge, the wide path was gravel, not dirt as I'd remembered. Rain hit the leaves of the plants along the path — laurel and ferns and wildflowers — so they did a gentle dance. Rain sank into the gravel. No mud. The path was not slippery at all.

"Wingate came here to meet me," Annie said sadly. "I thought he loved me. This is where he kissed me first. Up at the overlook. All the way up I knew he was going to do it." Her voice trembled.

I was startled. Annie didn't seem like the type of woman who would moon about where someone first kissed her. She was bold. Dashing. Also hard. Not the sort of woman who would anticipate a kiss all along a walk in the woods. But people have secret crannies, hidden soft spots. And Wingate created memories. I'd learned that. When had this happened? Before Hiram died? Or just lately? She didn't say.

Perhaps Annie had a hidden soft spot that could help me survive. God willing. "So this path has romantic memories for you," I said.

She didn't answer that. "Hurry up," she said. "It's getting late."

Late for what? I wondered. Late for me to still be alive? Annie walked so briskly and pushed me to stay in front. On our left I could hear a stream, purling along. Everything so peaceful, the plunk of rain, the smell of the wet woods.

We came to stumps at the edge of the path, cut off to be the height of stools. "You can rest a minute," she said. She sat down and looked around her. I sat down, too, watching her gun hand. It stayed alert. "I haven't believed in much," she said. "I heard somebody say that before I worked for Hiram I didn't have a pot to piss in. I often heard what they said when they thought I didn't." She gave me a pleased glance. Proud of herself. "By the time I met Hiram I was okay. I took care of myself."

I wished I knew how to take care of myself, to get away from this woman. My brain seemed paralyzed with fear.

"But as a kid, we were back-cove poor," Annie went on. "You wouldn't understand that! My father drank. I had an aunt who helped me out. Made me dresses to go to school. When I was sixteen, my father sold my best dress for liquor. I beat him up and left home. Yes. You heard that right. I beat up my own father." She glared at me as if I was going to judge her.

"It sounds like you had reason," I said, *and obviously,* I thought, *unusual strength.* "But I haven't hurt you." A red bird flew by. I wished I could fly. She kept telling her story: "I'm sure you've heard I was a hostess in a massage parlor. Hell! It paid. I worked my way through UNCA as a hostess, back when it was called Asheville Biltmore College. Hiram hired me as an office temp. I did that, too. Then he hired me as a housekeeper. He paid me well. We got on all right. I didn't expect him to be better than he was. He expected me to do everything he asked as long as the money was right." At least her autobiography was keeping me alive.

"Sometimes I slept with him. Sometimes I paid off his string of girlfriends. He said I was like a member of his family." She laughed. "But then he wasn't so good to the members of his family, was he? Except he left them that beautiful money. Each damn one got more than a million that should have been mine, because that sneaky Hiram changed his will. He divided his millions between eight people instead of nine. He broke his promise."

I was startled. The will left Annie ten thousand dollars. I thought that was right. That sounded like a lot to me. But she'd expected fifteen million! Compared with that, ten thousand dollars was a thumb of the nose.

She jumped up off the stool stump and snarled, "Come on!" She pushed me in front again.

The path was steeper and rockier. I was trying so hard to think of a way to get away that I forgot to watch my feet. I tripped on a ledge of rock, fell, and skinned my knee.

"Get up!" she yelled, as if I'd done it on purpose. Not this time.

"But why was Wingate killed nearly a year *after* Hiram changed his will, nearly a year after he died?" Somehow the worse things got, the more I had to know why. "I can see why you killed Hiram in hopes he wouldn't change his will, but why was Wingate killed?"

"Keep moving," she said.

"And then why try to kill Marietta and try to kill me?"

"All of you were snobs," she said, "and hypocrites. Laughing at me behind my back and trying to get me to help get favors from Hiram."

"I certainly never did," I said. "I'm not aware that Marietta ever did."

"No," she admitted, "but you two meant to get the sheriff stirred up. You meant to track me down. You were greedy like the rest. You wanted a luxury cruise, didn't you? Hypocrites, greedy fools, all of you! I meant to kill you for my pleasure and to see the terror in the ones who were still alive. And now no one will be able to prove whether you were pushed or fell. I like that."

I was to die like Wingate. That's what she planned. I remembered that breathtaking drop. I mustn't let my knees shake.

"So if you didn't kill Wingate, who did?" I asked. "And why?" Everything pointed to Annie. Why should she lie to me now?

"Wingate was the only one who treated me as if I was an important person — as if he cared about me. Always. A little while before Hiram died, we became lovers. I was so lonely. I was drained from looking after that sick old man. Wingate was my rock and my light at the end of the tunnel. I thought. But his damned hypocrite son found my message on his answering machine and ruined my life."

Yes. I knew that. "Your message," I said, "about love and money." The wet woods loomed dark around us. I almost tripped over a rock ledge.

"You mentioned Groucho Marx because Wingate always kept cash hidden in the frame of a picture of Groucho Marx. Back before Wingate had millions. You wanted Wingate to know that you'd talked Hiram into supplying the money for one of Wingate's projects, right?"

"You're too damn clever for your own good," she spat out.

The path came to some stairs down, and there in front of me was a squarish stone overlook with a low wall on three sides. I caught my breath. This was the place where Wingate was pushed over. I remembered the frightful drop straight down. To my left were the beautiful falls below, casting up white spray, but the long deadly drop was straight in front of me.

371

Annie walked around me, turned to face me, her back to the drop. Perhaps the sight made her queasy. I felt queasy. The gun still pointed at my heart.

"Wingate came here to meet me," she said, "just a little over two weeks ago." Suddenly she sounded as if she might burst into tears. Maybe she hadn't killed him. Maybe some coconspirator went overboard.

"Who else was here?" I asked.

She ignored that. "He said he wanted to meet me. He felt guilty about what happened. He wanted to figure out a way for me to get some of his money without his being ruined by the gift tax."

Gift tax! Was it possible this whole terrible situation had come about because of a gift tax? The ways of the wealthy are simply amazing. If I hadn't been scared silly, I'd have laughed.

"But why didn't you meet in his lawyer's office? Don't lawyers figure out how to get around gift tax?"

"I wanted to meet him here," she said. "He'd been so busy lately that I hardly saw him. I wanted him to remember how it had been between us."

She was a romantic. A cold-blooded romantic. I was amazed.

"Besides, I thought I knew of an easy way for us to share his money." Tears came into her eyes. "I was a damned fool. And he behaved just like always, as if I was the only person in the world, as if no one else mattered. He kissed me again right here, and I said 'Wingate, if you marry me, of course we'll share your property. We won't have to worry about any tax.' "

Then she almost choked on her words. "Then he showed what a bastard he was! He said I was just so damned wonderful, but that we wouldn't fit. I felt as if he'd hit me. I said he wouldn't stoop to marry his uncle's housekeeper — was that it? He was a millionaire, and I was nothing. Oh, no, he said, that wasn't it. He looked so virtuous I could have slapped him, and so handsome I could have kissed him again. And suddenly I knew. 'There's some other woman,' I told him. He said he wanted to be honest and not lead me on. The damned hypocrite! 'I've reached an age where I need stability,' he told me. He said his doctor told him he had high blood pressure and that he needed to take care of himself. He said he needed someone to help with that, so he meant to marry an old friend.

"An 'old friend'?" cried Annie. "I was an

old friend! I'd known him for thirty years!

" 'It's Suzie's daughter Mary Lou,' he told me. That damned girl who worked in the clothes shop, young enough to be his daughter. And I understood what I'd been — a way to reach Hiram, a way to milk Hiram, and maybe a good lay on the side."

I had the oddest feeling that we'd slipped back in time. Wingate or his ghost was standing with us.

"You wanted to buy me off!" she yelled. "To give me fifty thousand dollars cash instead of fifteen million dollars. To put the package in my hands so I couldn't resist." Then she shook herself and was back in the now. She lowered her voice. She glanced down at her hands. One was still pointing the gun. "And I took it all right, his silly bribe. I threw it on the ground and spat on it."

Boy, that must have been some big package. Or all in thousand-dollar bills?

She shot me a glance of challenge. Her voice trembled. "And I knew that's what he thought I was worth. A bribe. I was so angry." Her eyes flashed with rage. "And my hands reached out and pushed him." She paused. She shook her head as if to say no.

"He was so surprised. I was so surprised.

374

He grabbed at me. Almost pulled me over with him. He screamed all the way down. I have nightmares."

Her face contorted. "Wingate was the one who killed Wingate!" Annie cried out. "He showed me he was a sanctimonious son of a bitch. That he used me. That he wanted to buy off his conscience. He made me a killer.

"They all made me a killer. This whole damn family, which is rewarded for being greedy, and I get peanuts. I wanted them to be scared. I wanted them to know that someone was out to get them. And when they dragged you in, then you were one of them. I was so angry I didn't even care if I got caught as long as I scared those snobs good and took them down with me.

"Because what have I got? Not even memories.

"So now you know, and I have changed my mind. I do care if they catch me. I may be broke. I never saved my money because Hiram said I didn't need to. But I want to live."

"You thought Wingate really loved you," I said. "You thought he'd marry you and take care of you."

"Yes," she said, "when he kissed me here at the top of the world." A shiver ran through her. "I felt . . ." Tears came into her eyes. Her attention wavered. Her gun hand drooped.

I seized that moment to kick as hard and fast as I could and made contact with the gun just as it fired. I heard the whoosh of the bullet past my ear, but it missed me. I almost fell over backward. I'd kicked so hard and high that my foot knocked the gun in an arc in the air. No sound of it hitting the floor. And then I realized. I'd kicked so darn hard that gun went over the wall around the lookout. Of course I couldn't hear it hit the bottom of the gorge so far below. Adrenaline sure works. I don't have that kind of strength without it. I'd kicked so hard I almost lost my balance. My life depended on not doing that.

For a second Annie and I both teetered, equally amazed, and then I began to run. How I got back to the path from the lookout without falling, I don't know. She came after me, fast as the wind. Trees seemed to whir by me, my feet spread in great long flying strides, managing to avoid cracks between rocks where they covered the path, and then roots. She wasn't far behind me. I screamed, hoping someone might hear. If there were picnickers down below, maybe someone was up on the path. No answer. I needed all my breath to run. She was younger, but I was more desperate. Finally, right at the point where the paths branched apart, she caught my arm, then managed to push me down onto the path. I felt the grittiness against my bare legs. I struggled. I screamed again. Her hands went straight to my neck and began to squeeze. As I fought for breath, I raised my hands and gouged her eyes. She stopped choking me to protect herself. Then she banged my head against the path. I screamed again.

I heard running footsteps. Two rangers in uniform appeared above my head, a man and a woman. They grabbed Annie and wrestled her to the ground.

I sat up and felt for blood on the back of my head. My hand came back red. A lump would form soon. I looked at elegant Annie, pinned down in the dirt.

Annie had such iron self-control that she could kill her lover, hide her grief, and pick mushrooms with Brian for an alibi. She'd used her talent to destroy.

Of course this wasn't over gift tax. It was over love and jealousy and power, and a man who had a foolish flaw: a one-track mind, and no strategy to get around it. But money magnified those things into a crazy tragedy.

CHAPTER
35

A FEW DAYS LATER

What a day. Pop was about to leave for Arizona. Rich and Winnie had called to say they wanted to come see me and apologize, to explain why they'd omitted to tell me a few facts, and thereby nearly caused me to be pushed off a cliff. That was fine. I could give them a piece of my mind — since I still had a mind, no thanks to them.

Suzie called and said she had some advice for me. Suzie, Hiram's ex-wife who they joked knew more than God. I was curious to meet her and said, "I look forward."

I hoped we could avoid a traffic jam.

Rich and Winnie arrived first.

He sat down uneasily on one end of our living-room couch, and Winnie sat on the other. Rich was dressed in white shirt and dark pants, what the well-dressed teacher wears to apologize. Winnie was still jazzed up from her old self, wearing a denim skirt, a blouse covered with wildflowers, and multicolored sandals. I sat in the rocker and rocked, waiting to hear what they had to say.

"I'm sorry I wasn't entirely honest," he said in his schoolteacher voice. Winnie nodded that she was sorry, too. Rich switched to humble. "You see, when you said that Hiram was the most logical one to be murdered, I was suddenly scared that Hiram *was* murdered and that my father might be mixed up in that." He swallowed a lump in his throat. "Or at least appear to be. I knew he had fooled me in some way. I panicked. I wanted to think things out before I blabbed, and then it was too late."

"So you both knew that Hiram had heard from Goldie that the voice on the answering machine was Annie, and Hiram believed it. Even though Wingate swore it wasn't. You knew that Hiram threatened to cut Wingate and Annie out of his will. If I'd known that —" I stopped in mid-sentence. If I'd known that, it might have helped a lot — or not.

Rich ducked his head, very mea culpa. Then he looked me straight in the eye. "If my father had been mixed up in Hiram's murder, I was afraid it might even mean we'd lose our inheritance. I wanted to find out."

Winnie nodded again.

"Therefore," I said tartly, "we had a fifteen-million-dollar silence? No, a thirty-million-dollar silence, with the two of you taking part. Of course my life wasn't worth that much! Luckily I wasn't killed!"

"But I did help to save you — at least I could do that," Rich said sheepishly. "I beeped at you when I saw you with Annie. Boy, you had a long face. You looked scared, and it dawned on me that I couldn't keep my mouth shut any longer. Annie had as good a reason to kill Hiram as Wingate did. So I called Ted quick to warn him you might be in danger."

"Thank God for that," I said. "And thank God the giftshop woman found my wallet and remembered my wink. When she called my number, Ted was primed to tell her to get help up to the overlook quick."

"But on top of that, we'd like to do something to make your trouble up to you," Winnie said, smiling like a kindergarten sunflower. "At least as far as that's possible." She reached in her purse and pulled out a check with a flourish.

I didn't tempt myself by looking to see how much. "No, thank you," I said firmly. "The responsibility for Hiram's money is all yours, not mine. I feel like it's jinxed."

They both seemed to shrink.

"But you know how to lift the jinx," I said. "If you spend your money to help kids, Rich, and you spend it to help save the environment, Winnie — hey, that'll be a good thing. And I will probably forgive you when the lump on my head goes down."

Rich stood up straight, and that twinkle that reminded me of Marietta came back in his eye. "When you suddenly get fifteen million dollars," he said, "it's like God has called your bluff."

"Called your bluff?" What an odd thought. Had he gone a little balmy?

"Yes," he said. "You know how all your life you say I'd do this good thing or that good thing except I can't because I don't have the money? When you have the money, and no excuse, you have to face up to who you really are. So now I'm trying."

I wished him luck.

"Money," said a warm fruity voice behind me, "makes everything more so. More so good or more so bad. But if you kids are tired of yours. I'll take it!"

I jumped out of my chair. I turned around.

"I'm Suzie," said the woman in red standing in the front doorway. "Rich said he didn't think you'd mind if I came by and asked you to tell me firsthand exactly how Annie tried to kill you, and how you got away."

Rich jumped up, went over, and gave Suzie a hug. They were kin. She was his ex-stepaunt. "Have you been here long?" he asked. Of course he wanted to know how much she heard before we saw her standing there. If she'd cracked the door and waited — but perhaps she came right in.

Suzie blazed like the sun with a Ronald Reagan smile, and for some reason that worked fine in a bright-eyed feminine face. She had the blondish hair favored by women who cover gray but want to be subtle. Otherwise she was not subtle.

"Annie was always prepared," Suzie told us, "for any emergency. I admired her for that. She was also ruthless. She got rid of Hiram's friends she didn't like. Of course she didn't used to kill them. Just made up libel. A very talented girl. Killing is more dangerous. But these things escalate." She marched over to the wing chair near the fireplace. She sat down.

"But the stakes got higher," Pop said. Good grief, here he came in his wheelchair, all dolled up in red plaid pants and a red shirt for his airplane trip. Pushed by Max with hair like flax. "I might kill for fifteen or sixteen million dollars," he said. "On the other hand, I might not. Put my chair by that lovely lady," he told Max, waving toward Suzie.

"I'm glad I saw you before I had to leave. I've wanted to meet you, Suzie, and I'm off to go lose ten years. My wife has tried it and says it works, with minerals and vitamins and goodness knows what."

Of course he was leaving, now that the murders were solved. We were less exciting than Azalea's youth doctor. "Peaches doesn't need me anymore," he said, "now that Annie Long is behind bars."

Suzie caught me in her high-beam eyes. "How did Annie kidnap you?"

"She was a great stalker," I said. "I was almost never directly aware of being followed, but when she wanted to know where I was, she did. And she had nerve. I think now that she carried weapons — if you count bottles of alcohol and sulfuric acid, and finally a gun — in her shoulder bag. She was ready when a chance came."

"First she got you in a dryer," Pop crowed. "Boy, I'd like to have seen that!"

Suzie, of course, wanted every detail.

"And it was all Brian's fault," she accused after I told her.

"Brian," Pop echoed. "But he's a poet. What do poets know?"

"Hiram told Brian to take Annie Long with him when he traveled. Who do you think put Hiram up to that? Our Annie of course. Told Hiram that Brian might fall off of the world otherwise. If Brian had said no, Annie wouldn't have been on the *Ocean Queen*, much less in the laundry room."

I began to rock. There is something very healing about a rocking chair. This one had belonged to my mother. "But I thought Hiram liked to make trouble," I said. "Not keep his relatives safe."

"Mild trouble," Suzie said. "More like practical jokes. More like jabs to see if you could take it. Then he'd do something kind. A very confusing man. And more so as he got older. That's why I left him. That and the women. He said a man had a right to stray, a woman didn't. What a chauvinist! Wrong attitude — right, Rich?"

But that attitude had saved Rich's father fifteen million dollars!

Rich nodded. I could see he was still worried about what she'd heard about him, maybe afraid she'd ask him questions. He explained he and Winnie had another appointment, and off they went.

"I scare them." Suzie laughed. "Now tell me, Peaches, how did you get away from terrible Annie? Why aren't you smashed at the bottom of a drop?"

So I told her all the details. "But what's strangest to me," I said, "is that she worked out an elaborate alibi and then told me that she didn't intend to kill Wingate. She did it in a rage."

Suzie laughed. "That girl lied to herself and to anybody else who would listen. Of course she intended to kill him if he wouldn't marry her. That girl had depths of hidden rage."

Yes, I thought, and of course she used the alibi that chance brought her way, when Brian invited her to go and pick mushrooms. Poor Brian, who was never sure either exactly where he was or what time it was. That's what Marietta said. So Annie told him they were far away from Linville Falls, when they were close by. She made sure he was "lost" for a while at the time she met Wingate. So twice she picked mushrooms, once when she intended to poison Hiram, and then saw he was so near death that she could smother him and get away with that, and once when Brian offered her an alibi. She always used what chance brought.

"And yet," I said, "I think she did love Wingate in her way. That's why her focus on me wavered, and I had a chance to kick the gun. In a way love did her in."

"Love can move mountains," Pop said. "Thank goodness it saved you, Peaches. It's taking me to Arizona."

Ted had come in to help move Pop's bags out to the car. Pop hugged Suzie good-bye. "Till we meet again," he said. He wasn't about to lose such a good source of gossip.

I was going to the airport, but I knew it would take a few minutes to get Pop and his baggage settled in the car. I sat with Suzie a little longer.

"So what do you think of Marietta's money manager going bankrupt?" Suzie asked. "I hope he only lost his shirt, not hers, but she'll manage no matter what. Marietta is like that."

Before I could say a word, she added: "And do you think that Goldie will marry that environmental type? The one who wants to start some offbeat paper mill?

Imagine Goldie getting earnest. I don't think it will last."

I opened my mouth to speak again, but Suzie was too quick for me. "And Brian entering a monastery! That won't last three days. But thank goodness Lillian has joined AA." With Suzie on the job, that would hardly be anonymous.

"And is it true you've sworn off murders?" Suzie asked me. She made it sound as if I'd resigned from the Mafia.

"I've promised Ted," I said, "that I'll try not to get mixed up in dangerous situations. It's not fair to make him worry so much."

"That's what I heard!" she said. "You should be a reporter! That's a safe way to snoop. Did you know the weekly paper over in Madison County is looking for a reporter to cover murder trials? And other stuff, too? I know the editor. You'll like him."

"You want me to apply," I said, stunned. How did the gossip hotline know what I'd promised Ted? Well, of course, through Pop.

"You wrote a book," Suzie said. "You've solved murders. You live thirty-five minutes from the paper. If there's anything you don't know, you're married to a journalism professor. Think about it."

"So I can tell you all the dirt in Madison County?" I asked.

"Of course." She winked.

"Does the gingko extract from Marietta help you to remember?" Suzie asked. "Reporters have to remember."

"The what?" I was caught off guard by her sudden subject change.

"The gingko extract to jog memory."

I had to admit I'd forgotten to take it. "I'll start today," I said.

Suzie jumped up. "Good! Now, I have a lot more to do this morning. Maybe I'll see you in Madison County." Her eyes said mission accomplished. She charged out as suddenly as she'd come in.

Ted and I went off to the airport with Pop.

We came home to a silent house, to our house just for Ted and me. Wonderful to be alone. We sat down on the couch, and I kicked off my shoes. I contemplated the antique log-cabin quilt that hung on the wall. My grandmother made that. I looked at the silver cup on the mantel that Ted had won for a series of stories on migrant workers, at the copy of *Editor & Publisher* magazine on the coffee table.

"So what do you think of Suzie's idea?" I asked.

Ted reached over and took my hand. "Maybe," he said, "if instead of getting involved with murders by mistake, you were a reporter on purpose — you'd be safer." He kissed my hand. Very continental. "Perhaps no one would try to kill you. I would like that."